"I'm going to kill Jules for setting me up," Kansas said.

"Baby, if anyone was set up, it was me. Sydney knows I'm determined to retire from the Bureau. Throwing you into my bed is no doubt a clever attempt to give me a reason for staying."

"That's ridiculous!"

"I agree. Nothing could make me stay. Not even great sex."

"Rio—"

"I know, I know. I think we're both in agreement about that."

"Which is...?" she asked cautiously.

"Physically attracted, but no interest in pursuing any kind of relationship."

Good. That was exactly how she felt. So why the sudden churning of disappointment in her stomach? "Right. So, what are we going to do? Because this isn't working."

"The way I see it," he said, "we go back in the bedroom, take off our clothes and get rid of the tension so we can concentrate on the job."

Dear Reader,

I hope you've had a warm and cozy holiday season, and are ready to sizzle up the New Year with some fabulous reads from Silhouette Intimate Moments. I sure am!

It's so exciting for me to be able to launch into 2006 with this fast-paced, edgy story. The idea for *Enemy Husband* was born several years ago when I saw the movie *Entrapment* with my own husband. I just loved that opening scene. I wanted my heroine to do that! But yikes, a thief? In an Intimate Moments book....? Sass had better have a darned good reason for stealing that computer disk! And Rio, what can I say? He came out of the shadows, surprising me as much as Sass with his (un)timely appearance. That's the great thing about terrific characters. They really have minds of their own. We authors might think we're in charge, but it's really them....

Enemy Husband will take you on a nonstop thrill ride from Washington, D.C., to the sea islands of South Carolina. Hope you enjoy it! And later this year, please look for my next Intimate Moments book, *Royal Betrayal* (July '06), book 4 of the exciting CAPTURING THE CROWN continuity series, which starts in April.

Good reading!

Nina Bruhns

NINA BRUHNS
ENEMY HUSBAND

Silhouette®

INTIMATE MOMENTS™

Published by Silhouette Books

America's Publisher of Contemporary Romance

SILHOUETTE BOOKS

ISBN 0-373-27472-6

ENEMY HUSBAND

Visit Silhouette Books at www.eHarlequin.com

Printed in U.S.A.

NINA BRUHNS

credits her Gypsy great-grandfather for her great love of adventure. She has lived and traveled all over the world, including a six-year stint in Sweden. She has been on scientific expeditions from California to Spain to Egypt and the Sudan, and has two graduate degrees in archaeology (with a specialty in Egyptology). She speaks four languages and writes a mean hieroglyphics!

But Nina's first love has always been writing. For her, writing for Silhouette Books is the ultimate adventure. Drawing on her many experiences gives her stories a colorful dimension and allows her to create settings and characters out of the ordinary. She has won numerous awards for her previous titles, including the prestigious National Readers Choice Award, two Daphne Du Maurier Awards of Excellence for Overall Best Romantic Suspense of the year, five Dorothy Parker Awards and two Golden Heart Awards, among many others.

A native of Canada, Nina grew up in California and currently resides in Charleston, South Carolina, with her husband and three children. She loves to hear from her readers, and can be reached at P.O. Box 2216, Summerville, SC 29484-2216 or by e-mail via her Web site at www.NinaBruhns.com or via the Harlequin Web site at www.eHarlequin.com.

For my own wonderful husband, Tim, who is the embodiment of all my heroes in one perfect man. I love you.

Chapter 1

Washington, D.C.

She went in through the window this time.

That was something they probably weren't expecting, considering it was thirty stories up and, technically, wasn't supposed to open at all.

Kansas Hawthorne allowed herself a good chuckle as she lowered herself another few inches on a thin metal cable against the side of the building, and finished tightening the last of the two-foot-long bolts inserted in the holes she'd drilled through each of the corners of the target office window. Then she wedged the heavy pane away from its casing—not a simple task, but she managed, as she'd known she would. It had worked fine on paper, after all.

Damn, she loved breaking and entering! It was something

you could count on. If you planned carefully and followed the plan meticulously, things always turned out as they were supposed to. Unlike life in general.

She checked her watch. 2:00 a.m. exactly. Right on time.

Squeezing through the eighteen-inch gap provided by the bolts she'd rigged, Kansas quickly flipped down her infrared goggles and studied the motion-detecting laser beams crisscrossing the dark, night-empty office she was breaking into. *Complicated, but not impossible.* Most of the red beams in the matrix were concentrated around the outer door and the ventilation shafts in the ceiling.

Shaking her head, she directed a silent *tsk, tsk, tsk* at her adversary, the handsome but obviously unimaginative ANSIR—Awareness of National Security Issues and Response—agent, Stewart Rio. This was going to be easier than she'd thought. He'd be eating crow big-time over this one. Her mouth curved up at the thought.

Earlier, during business hours at the well-known beltway defense contractor, she'd slipped into the building's basement and hacked into the wiring to the surveillance camera to freeze-frame at 2:00 a.m., but for only six short minutes. So once she was in, she went straight to the safe, cracked it and extracted the top secret government software CD that was her objective.

She checked her watch again. Two minutes. Excellent.

She headed around the big wooden desk in the center of the room and back to the window. Trying to avoid one of the laser beams, she banged her leg against the desk's corner.

"Damn," she cursed crisp and low and reached for her throbbing knee. Her hand knocked the out-basket off the desk, spilling its contents onto the floor and missing the red beam by millimeters.

Again she swore roundly, then bent awkwardly to gather up the files and envelopes, stacking them neatly back in the out-basket. Straightening, she unzipped her black catsuit, swiftly tucked the CD under her breasts—against her rib cage—and zipped it back up, snug and secure. She hurried to the window.

Thirty seconds left.

Her heart was pounding like a jackhammer by the time she'd repositioned the window and replaced the temporary bolts with taps so everything would look normal in the morning.

She raised her fist in glee. What a rush! Everything had gone perfectly.

Oh, yeah, she'd give half her month's paycheck to see that insufferably arrogant, unflappable Stewart Rio's face tomorrow when he realized she'd beaten him.

Again.

Laughing out loud, she pulled the band from her ponytail and tossed her head, letting her long hair fly wild and free, then with a squeal she released the brakes on the pulley-reel holding the cable she was dangling from, thirty floors up.

Downward she plunged, fast and reckless, using her soft boots to rappel off the building in graceful arcs so she didn't cream herself on the way down. She shouted a rebel yell at the top of her lungs out of sheer exhilaration, knowing the sound of her voice was swallowed up by the height and the dark, fathomless night, her blood pumping to the primitive beat of pure adrenaline.

This was what she lived for!

Some might prefer tamer pursuits, like stamp collecting or falling in love. But for Sass, there was nothing more thrilling than the danger of pulling off yet another impossible job.

Her feet hit the springy grass of the manicured grounds surrounding the posh office building, and she flipped a switch on the reel in her hand, sending it back up the wall to the roof where she'd attached the apparatus earlier, winding up the microthin cable as it went. Just one more small maneuver left, and she'd be home free.

With immense satisfaction, she watched the reel and cable disappear from sight, and murmured, "Take that, Stewart Rio."

"Thank you," a deep voice rumbled directly behind her. "I believe I will."

Kansas spun. How the hell had Rio managed to find her so quickly?

"Special Agent R-Rio," she stammered, suddenly harrowingly unsure if she could actually pull this mission off.

"Well, if it isn't Special Agent Hawthorne," he returned politely. Even in the dark, she could see the gleam of straight white teeth between sensually chiseled lips. "How nice of you to…drop in."

She clenched her jaw. "Very clever."

The silhouette of his broad shoulders lifted negligently, and he moved in closer. Within inches.

"I've had a lot of experience," he said modestly.

She stifled the urge to step back. She'd cracked safes only a handful of specialists could breach, faced blazing guns and two-hundred-foot drops without blinking an eye. This man would *not* intimidate her. He hadn't before, and he wouldn't now. She had to stay focused on the task at hand.

"Is that so," she said, reaching out to run a finger down the front of his black FBI T-shirt.

She sensed his body stiffen, and then relax a fraction. Yes. She could do this.

There was no way she'd let Stewart Rio best her. Not a chance. Covert Ops was counting on her to bring home the trophy in their annual informal intra-agency competition—for the second year in a row. Rio was the Special Agent in Charge—or SAC—of an elite FBI squad within its ANSIR division. His squad was responsible for preventing the theft of top secret government assets throughout the country— In other words, exactly this kind of burglary. But within a year of joining the Bureau, Sass had become the FBI Covert Ops squad's newest weapon, and an annoying thorn in Rio's over-bearing butt. She had no intention of disappointing either side this time around.

He was the enemy.

Besides, she liked winning. Too much to be bested by this man.

Rio held out his hand. "Give me the disc, Sass."

She lifted a brow at his use of her nickname. It was the first time she'd ever heard him use it. Usually his dealings with her were as stiff as his own neck, and always by-the-book formal, same as with all the women agents he knew. What had changed now?

"Come get it," she replied, smiling coyly, gratified when his eyes widened in surprise.

Taking swift advantage, she shoved hard on his chest and crooked her foot around his legs, hitting the backs of his knees as hard as she could. He fell like a sumo wrestler and she took off running.

She got as far as the bushes at the edge of the property. He tackled her from behind, knocking her to the grass face-first and landing on top of her.

"That wasn't nice, Special Agent Hawthorne," he scolded in her ear.

"Sorry," she muttered, spitting grass out of her mouth. "I don't like losing."

"Me, neither." He lifted up and turned her none too gently to face him, and settled back on top of her. Giving her an even look, he said, "Now, are you going to give me the disc, or am I going to have to take it from you myself?"

For some unfathomable reason, her pulse doubled at the prospect. She squirmed under him. Big mistake. Her catsuit was thin, a scant ounce of body-clinging fabric. His long, hard frame pressed firmly into her curves, reminding her of things she'd rather not think about. *Especially* under these circumstances.

Stick to the plan, Sass.

When she didn't say anything, he gathered her wrists in one of his big hands and pulled them over her head. "All right, have it your way."

She squeezed her eyes shut as he took hold of her catsuit's zipper tab and started pulling it down her chest.

Okay, easy now. She chewed her lip, waiting, silently willing her unruly body not to respond.

It did anyway.

She stifled a groan. Just as well. It would make what she was about to do all the more believable.

Taking a steadying breath, she ignored the blood pounding in her ears. "Listen, uh, I was wondering…"

She opened her eyes to find him gazing at the large expanse of pale flesh exposed between the open zipper, which had stalled just below her bare breasts. She could see the valley between them gleam in the moonlight, along with a few inches of lush slope to either side. She had deliberately left her bra off tonight, in anticipation of this very moment.

Rio tugged the zipper down a bit more and faltered again when the ultrastretchy black fabric threatened to snap to the sides and expose her completely. He changed tactics and tentatively slipped his hand into the opening, just above her breast, ostensibly probing for the disc.

He seemed fascinated, yet at the same time horrified by what he was doing. Undoubtedly, he knew exactly where it was.

"Rio?" she prodded, waiting for him to acknowledge her query.

"Hmm?" he mumbled, obviously not concentrating on the conversation too well.

"Any chance we could make a deal?"

That jerked his wary attention back to her face. Disconcertingly, his hand halted, over her breast.

"What kind of a deal?"

In the position they were in, neither of them could miss his growing arousal. It was probably as involuntary as her own body's response, but nevertheless, it was good to know she turned him on, if only on that instinctual, primitive, male-female level. She lay still for a moment, allowing the hard ridge to swell bigger between them.

His fingers tightened on her breast and she swallowed heavily, suddenly completely unnerved. Had she gravely misjudged the man lying on top of her?

Too late now.

She cleared her throat. "I'm up for my two-year review in a few weeks," she said. "I really want this win on my record."

He stared at her levelly. "And?"

"And I'd be willing to trade for the disc."

His gaze narrowed. "Trade what?"

Her throat was so dry she could scarcely squeeze the words out. "Surely, there's something you can think of."

Wariness flitted through his eyes, followed closely by something else. Something more predatory, and calculating.

She stifled a gasp when his hand moved slowly around her breast, touching her deliberately and thoroughly. Unwillingly, excitement zinged through her like a jolt of electricity.

She bit back a murmur of protest when his hand continued its travels downward, hitting the edge of the CD hidden against her rib cage.

He pulled out the disc and looked at it consideringly. "You must want to keep this very badly."

"I do." She held her breath, her heart hammering like a tommy gun.

He tipped his head. "I think we both know just how…interesting…I find your offer." For a heart-stopping, terrifying moment she thought he would actually accept. "But I must regretfully decline."

Her breath whooshed out in relief. But before she could feign a protest, the sound of soft footsteps padding across the grass grabbed their attention. Rio quickly slid her zipper back up, released her wrists and leaped to his feet. She couldn't figure out why, but when she tried to do the same her legs would barely hold her. What the hell was it about this man that suddenly made her feel so unsettled? Rio grasped her arm and held fast as he turned to the approaching man.

"Find it?" Rio asked.

"Sure thing, boss," the man answered, and held out a cardboard Priority Mail envelope for his inspection. "Right in the out-basket, just like you said it'd be."

Taking the mailer, Rio ripped it open.

"Tampering with the mail is a federal offense, you know," she said through gritted teeth.

As he extracted a CD—identical to the one he'd taken from her—he looked down and smiled. "Nice try, Special Agent Hawthorne."

She scowled and folded her arms over her chest. "How did you know?"

"Oldest trick in the book. And you should have covered your tracks a bit better when you rerouted the surveillance camera through your freeze-frame timer. We were watching you for the whole six minutes in the office. Nice safecracking, though. Where'd you learn that?"

She swore lightly and ignored his question. If he didn't know about her father, she certainly wasn't about to tell him.

"Sure I can't change your mind?" she asked instead, raking him with a bold look. "I'd make it worth your while."

"I've no doubt you would, Special Agent Hawthorne." He tossed her the disc he'd taken off her just moments ago. "Keep it. A souvenir to remind you to do your research next time. You should know better than to try to bribe me—with *anything*."

She lifted her chin at his smug parting salute, barely resisting a smirk of her own.

Oh, she knew better all right.

He and his compadre strode away over the grass leaving her standing alone in the night.

"To remind you to do your research next time," she mimicked in a high-pitched voice at the CD in her hand.

She rolled her eyes. What an insufferable boor. Everyone on the planet knew he was totally incorruptible, and never, ever dated other agents. Stories of those who'd tried and failed were legion.

Her face broke out in a broad grin. And that's just what she'd been counting on. Naturally he'd come through like an ace, mistaking her for a rookie female who used her body rather than her brain. Typical.

Men were so damned predictable.

She'd hit Rio exactly where she knew he'd react—his male ego—and he'd walked right into her trap, giving her precisely the knee-jerk response she'd been looking for.

She was in a man's world, playing a man's game. But she was anything but predictable. And that's what made Special Agent Kansas Hawthorne so damned good at her job.

She tossed the disc up in the air and caught it between two fingers. Oh, yeah. She couldn't wait for tomorrow.

Stewart Rio smiled good-naturedly at the ribbing he was getting from the squad as they walked down the hall toward the fifth-floor conference room. Both ANSIR and Sass's C-Ops team were located at the FBI headquarters in downtown D.C. The authentication meeting and informal trophy ceremony for their little intra-agency competition was always held there. He grinned. "I'm telling you, boys, it was strictly business."

Being caught in a compromising position with Sass Hawthorne was something most men only dreamed of. And to be honest, he'd had his share of intriguing fantasies thinking about her proposition once he'd finally climbed into bed last night—alone.

There was no doubt she was hot—long blond hair and a body that wouldn't quit. But he wasn't interested in Sass, or any of the other female agents who'd come on to him over his fourteen years at the Bureau. When he closed the big case he'd been working off and on for the past thirty-six months, he'd be out of Washington D.C. like a shot. Down to some lazy Southern beach community, to buy a house and a fishing boat and open his own charter business, hiring out relaxing vacations to all his overstressed buddies from Washington D.C. Then he'd find himself a nice, quiet woman who'd give him a passel of rascally kids. A homey, unassuming, gentle woman. A woman not accustomed to being shot at for a living. And definitely not a woman who worked as a thief, even if it was for the Bureau in Covert Ops. Steward Rio with a thief of any description was never going to happen. Not in this lifetime or his next hundred lifetimes.

Still, he was a man, and if the squad wanted to think the sexy C-Ops rookie had put some serious moves on him, who was he to disappoint them?

"Sure, boss. Strictly *monkey* business," one of the guys said.

They guffawed, obviously not believing a word of his denial.

Still grinning, he glanced at the wall clock—7:55 a.m. He and his team always ate breakfast together, but he made sure they rolled into the office by 8:00. Today he definitely didn't want to be late.

Poor Special Agent Hawthorne. He almost felt sorry for the woman, having gone to such lengths to win. Almost.

He strode confidently into the conference room. A long, polished wood table with chairs ran down the center of the space; a coffee table and two oversize leather wingbacks were grouped in front of the window. One of the leather chairs was placed with its back to the door.

Rio's team spilled into the conference room after him, poking each other in the ribs.

"Next year let *me* tackle Hawthorne," Gordo, the one who'd seen him lying on top of her, said with a snicker. "I'll show her the business."

"No way they'll use her again next year," another team member said. "Not after this."

"Anyway, it'll be good to have that trophy back where it belongs," a third man said.

"That's what C-Ops gets, sending a girl to do a man's job," Gordo muttered.

Rio shook his head as agreement sounded all around from the men. Sometimes his all-male team could get an attitude. One of these days it would be their downfall.

"Woman," corrected Rio setting his cup of coffee and a manila envelope down on the conference table. He pulled out a chair. "And she's better at her job than half you jokers."

"Hey!" the guys protested. "No way."

Suddenly, he caught sight of Special Agent Hawthorne's reflection in the plate glass window. One brow raised, she sat watching him from the wingback chair with its back to the room, only her mirrored image visible.

Figured she'd chosen that chair. Or maybe she'd put it there deliberately. Some old tricks stayed in the book because they worked. *Usually.*

"C'mon, boss!" Gordo exclaimed. "We had her nailed from the git-go. Hell! She left the old code in when she reprogrammed the security camera! How amateur is that?"

"Yeah, well," said Rio, holding her gaze in the reflection. "That was one mistake in an otherwise flawless plan. If she'd scheduled an extra minute to type the code back in after she got out, we'd never have been on to her. Let that be a lesson to you all."

There was a general grumbling of disagreement and the conversation took off on all the other things the men thought were wrong with her plan.

He strolled over to the chair where she sat, and stood behind it, folding his arms across his chest.

"So it was the code that gave me away, huh?" she asked in a low voice meant just for him.

He gave her reflection a half smile. "Common mistake. Rookies think a job has to be fast and furious to be successful. Experience teaches you to take all the time you need to be thorough."

"And do your research," she added, echoing his words from last night.

"Yeah. And do your research." Next year he was pretty sure she wouldn't let a stupid error ruin her run. He'd have to be extra diligent to catch her. But he would. This was one thief he could easily take revenge upon. Unlike the other…

She steepled her fingers. "Did you do your research?" she asked. "About me?"

"Of course."

"And what did you find?"

He thought for a moment, then recited from memory, "Graduated from Quantico two years ago top of your class, immediately assigned to Covert Ops where you've specialized in…information and evidence retrieval."

She chuckled softly at his euphemism for common thievery. Apparently what she did didn't bother her.

"You have friends but prefer working alone. You don't like to follow orders and never do anything the way it's expected. You love taking risks—the crazier the better." He tried to dampen the obvious note of disapproval in his tone. If she were on *his* team she'd last maybe a minute. He didn't like loose cannons. He worked hard to achieve perfect teamwork among his men.

But he granted, "You've never failed at an assignment." His gaze dipped involuntarily to her breasts then up again. "Until yesterday."

Color flashed briefly through her cheeks. "Not bad. In fact, I couldn't have done better myself."

"Just thorough research."

She tipped her head. "Tell me, Special Agent Rio, do I sleep around?"

He frowned. "No."

"Ever?" She carefully watched his face in the reflection.

A prick of foreboding streaked through him. "No. Not that I've—" And that's when the realization hit him right between his eyes.

He should have known last night was too easy. That *she'd* been too easy. But he hadn't been thinking with his brain.

Damn, damn, *damn*.

Last night he'd turned down her offer.

But he had the sinking feeling she'd screwed him anyway.

Chapter 2

Rio clamped his teeth together. This couldn't be happening. He had to be wrong. How could she possibly have—

Hawthorne stood up and stretched. "Maybe I'll buy you breakfast after the ceremony. Seems appropriate for the morning after." She winked. "Oh, that's right. You've already eaten."

Rio felt a muscle twitch in his cheek. Usually a consummate gentleman, under his breath he made a very rude suggestion. She just grinned.

He was so screwed.

Just then Jules Mannheim, Hawthorne's SAC walked into the room along with Rio's own boss, ANSIR director Paul Sydney. A third man accompanied them, whom Rio didn't recognize.

Sydney and Mannheim sat jointly at the head of the conference table, where a laptop and the cheesy imitation brass trophy stood waiting. The other man sat on Sydney's right. Sass Hawthorne took a seat next to him, so Rio grabbed a chair on the other side of the table, followed by his men.

"Well, let's get this show on the road," Sydney said cheerfully. "May I have the disc?"

Rio glared at Hawthorne. She didn't move.

"Sure," he said.

He slid the Priority envelope over to Sydney, who extracted the disc from it, plunked it into the laptop's drive and punched a few keys. Everyone turned expectantly to the large plasma screen on the wall.

The image of Sass's annoyingly pretty face appeared on the screen, her full lips curving in a bow. She leaned in close to the camera and whispered just one word.

"Gotcha."

Stunned, the whole team stared at the screen in disbelief. The disc whirred and rebooted itself, repeating the short, stinging message.

It cycled two more times before Rio reached over and ripped it from the drive. With a scalding curse, he hurled it into a nearby wastebasket.

"I believe this is what you're looking for," Hawthorne said, passed Sydney the disc, then turned back to Rio. "Rookie mistake," she said sweetly, "underestimating your opponent. That priority mailer? Just a decoy. I had the real disc all along."

Anger spiked in him, hot enough to spit hollow points.

She'd gotten him. *Two years in a row*. It didn't bear thinking about. Before that, the trophy hadn't been out of ANSIR's hands for all the years since the division was formed and the competition began. There had never been a thief who'd bested them before this…woman.

Damned vixen. Where the hell had she come from, anyway? And how had she learned all those sneaky tricks?

"You—" he pointed an accusing finger at her "—play dirty."

And he'd get even with her if it was the last thing he did.

She just grinned and accepted the trophy from a beaming Mannheim. "Hell, Rio, all that research, you should know, dirty's my specialty." Mannheim chuckled. She rose. "Well, boys, see you next—"

"Hang on, Special Agent Hawthorne," Sydney interrupted. "There's something else."

She halted. "What's that, sir?"

Rio cleared his throat. "Sir, if you're waiting for me to congratulate—"

The ANSIR director waved his hand dismissively. "Goes without saying. She beat us at our own game, and did an admirable job of it. I'm just glad she's on our side."

Rio's jaw clenched.

"Thank you, sir," she said, obviously surprised at the praise.

With good reason. Last year Rio's boss hadn't been nearly as magnanimous in defeat. Now he was actually smiling— well, a pretty good imitation anyway. "Rio, you stay. The rest of you men get back to work," he ordered. "And let this be a lesson to you."

Mannheim, Hawthorne's SAC, silently pointed at her empty chair and she sat back down, plunking the trophy onto the table.

Now what? Nerves jangling uneasily, Rio took the seat next to her and waited for the boom to fall.

"So, Rio," Mannheim said when just the five of them remained in the room—including the man who'd walked in earlier with the two bosses. "What do you think about our Special Agent Hawthorne, here? Pretty sharp, eh?"

It's not as if he could deny it. The evidence was fairly clear on that point. "As a stiletto," he grudgingly said.

Hawthorne's SAC flashed a grin. "Good, good. I'm glad you feel that way." He paused. "Since she'll be working closely with you on the Dawson case."

Rio's universe came to a screeching halt. "Excuse me?"

The Miles Dawson case was ANSIR's case. *His* turf. He didn't want C-Ops horning in on it. Especially not with an upstart agent as irritating and distracting as Sass Hawthorne. Not only was she a royal pain in the backside, but being around her more than one day a year might tempt him to forget about his strict rule against—he swallowed. Well, against being tempted. Thief or no, she was too sexy for her own good. Or his.

"My team has been working that case for nearly three years," he protested angrily. "Sharp or no, I don't need Special Agent Hawthorne's help."

He glanced at her. She seemed as shocked as he was by this unwelcome twist. There was hope.

"You may change your mind when you hear the latest," Sydney said, and introduced them to the silent third man. "This is Agent Cory Macon of The Department of Homeland Security. He's brought us some interesting intel on Dawson and a request for help."

Macon nodded and pushed a file folder across the desk toward Rio and Sass. "This came in to us from U.S. Customs early this morning."

"What is it?" Sass asked. "And who is this Dawson?"

Sydney answered her. "Miles Dawson is an international fence for stolen technology and weapons. He started out small, back in the seventies in Chicago, then moved up to working out of Seattle dealing stuff from the local aerospace companies."

"Now he's gaining a reputation as a procurer of stolen government and military commodities for terrorist organizations all over the world," Macon said. "Dawson's high on Homeland Security's watch list."

"And every European country's list, as well."

"Unfortunately, he's very good at covering his tracks," Rio added. "He moves around frequently, never staying in one place more than a few months. And there's never been enough evidence to arrest him for any of his activities."

Rio knew the frustration firsthand. Every time Dawson was within jurisdiction they tried to build a good case against him. Hadn't succeeded yet.

But what was even more frustrating, there'd been rumors Dawson was somehow involved in the last case Rio's dad had worked for the Bureau. The case that had gotten him killed.

Rio wanted Dawson bad. Real bad.

"Well, this time we caught a break," Macon said, tapping the file. "A Customs patrol off Florida stopped a Cayman registry sailboat this morning for a routine drug search. They found evidence its two occupants were heading for Dawson's next auction. As proxy bidders for the Al Sayika. The auction's in three days."

Rio's head jerked up. "Al Sayika?" One of the nastiest terrorist organizations in the world, on everyone's list. "And these people talked?"

Macon shrugged. "At our urging the Customs guys used a little *friendly persuasion.*"

"This is all very interesting," Hawthorne interjected. "But what does it have to do with me?"

Ignoring her, Rio frowned. "Does this auction have anything to do with the vial of smallpox that went missing in Paris a couple of weeks ago?"

The theft of the deadly virus had had law enforcement officials everywhere scrambling to tighten security. If it was released, whether deliberately or accidentally, millions would die.

"No, thank God," Mannheim said. "It's not the smallpox. On the block is a prototype nuclear triggering device stolen from a Department of Defense subcontractor a few months ago. Highly classified. It's as valuable as the nuclear bomb itself, and worth ten times more than the plutonium."

Rio whistled. "We got a location?"

"A private island off the South Carolina coast."

"Great." He surged to his feet. "My team will be ready to roll within the hour."

Sydney held up a hand. "Not so fast, Rio. Your team won't be going in."

Rio halted on his way to the door and turned to his boss in disbelief. Surely this wasn't punishment for losing the dumb trophy. "Why not?"

"Because *I* will. Right?" Hawthorne said, a smile starting to form on her lips.

"In a manner of—"

"You want me to steal back the triggering device. Piece of cake. When do I leave, sir?"

"It's a little more complicated than that," Macon said, leaning back in his chair.

Sudden apprehension tingled down Rio's spine. "How so?" he asked, and Sydney and Mannheim glanced at each other.

What the hell was going on?

"You and Hawthorne are going to pose as the two arrested bidders, Rafe Gerard and Gun Sundstrom. Take their place.

We want you to attend the auction and gather enough evidence to arrest Miles Dawson and his cohorts so we can close them down once and for all."

Hawthorne shot out of her seat. *"Rio and me?"*

"That's correct."

"Why not a Homeland Security team?"

"We don't have anyone with your skills or as up to speed on Dawson as Special Agent Rio. Together you two are our best shot."

Like hell. Instantly Rio's mind came up with a million reasons going undercover with a woman, especially this particular woman, could backfire.

"With all due respect, sir," Rio said, wiping his hands down his slacks, *"no damn way.* Hawthorne's specialty is breaking and entering, not undercover operations." And Sydney knew damn well how he felt about thieves. How could he be asking him to work with one?

"I can do this," she countered quickly. "But not with him. I work alone. In and out, under cover of darkness. A simple second-story laydown with no company to mess things up."

Rio shook his head emphatically. "Too risky. His security is always on high alert and usually lethal," Rio argued. "I'll go under and attend the auction, but I'll take one of my own men instead."

Macon cut off their protests. "Not possible, I'm afraid. Even if there were someone on your team with the necessary safecracking skills—which I understand there isn't—it has to be a woman."

"And why's that, sir?" Rio asked. He had a terrible sinking feeling in his gut. Just like the one he'd had right before viewing that damned CD.

Sydney looked from one to the other. "Gun is short for

Gunilla. She's a woman. You and Hawthorne will be going in as a couple."

Hawthorne froze in her seat as did Rio. "A couple? As in—?"

"As in together," Mannheim said calmly, his expression immovable as a brick wall. "Rafe Gerard and Gun Sundstrom are married. You're going in as husband and wife."

Chapter 3

Sass was still reeling. How could this have happened? Of all the people to be sent on her first undercover gig with, why did it have to be the only man in recent memory capable of making her hot and bothered with a single look?

She was in major trouble. She couldn't blow this assignment. She loved her job and had a perfect record. She couldn't let any man, regardless of how sexy he was, distract her from achieving another success. Her job was all she had in the world. She couldn't risk it on hot and bothered.

Hot and bothered usually led to sex. Which usually led to relationships. Which usually led to questions. Which always led to being dumped. So she'd given up hot and bothered a long time ago. Which worked out well, because a *really* long time ago she'd given up the notion of ever settling down. Bad things happened when she tried settling down. *Very* bad things.

First her mother and sister had died. Then her dad had been put in prison....

Determinedly, she swept away the bad memories. All that was beside the point. The real point was that she could not let Stewart Rio distract her from doing her job.

So she wouldn't let him.

She was good at her job—and even better at not becoming distracted. Hadn't the past eleven years proven that?

She could definitely handle Special Agent Rio for a couple of days.

Besides, she had nothing to worry about from him. The man was so rigid he'd snap in a stiff wind. Witness last night. Hell, maybe he was even gay.

Yeah, no problem. She could do this.

After the meeting, Jules Mannheim had given Sass an hour to get ready. When she finished packing, she decided to use her last few minutes to call her father in prison and let him know she'd be gone for a while, and the gist of why. She knew she could trust him to keep his mouth shut. He'd always told her about his jobs when she was a kid, listening to her ideas no matter how dumb or naïve. Now she liked doing the same thing with him. Working with a longtime professional gave her an edge no one else had.

"Well, at least I get to be Gun," Sass said wryly. The Swedish name wasn't pronounced the same as the English word—more like the "Poon" in Punjab, India—but it still looked tough as nails on paper. She liked that.

Unfortunately, her dad read something different in the situation. "Think of it as an adventure, Kansas. And a golden opportunity to snare yourself a nice, steady man."

A real comedian, her dad. "Yeah, that'll happen. Right after you go straight."

Her dad chuckled. "Tell me about this guy you'll be married to."

"Rio?" She played with the strap of her small overnight bag. Jules had told her to pack light, just the necessities, because she'd be using Gun's clothing from the boat. They were close enough in size that the clothes would work. "Rio's a pain in the butt."

Her dad laughed again. "A good match, in other words."

"You're a riot, Clive."

"Is he good-looking?"

After a slight hesitation, she reluctantly said, "Yeah."

"Interesting?"

She sighed. "Moderately," she admitted, only because Clive always saw through it when she tried to con him.

"Smart?"

But enough was enough. "Dad, I just beat him at what he does best."

"Uh-oh. Is he going to hold that against you?"

"Of course."

She heard him grunt. "Try not to be too hard on him, poppet. A man's ego is a fragile thing."

Wasn't that the damned truth. She didn't understand what it was about the creatures that made them incapable of handling a woman like her. Usually they blamed her background, but she knew that wasn't the whole story. A jailbird dad and a few years in juvie couldn't totally explain the fear of getting involved she'd experienced from the men she'd dated. It was fear of her and her crazy lifestyle.

Which, given her circumstances, was just as well. But it just made for a bit of a lonely life.

"Sure, Daddy. I'll go easy on Rio." *In some alternate universe.*

"So, what did you say his first name is?" he asked far too casually.

"Stewart. Why?"

"Not Spencer Rio?"

"No. Dad, what's—"

"By any chance was Rio's father, or brother, a Fed?"

She thought she remembered hearing something like that. "Yeah, I think so. His dad. Years ago. What's this all about?"

She thought she heard a whispered curse. "Nothing. Just a name I ran across once." Then he went quiet.

Apparently that's all she was getting. She knew better than to try to pry anything more out of him. She'd have to check into that later.

"Listen," she said into the lengthening silence, "have you ever heard of an import-export specialist named Dawson?" Her dad knew just about every big name in the fencing biz, if only by reputation, so Sass frequently dipped into his store of knowledge.

There was a pause. "Who?"

"Miles Dawson. He's involved in international stuff now, but started out as a small-time Chicago fence. Thought you may have heard of him somewhere along the line."

She waited.

"Yeah. I've heard of him. Dawson's bad news, Kansas. Real bad news. This job you're going on, does it have anything to do with him?"

"He could be mixed up in it. Any advice?"

"Don't go," Clive said with surprising vehemence. "The man's dangerous and unpredictable. *And* a pervert. Sweetheart, please tell me you won't even be in the same state as Dawson."

"That could be tough," she sidestepped.

Clive muttered something that could have been a swear word, then wheezed out a long cough. "Did Jules Mannheim have anything to do with this Dawson assignment?" he demanded.

"Jules is my boss, Dad."

Sass had a special affection for Jules, and her father's dislike of the man had never sat well with her. Jules was the one who'd dragged her eighteen-year-old butt off the streets when she'd had nowhere to go and no one to care, straightened her up and made sure she went to college and graduated. He'd even helped her expunge her juvenile record and legally change her last name, so she could leave the stigma of her past behind completely. Not that she had. Some things were impossible to leave behind.

But she'd tried.

After college she floundered around in dead-end jobs she was overqualified for, learning that architects who trusted female structural engineers were few and far between. Jules was the one who recognized she was on the verge of going back to her old life and recruited her for the FBI, writing a glowing recommendation to offset her shaky background.

He was also the one who'd put her father in jail.

Which might have explained why he'd done all that except that Jules was a genuinely good person who had helped other kids out of hard places, not just her. It was his calling. Just as being a thief was hers.

This time she plainly heard her father's curse. "I'll kill him. He swore to me…"

"Swore what?"

Instead of answering, her father was seized with another long, racking cough, courtesy of twelve years behind bars with nothing to do but smoke cigarettes and watch TV. Clive wasn't into pumping iron.

"Kansas, I'm serious," he finally said when he was able to speak again. "Promise me you won't go near Dawson."

"I promise," she lied. She didn't want her dad worrying about her, possibly calling Jules and making a fuss. She doubted the FBI would approve of her consulting a convicted felon about her cases. "I'll be fine, Daddy."

After an affectionate goodbye, she hung up.

A horn honked outside.

Showtime.

Sass picked up her bag, gave her sparsely furnished apartment a last check, took a deep breath and strode out to the waiting car.

Yeah, she could do this.

"Nice digs," Rio remarked when she slid in next to him in the backseat of a gray, unmarked sedan. Macon was in the front seat with the driver, Jules on the other side of Rio. She thought briefly about going around to the other door and making them all slide over, but decided it would make her look like she was scared of him.

"Thanks," she said, then studied the view out the window, squishing up as close to the door as she could. She wasn't about to make chitchat. Or touch him if she could help it.

Too bad her plan was spoiled when Jules said proudly, "Sass picked up her town house at a government foreclosure for a buck. Can you believe it? Fixed it up herself."

"A *buck?*" Rio turned to look at her and his leg settled against hers. Thank God she'd worn long pants.

"The neighborhood wasn't quite so hospitable in those days."

The understatement of the decade. Jules had been justifiably horrified when she'd told him about it. But she'd convinced him she needed a place to live while attending George Mason University across the river, and she didn't have the means to pay rent. Despite the bars on all the windows, free was as good as it got. Of course, she'd had to agree to the bank's stipulation that she improve the property within a certain amount of time. Which was fine. She'd been going for a degree in structural engineering, so the rehab had given her lots of practical application and fodder for several term papers. Now the place was worth more than a quarter million and situated in the middle of a trendy, gentrified area that catered to midlevel government workers.

She'd actually been thinking of moving.

"Not a bad deal," Rio said, as they drove by more newly renovated brick town houses.

"Yeah," she said noncommittally. Jules shot her a "be nice" frown and she resisted the urge to stick out her tongue at him. "So, where do you live, Special Agent Rio?" she asked in her nicest tone of voice, pretending to be interested.

"On the river."

"The Watergate?" She could see him there, in some hoity-toity condo.

He gave her a lopsided smirk. "No, I mean literally. I have an old tugboat tied up by the fishing wharves."

She just stared.

"Slip fees are cheaper than rent in D.C." He shrugged. "And I like boats."

"You live on a tugboat."

"Yep."

"All year? Doesn't it get cold in the winter?"

"I have a heater. Electricity and running water, too."

She shook her head in amazement. "I've never met anyone who lived on a boat before."

"I've never met anyone who bought their house for a buck before."

Jules chuckled. "There now, see? You two will have loads to talk about. In the meantime, we'd better go over these interviews with Rafe Gerard and Gun Sundstrom. Agent Macon?"

Macon passed the suspects' Dept. of Homeland Security jackets over the seat. Sass dutifully read through Sundstrom's file while Rio leafed through Gerard's.

There were several grainy prints taken from their videotaped interview. Sass didn't resemble Gun all that much. About the same size, but Gun had short, dyed-black hair, while Sass's was long and blond. Gun's face was cold and hard, except when she looked at Rafe—then her mouth softened and her eyes went all puppy dog. A woman in love.

Shifting nervously, Sass glanced at Rio. His jaw was tight as he studied a photo from his file—Rafe and Gun kissing goodbye as they were ripped from each other's arms by the arresting Customs agents. If they weren't terrorist mercenaries Sass might have felt sorry for the lovers.

Which brought her back to reality with a jolt.

Lovers…Kissing…Which meant—

Damn. Would she have to…?

The thought of kissing Stewart Rio was more unsettling than stealing back the nuclear triggering device right from under Dawson's nose, or even getting caught doing it.

"I take it Dawson has never met these two?" she asked Macon, crossing her legs to escape Rio's warm thigh against hers.

"No, but you can be sure he's investigated them and knows all about their relationship," Macon replied, as though reading her mind. "Luckily there don't seem to be any pictures of them at any of the usual sources. We're hoping Dawson didn't find any, either."

Rio didn't comment, but continued to peruse the file in his lap. "I guess we'll find out soon enough if he did."

Sass noticed that the muscle in his cheek was twitching again, and found comfort. He wasn't liking this any better than she was. Surely they could come to some kind of understanding about the kissing thing. She'd be much happier skipping that whole part, thanks very much. And definitely anything more than that. Judging by his reaction to the photo, he would, too.

She leaned back in the seat and closed her eyes, willing herself to be calm.

"What about her hair?" Rio asked.

"Touch the hair and I bail now," she muttered.

"But—"

"Forget it. I don't do Goth."

"That's not a problem," Macon interjected. "Gun Sundahl changes hair color like she changes outfits. There's also quite a collection of wigs on the sailboat."

Sass lifted an eyelid. "Disguises?"

"Maybe."

"Do we know what else these two do besides act as intermediaries for terrorists at weapons auctions? I'd like to know how a woman ended up working for an Arab outfit," she said.

"We're looking into it all and will give you a full report tonight, before you get to Dawson's mansion tomorrow."

"How, exactly, is this all going down?" Rio asked.

Macon passed them each a memo and a map. "Here's the working plan. You'll fly into Jacksonville where Gerard and Sundstrom's sailboat, called the *Mermaid*, is being held for you. From there it's just a few hours' sail to the private island off the Carolina coast where Dawson is staying. But you're not expected there until tomorrow morning. That should give you enough time to acquaint yourselves with each other and your cover, and us enough time to fill in any blanks on Gerard and Sundstrom, and get you the dummy device."

"How will we get this stuff?"

"Head for Seven Moon Island, located several miles south of Dawson's place. It's marked on the map. Tie up at the Seven Moon Island Charters dock. I'll arrive there later with the update and last-minute instructions. By the way, the owners are civilians. They know nothing of the operation."

"So essentially," Sass asked wanting confirmation, "my part of the assignment is to locate and steal back the trigger before the auction, right?"

"Not steal," Jules corrected. "Exchange. We'll be supplying you with an identical dummy device which we want you to substitute for the real one."

"How do you know it's identical?"

"The DOD subcontractor the technology was stolen from is supplying it. Everything will be exactly the same as the real equipment, except for one critical connection, rendering it useless. Plus, a homing device will be embedded in the built-in software."

"Which will lead you to the purchaser," Rio said.

"Correct. And we can eliminate another nest of terrorists plotting against our country."

"And my job will be looking for anything incriminating on Dawson, so we can arrest him," Rio verified.

"Preferably hard physical evidence linking him to his crimes. But be sure to leave everything in place. We can get a search warrant based on your say-so, but we want all evidence to be seized legally and in the presence of a federal prosecutor. Dawson isn't going to slip between our fingers this time on a technicality."

Rio raked a hand through his hair and looked grim. "Got it."

Apparently he'd been down this path before. She'd have to ask him about his investigation. Three years was a long time not to catch a man everyone in the world seemed to know was a major bad guy.

They arrived at a small government airport and grabbed their gear from the trunk. Rio had considerably more luggage than she did; he must not be the same size as Rafe Gerard.

"You'll be hitching a ride on a Customs plane," Macon informed them on the way to the hangar. "They'll take you to Jacksonville."

After introducing them to the Customs Chief, who in turn introduced them to their pilot, Macon said, "Oh! One more thing." With that he handed each of them a small item.

She looked at her palm and felt the blood drain from her face. A wedding band! Panic nearly got the better of her—until she saw the look on Rio's face. He looked like he was about to choke.

"See you tomorrow night," Macon said.

Jules gave her a hug. "Good luck. Watch your back, eh?"

With a wave, they both departed.

Crap. No turning back now.

Rio was watching her consideringly. "Your SAC always hug his agents before sending them on their missions?"

"Shut up, Rio," she said. "We go way back. He's a friend, okay?"

He held up a hand. She noted he was already wearing his ring. "Just checking if my wife is cheating on me already, that's all."

She ground her teeth and slid hers on, too. It was a perfect fit. "Well," she said conversationally, as they followed the pilot onto the tarmac and clambered into the waiting plane. "I don't s'pose they serve drinks on this thing?"

The pilot grinned over his shoulder. "Sorry. Only peanuts."

"Figures," she mumbled. The one time she could really use a shot. Make that two. Anything to kill the herd of butterflies flying stunt tricks round and round her stomach. All because of the man buckling in next to her.

Her husband. Lord.

Hell, she hadn't been this nervous since her first job interview after college. At least until she'd shown the silver-haired architect her shiny new engineering degree and he'd just laughed and called in the next applicant. After that, she'd just been plain angry.

Maybe she could go for anger now, too.

She tried to come up with a reason. Unfortunately, there was nothing she could think of to be angry about.

Switching the trigger was a good plan, and she was the best person to pull it off.

The only thing she was unhappy about was being sent on this assignment with Stewart Rio. Sure, Rio's extensive knowledge of Dawson would be valuable. But he had pegged her exactly right in his research. She always worked alone on a laydown. She preferred it that way. She didn't like the complications a partner presented.

Never mind pretending to be that partner's *wife*.

Her eyes slid down to the golden band on her finger. Exactly how cozy were they expected to get?

Never mind. She was a professional. She could deal with it. She simply had to make her position clear to him. They might have to pretend to be married and in love, but that's all it was—make-believe.

Just because they felt a little chemistry with each other didn't mean they had to act on it.

She glanced at him and found him looking at her with a

steady gaze. His blue eyes had darkened to the color of winter storm clouds and his perfect lips were poised in that same searching, calculating line as last night—when he was exploring her body with his hand.

She squelched the urge to grab the nearest parachute and leap from the plane.

No. The man was *not* going to unnerve her.

She was in control.

She just had to get things straight between them.

Soon.

Very soon.

Before those tempting lips had a chance to say something…or do something…to change her mind.

Chapter 4

Okay, this was not going well.

Rio was a seasoned sailor and could probably handle the *Mermaid* all by himself the way it was rigged, but the DHS files had stated both Rafe and Gun knew their way around a sailboat. Sass had never even set foot on a rowboat before today, much less a boat like this. He wanted to teach her the basics on the trip to Carolina, just in case.

But it wasn't easy when every time he touched her she jumped a foot in the air and looked like a deer in headlights. And sailing was practically a contact sport, at least to learn.

"Listen," he said, taking the line that dangled from her fingers as she hopelessly tangled it in an attempt to coil it onto the deck. She jolted when their hands brushed.

He clamped his jaw and started again. "Listen. This is not working. You have to relax. I don't know what you think I'm going to do to you, but whatever it is, you've got it all wrong."

She had the grace to look embarrassed. "I have no idea what you're talking about."

Yeah, right. "Get over it, will you? Touching your body was not such an orgasmic experience that I'm interested in endangering this operation in order to repeat it," he said gruffly, cutting to the chase.

Actually, that was a lie. His palms had been itching all day with the memory of her soft curves. She was a thief, he'd reminded himself repeatedly, and a colleague, but it hadn't helped. He was still attracted to her.

But she didn't need to know that.

Her face turned scarlet for a brief moment, then her spine straightened. "Good. Because you won't."

"All right."

"All right." She looked down at the mess at her feet and kicked it. "And as for this sailing stuff, I'll find a way to get out of it if it comes up with Dawson. I'm just not cut out to be a sailor."

Truer words were never spoken. "Fine," he agreed. Hell, at least she wasn't seasick. "I'll just start the engines and we'll go under power instead." A shame, really. The *Mermaid* was probably a dream under full sail. But at this point he'd do anything to get her out of his hair.

"Thank God," she muttered, and tromped away down the deck.

As soon as she was gone, Rio's smile returned. Securing the boom he made for the cockpit, forgetting all about his irritation.

The sailboat was a real beauty. All wood and titanium and sleek lines and so yare she almost gave him a hard-on. With every bell and whistle imaginable, the *Mermaid* had to be worth a fortune. More than he'd ever see in a lifetime.

Not that he had ambitions to own anything this fast and fancy. The fancier the boat, the more the upkeep, and the more worry about every little ding and scrape. Give him an old, ugly but reliable vessel any day. He didn't need speed or flash.

No, his life's dream only involved a used fishing boat and a peaceful island off the Southern coast, nothing more elaborate. And he planned to retire just as soon as the Dawson file was closed and he'd solved the mystery of his father's last case. The fact that the day was suddenly looming much sooner than anticipated lifted his spirits immeasurably.

He liked his job, and he was good at it. But it had never been his dream to work for the Bureau. That had been his dad's wish—that the son would follow in the father's footsteps. Dad had been a hero, a special agent superstar, who loved the edge-of-your-seat danger of working undercover. Danger that, in the end, had proven deadly.

The danger didn't scare Rio, but he didn't crave it, either. Not like his father. Rio was more of a kick-back than a kick-ass kind of guy. And he was sick of always seeing the potential for evil in everything.

Nearing forty, what he wanted was to start smelling the roses. And the salt air. And the aromatic scent of wood shavings as he routed pickets for the fence around his own beach-side cottage. Even the sweet perfume of a soft, pretty woman to share his bed, permanently.

"Ow! Damn it!" Sass's curses came piercing through the soft sea breeze and he sighed.

One thing was for damn sure, the woman he picked would be *nothing* like Kansas Hawthorne.

"What's wrong?" he called patiently from where he was adjusting the satellite navigation instruments on the panel, one of the cooler features of the vessel.

"Not used to stuff sticking up from the floor," she grumbled. "I stubbed my toe."

"Deck," he corrected. He finished his fine-tuning and flipped on the autopilot, heading north. Even aside from the thief thing, Sass Hawthorne was way too high maintenance. Too sharp edged, career oriented and mouthy.

"I'm bleeding," she announced with a mixture of annoyance and incredulity. "This is ridiculous. I never get hurt on jobs!"

With a last visual check of the horizon, he sauntered toward her, swiping up his duffel bag as he went. Still, the woman was a sweet drink of water to look at. "Come on. There must be a first aid kit below deck. We should check it out down there anyway."

They hadn't had an opportunity in Jacksonville to take the whole tour of the boat because they were rushed to get underway, nor since, because of Sass's sailing lessons.

After wrapping her toe in a tissue from her overnight bag, she followed him down the half ladder into the cabin. "Wow," she said, echoing his own reaction.

"I'll say."

There were two rooms below, a galley-salon combo midships, and a separate stateroom in the forward area. The galley was tiny, but still looked as if it could be in a restaurant, with stainless steel appliances, real china and sparkling crystal goblets firmly secured in the glass-fronted cupboards.

But it was the salon that caught his breath. Though very narrow because of the shape of the boat, its appointments were luxurious. Dim lights, a plush Oriental carpet, buttery soft leather cushions covering the sprawling banquette and matching easy chair gathered around a low mahogany table. There were fur throws on the banquette—real fur—and a compact but extensive TV and stereo system graced narrow mahogany bookshelves lining the bulkhead.

The place oozed of lazy, sinful pursuits.

He couldn't wait to see the bedroom.

"I'm not finding a medical kit," Sass said, poking around in the galley. "Oh, well. It's only a stubbed toe. I'll just wash off the blood." With that, she hoisted herself onto the counter and turned on the water.

Rio sauntered over and inspected her toe. "You'll live. Here. I found some antiseptic." He lifted her foot into the sink where he stuck it under the water.

"Hey, what's your deal? I really don't appreciate you manhandling me and—"

"I'm taking care of you," he corrected, spraying the wound with antiseptic. "As the agent in charge of this mission, that's my duty."

Her mouth opened again, but he cut her off. "And I'm also supposed to be your husband. That's the kind of thing a husband does for his wife." At least he assumed it was. His mom had died when he was little, so he really didn't remember much of her interaction with his dad. But he'd seen reruns of *Happy Days*. "We have to pull this ruse off. So get used to the idea."

Sass was staring at him with an alarmed expression. He realized he had straightened and was now leaning into her, toe forgotten, standing between her knees with his hands anchored on the cupboards on either side of her shoulders. It was an aggressive stance.

A sexual stance.

And just like that he was back on the dewy grass in the dark, lying on top of her, sliding his fingers inside her catsuit, feeling her silken flesh quiver with his touch. Wishing she'd wrap those long legs around his waist…

She was back there, too.

He could see it in her eyes.

He took a big step back. He was not ready for this potent attraction springing to life between them. He'd spent his entire adult life devising ways to catch thieves and put them behind bars. He wasn't about to fall for one himself, even if she was an FBI agent. Hell, *because* she was an FBI agent. She was off-limits on all levels.

"Sorry," he said. "I didn't mean to get in your face."

She swallowed, then shook her head. "No. You're right. If this is going to work, I need to get used to you being close to me."

"Am I that bad?" he asked, knowing he sounded defensive. He wasn't used to women running away from him.

She blinked, her cheeks coloring. "That's not what I meant. It's just—"

He waved off her explanation. "Whatever." Her opinion of his appeal didn't matter, he told himself. "Anyway, we're not at Dawson's place yet."

"Still, it's best to be prepared. That's no doubt what Jules and Sydney had in mind by sending us on this little cruise first."

He shifted, uncomfortably aware of the ring on his finger. "No doubt." He'd have a thing or two—or five or six—to say to Sydney next time he saw him.

"But we need to get something straight," she said.

"What's that?"

She regarded him soberly. "Whatever we have to do on this mission, we can't take it personally. It's just business. Part of our cover."

Surprised at her candor, he allowed her a wry grin. "You mean if you have to kiss me, or something awful like that?"

"Yeah," she said, quickly turning away. "Something awful like that."

His smile widened. Had she blushed? Doubtful. He must be imagining things. That would have made her seem almost—

Like something she wasn't, he reminded himself pointedly, and turned to fetch his duffel. He really needed some distance. Quick.

Striding to the stateroom, he said, "I'll just stow my gear," but halted at the threshold. He was practically blinded.

"Jeez, Louise."

She came up behind him and he heard her gasp softly. Everything in the microscopic stateroom was in shades of red, from bright fire-engine red to dark cranberry to transparent cherry cotton candy. Not that there was a whole lot of stuff in there. In fact, aside from the mirrored built-in closet taking up one side of the bulkhead, there was only one single piece of furniture.

"Oh, God," she murmured.

He should have known. But because his tugboat was so spacious, he'd never even considered the obvious downside to a sailing vessel.

"There's only one bed."

Sass tried to act like a worldly adult. The professional she was. Somehow she managed to get herself together, despite Rio's disturbing presence shoulder to shoulder with her.

"I'll sleep in the salon," he said evenly.

"No," she quickly countered, surprising both of them. Most of all herself. "That won't be necessary."

She was twenty-nine years old, hadn't been a virgin for quite some time, and though she had no intention of having sex with Stewart Rio, she was far from being a prude. Her body's uncharacteristic reaction to him was throwing her for a loop, but she could handle it. She'd just been single for too long.

He glanced at her sharply, assessingly.

"Surely, you've shared a bed with a woman before and not had sex?" she said.

Rio looked at her as if she was from Mars.

Okay, so much for that.

"Well, then," she said as businesslike as she could muster. "I guess this'll be your first."

"Sass, I don't think—"

"We're supposed to be married. You don't think Dawson will give us separate rooms, do you?" When he just stared, she added, "Chances are there'll only be one bed. We're all adults here, right? Let's try to act like it."

With that, she got out of there, hurrying topside. She needed fresh air. Air that wasn't scented with Rio's musky, exotic aftershave.

Hell, *what had she done*?

The best thing for the mission, that's what. Her father had warned her about Dawson, that he was dangerous and unpredictable. And to have eluded law enforcement this long, he was obviously highly intelligent, too. If she and Rio were going to pull this thing off, they needed to act like a *real* husband and wife. And that meant not balking at physical closeness with each other. Sharing a bed might be one way to get over this weird chemistry zinging between them that had her acting like a silly teenager.

With any luck Rio snored and wore polka-dot pajamas. That would cure her real fast.

Dragging in a lungful of fresh-scented sea air, she felt immediately calmer. What was it about the salty, sultry breezes that was so soothing? The whole concept of the lazy, tropical South was completely foreign to her tough urban upbringing, but for some reason she felt almost at home in this environment. Strange.

Rio joined her on deck, and went about rechecking the gauges and tinkering with the various mysterious things that made up the sailboat. Studiously avoiding her.

He obviously knew his way around a boat. She'd be lucky to do as much as pick out the mast and sails. Show her a building and she could name every single part of it, from the footings to the cornices. But in this watery world she was at his mercy.

Considering that up until several hours ago, Rio had been her nemesis, the thought rankled.

She watched him work, reluctantly admiring his smooth efficiency…along with the breadth of his shoulders, the leanness of his hips, the rippling slab of muscles in his chest and abdomen. Nothing about the man before her resembled the distant, uptight, by-the-book professional she'd known from work. He had stripped to his cobalt blue swimming trunks and the sight made her slightly dizzy.

Actually, it was probably the sun getting too warm for her. So she moved under the canopy over the cockpit—the biminy, Rio had called it—and took the passenger seat, grabbing a bottle of water from the cooler.

"Any beer in there?" he asked, joining her, collapsing into the captain's chair. "Hard work, all this relaxing."

She smiled, struggling to keep her eyes off his sweat-damp body. "I think so."

She pulled an icy bottle out and opened it for him.

"Thanks." As he took a long pull, he eyed her modest khaki slacks and aqua T-shirt. "Aren't you hot?"

She decided against the obvious comeback. "I didn't bring a bathing suit." *Thank goodness.*

"I'll bet Gun has one. You should go through her clothes. Try on some things. To get comfortable in her skin."

He was right, of course. But a bathing suit was probably not her wisest first choice. Skin being the operative word there.

"Maybe."

Exposed skin. Like the tan, hair-sprinkled skin of his muscular legs and strong, corded arms that contrasted so nicely with his sunstreaked brown hair. He must work out regularly at the gym. And spend hours on his tugboat home with no shirt on and—

She leaped to her feet. *Damn*. "Yeah. Good idea. In fact, I think I'll go try on some things right now."

Scrambling down the ladder, she silently upbraided herself for her lack of backbone. It was just a male body, for crying out loud. Granted, it was a good one. A *very* good one. But she had to remember it belonged to her enemy. The irritating, arrogant Stewart Rio.

True, his edges seemed to have softened a bit under the influence of the wind and sails. And the way he looked at her made her think…

No. He wasn't interested in other agents. Ever. Even aside from his well-known reputation, he'd made it crystal clear twice now. It was just that instinctual, primitive, male-female thing happening again, brought out because of their coming masquerade as husband and wife.

And all that skin.

The way he was looking at her meant nothing. Those languid, half-lidded bedroom-eyes did not mean he was thinking about sex. With her, anyway.

And she'd better stop thinking about it herself, or she wouldn't get a wink of sleep tonight when they shared that all-too-cozy crimson bed. Better by far to concentrate on her wardrobe.

Opening the mirrored closet door, she took in the contents.

Everything in it looked tight and short and sexy. Along the top shelf was a row of round stands bearing wigs of all lengths and colors. Okay, that could be fun. It would be like playing a role on one of those kick-butt spy TV shows.

She picked out a short wig, red, and an even shorter black miniskirt and halter top. Take that, Stewart Rio. This should knock his socks off.

Grinning, she shed her boring slacks and T-shirt and donned her new persona. Gazing in the mirror, she was astounded at the change. Definitely a new look for her.

From her overnight bag she pulled out her makeup and darkened it, in keeping with her new image.

Actually, she kind of liked what she saw. The woman in the mirror was just the type who'd enjoy cracking safes and rappelling down thirty-story buildings. Hmm. Maybe she should seriously consider a permanent makeover.

"The name's Gun," she told her reflection in a throaty James Bond imitation. "Gun Sundstrom."

"You take yours shaken, or stirred?" came an amused male voice from the doorway.

She whirled. Rio was leaning negligently against the door frame, watching her with a crooked smile.

"How long have you been there?" she demanded.

"Not quite long enough," he said, taking in her new outfit with a lazy but thorough inspection.

"I could have sworn I closed that door."

"You might have," he admitted, his smile growing even more disreputable. "Probably a faulty catch." He stepped into the narrow space between the door and the bed.

Her heartbeat doubled.

"Rio…"

He regarded her for a long moment as her pulse raced, then

said, "Just came in to get a fresh shirt. We're almost to Seven Moon Island."

Relief whooshed through her. "I'll just change back—"

"No time. I need you on deck ASAP to help dock. Besides, I like what you're wearing. Though the wig'll take some getting used to." He snagged a polo shirt from his duffel. "Come on. Let's see if we can pull this thing off."

The island they approached was like nothing Sass had ever seen before. Hauntingly beautiful. Lush with every shade of green imaginable, the low-lying land was covered with a jungle of trees and shrubs, grasses and vines. But most surprising was the mix. There were tall swaying palms sitting among broad, stately oaks that trailed long beards of Spanish moss. Thick vines tangled with the underbrush, covered with a multitude of bright yellow blossoms that swayed and winked in the bright sunlight. She could smell the earthy scent of fecund soil and fragrant vegetation even from the deck of the *Mermaid*.

There was a rickety old dock jutting out into the water that looked like something out of one of those black-and-white gangster movies from the forties, where the bad guys came to a place like this to hide out. It also looked as if it would fall apart any minute.

"Are you sure we're in the right place?" she asked, glancing at Rio for the first time since she'd fled the stateroom.

He didn't answer but instead used his chin to point to an equally dilapidated shanty sitting on stilts where the dock met the land. There was an ancient, crooked sign that read Seven Moon Island Charters.

This was the right place. Jeez, these people could sure use a decorator. Or a structural engineer.

She looked back at Rio, then did a double take. The expression on the man's face was nothing less than awestruck.

"I love this place," he said as though hypnotized.

Her brows shot up. "You've got to be kidding. The place is—"

He waved off her objections, easing the boat close to the jetty. "It needs a bit of work, I'll grant you. But look at it. It's perfect!"

She rolled her eyes. "Snap out of it, will you? You're scaring me."

The spell broke and he gave her an unrepentant grin as he passed her the end of a rope. "Hop onto the dock with this. I take it you don't see the considerable charm of the place?"

"What can I say? I'm a city girl through and through," she called flippantly as she made the easy leap to the wooden surface, praying it wouldn't disintegrate when she landed. The inlet looked clean and fairly clear, but she didn't feel like swimming. She'd heard there were alligators in South Carolina.

"Tie the line to the cleat," he directed.

She stared first at the big metal thingy on the dock, then at the rope—er, line—in her hands, but before she could decide how the heck to join the two, a female voice next to her said, "I can do that for you. Y'all must be the Gerard party. The *Mermaid*, right? We have your reservation."

The young woman wasn't at all who Sass expected to be running a boat charter company. She looked more like a skinny kid than a woman. Her blond hair was in two pigtails sticking out from a backward baseball cap; she wore denim overalls that were three sizes too large and covered in oil stains, along with a turquoise T-shirt, equally stained. No makeup, but her face was cute, her perky nose and rosy cheeks covered with a dusting of freckles.

She stuck out her hand to Sass. "I'm Jenna. The grease monkey around here."

Sass smiled. "I think I could tell. I'm...Gun Sundstrom." She did a mental grimace because she'd almost used her real name. *Nothing like blowing it in the first thirty seconds, Kansas.* "This is Rafe." She smiled as he joined them. "Darling, this is Jenna."

He didn't even seem to notice the endearment, but slid his left arm around her waist as he shook Jenna's hand.

"Great place you've got here."

Jenna gave him a skeptical glance, then shrugged. "Wanna buy it? It's for sale."

At least, that's what Sass thought she said, but wasn't quite sure. She was too busy freaking out because Rio's hand was brushing slowly across the bare skin of her midriff.

"Yeah?" he said. "Why's that?"

A halter top with a low-slung mini had been a bad choice. Very bad.

He started caressing her with his fingers.

Omigod.

Omigod.

Sass only caught bits and pieces of Jenna's explanation as she struggled to remain unaffected by Rio's hands on her. *Stay professional.*

"...inheritance...best friends since grade school...great fun...unfortunately none of us had any business experience..."

Sass stood absolutely still with a smile frozen on her lips as Rio stepped behind her and put his other arm around her, too. And entirely missed his reply to Jenna. She didn't give a darn about their failing charter business. What she wanted to know was, why on earth did his arms around her feel so darn...good?

"Gun?" he asked. Both of them were staring at her expectantly.

Gun? Aw, hell, that was her!

"What? Um, sorry. I was, um—" She spotted another shanty, next door to the Seven Moon office, but this one had tables scattered around the wraparound porch deck. There were people sitting at them. And drinking. "—thirsty," she blurted out. "And hungry. Does that place serve food?" She pointed to it, extracting herself from Rio's embrace as Jenna nodded.

"Sure."

"You okay, baby?"

"Low blood sugar," she said, waving her hand around in a nervous gesture. Then smoothing it down her abdomen. "Sometimes I zone out." Trying to extinguish the flash points on her skin. From his touch.

She could tell by the smug curl that appeared on his lips he wasn't buying her excuse. He knew he'd flustered her.

Which was just enough to bring her back to reality.

She straightened.

"There's some quick paperwork to get you berthed and the electrical hooked up like you ordered," Jenna explained.

"No problem." Sass looped her arm through Rio's. "I'll keep."

The three of them walked up the pier to the office, where a second young woman was seated behind a scatter of ledgers piled on a massive counter which was carved from what looked like a single piece of driftwood. Rio ran his hand over it as though it were a piece of priceless artwork.

"Nice."

The woman behind it glanced up in surprise. "Oh! I didn't hear you come in!"

"Fighting those books again?" Jenna asked with sympathy in her voice.

"A losing battle, I assure you."

"Bobby Jo, the Gerards are here." She introduced them.

Bobby Jo was a quiet beauty, dark-haired with full lips and wide green eyes, at the moment, filled with frustration. Sass immediately liked her, too.

Probably because she didn't give Rio a second glance.

Not that *that* would matter.

Bobby Jo sighed and riffled through a cluttered box on the driftwood counter, finally pulling out a bad copy of a printed form, which she slid across to Rio. "Just fill this in and you're all set."

Sass wondered what she'd do with the form after it was filled in. Lose it, probably. There wasn't a file cabinet in sight, she noted, as she scoped out the exits and layout of the room, just in case.

"Maybe I could help," Rio said to Bobby Jo. "What part of those books are giving you trouble?"

Sass was so not interested in these people's books. But the shack was fascinating. From a structural point of view. However, she couldn't resist tormenting Rio, so she casually stepped behind him, turned and leaned her back against his as he stood at the counter writing and chatting with the ladies. His spine stiffened under hers, but his backside felt nice. Very nice. Firm and tight. Not too big, not too flat. Just right. Suddenly, his spine relaxed and his bottom wriggled against hers, almost imperceptibly.

For a moment she forgot her habitual visual reconnaissance of the structure—especially the strange exposed beams in the walls and ceiling. But only for a moment.

Then Jenna noticed the direction of her stalled gaze, and said, "The office was built of lumber salvaged from old shipwrecks," and Sass snapped back to the present. "The windows, too."

There were two windows, one on each side of the front door, both mullioned, the small rectangles inset with thick, wavy panes of glass.

"They're lovely," she said, remembering to lay on the Swedish accent she'd practiced on the sailboat. "I thought the beams looked big for this size place." They'd probably support two more floors and a built-in pool on the roof. What looked rickety from the outside was just the weathered shingles, artfully hammered on every which way. Very deceptive.

As she casually studied the building, she thought about Rio. He was very deceptive, as well. His exterior was stiff and aloof, but she was quickly realizing that that might be a false facade, too, hiding his real personality. This Rio didn't seem to be aloof at all. He seemed to like being close to her. Real close. In fact, he hadn't stopped touching her since they'd gotten off the boat.

Then again, they *were* supposed to be married. And despite the fact that there were only four people in the room, *anyone* could be watching.

He moved, turning to drape his arms over her shoulders from the back. "Ready?" he asked, his warm breath fanning over her ear.

And suddenly, she was scared to death.

Ready for what? she wanted to ask him. But she didn't dare.

She'd been worried because of her own unwanted attraction to Rio. Now she was worried because she feared he was just as attracted to her. Not good for the mission. And not good for her own well-being.

She swallowed. "I think I could use a drink."

She had to keep this crazy thing between them under control. Because if she didn't, Stewart Rio could prove just as dangerous to her as Miles Dawson.

Chapter 5

"Cute, but goofy," Rio pronounced about the owners of the Seven Moon Island Charters as he and Sass walked up the overgrown path to the casual eatery next door. "And apparently there's a third."

"Third what?"

"Owner. She's the boat captain. Out with a bunch of fishermen today."

"Oh."

Sass seemed a little preoccupied. Had been since they'd walked back to the *Mermaid* to secure her before strolling up to grab a bite to eat.

Rio had a feeling it might be because of the arm he'd slung around her shoulders and refused to remove. The sexy high heels she'd slipped on onboard put her at exactly the right height to fit snugly under his arm.

"Change your mind?" he asked.

"About what?"

"Getting close to me."

She stopped walking, forcing him to halt and face her. A warm breeze whispered over them, bringing with it the piquant smells of jessamine and frying seafood. He still didn't remove his arm. He simply put the other one around her, too.

She sucked in a breath. "I just wish I knew what that involves. Precisely."

"Does it matter?"

"Of course it matters!"

He wondered. "Last night you were willing to give me anything I wanted, to win the competition."

Her jaw dropped. "Rio, that was never going to happen and we both knew it."

"Did we?" He moved in a little closer. "What if I'd accepted your proposition?"

She backed away. "Don't be ridiculous. You'd die before taking a bribe or losing on purpose."

Whoa. She had him pegged to a convenient T.

He frowned. Why was that so annoying? Why did it suddenly bug him that the point spread in any given FBI office pool would be a million-to-none that he'd always choose honor and professionalism over a night of limitless sin with a beautiful woman? Was he that square? Uptight? Unimaginative and predictable?

Maybe it was time to change his image.

Sass might be the opposite of his type of woman, but she was still attractive as hell. An undercover fling wouldn't be so bad. In fact, it might be downright pleasurable, if she could be convinced….

He spread his hand over her bottom and pressed her body into contact with his. Her eyes popped.

It was fun seeing the ice princess so unsettled.

"Maybe. I wouldn't normally take a bribe," he said. "But we're not in that situation now, are we? We're on an op. And us getting close will only help our cover."

Color crept up her neck. She swallowed. "Who are you, and what have you done with Stewart Rio?"

"Rio's long gone, baby. The minute we left Jacksonville I became Rafe Gerard. The question is, who are you? Kansas or Gunilla?" *Thief or seductress*?

She tried to step back again, but he wouldn't let her.

"I'm *pretending* to be your wife, Rio. I didn't sign up to play the part in real life."

He couldn't read the look in her eyes, so he pulled her into a full-body embrace, holding her tight, lowering his mouth to her ear. The scent of her spun through his senses, pushing out everything else. Making him dizzy with the possibilities.

"How bad do you want to win, Sass?" he whispered.

In answer, a tiny tremor shivered through her body. Her throat made a quiet mewling sound. "I—"

"Mr. Gerard and Ms. Sundstrom?"

The businesslike voice of Cory Macon sent Sass jumping out of Rio's embrace like a guilty teenage girl caught with a college boy. Damn. He'd forgotten Macon was coming tonight with the updates on Gun and Rafe.

Rio stifled a silent curse and turned to their Homeland Security handler. "Hey, man. What's up?"

"I've got that engine part you ordered." Macon jerked his thumb back toward the *Mermaid*, next to which a ratty cardboard box sat on the dock. "Wanna check it out? I also brought dinner." He hefted a large paper bag in his hand and grinned. "Fried shrimp and oysters, side of grits and a six-pack."

"Grits?"

The agent shrugged unrepentantly. "When in Rome and all…"

Rio had no choice but to go along, but not before he'd given Sass a piercing we're-not-done-with-this-conversation look.

"Hope you brought plenty. We're both starved," he said, banking his frustration for later. When they were alone again.

After they'd all arranged themselves around the sleek, low coffee table in the salon of the *Mermaid*, Macon pulled out a short stack of files, papers and photographs. "This is everything we've dug up on Gerard and Sundstrom. There's some deep background—" he slid a couple of manila folders to each of them "—the relevant data we retrieved from their computer hard drive, and a few other tidbits, including their online shopping habits, gleaned from a couple of spyware companies who've been cooperating with us. Very interesting reading."

Rio popped a fried oyster into his mouth, took a sip of beer and flipped open the background file on Rafe. And nearly spewed. "What the *hell?* Gerard's an *Interpol agent?*"

Sass's jaw dropped as far as his. "Are you kidding?"

Macon calmly dished a scoop of buttery grits onto his plate. "That's an affirmative. As soon as he was separated from Gun he started throwing his Interpol credentials around to anyone who'd listen. We checked it out with their headquarters. He is an undercover investigator, but he's *not* working a case against Dawson. This whole trip seems to be extracurricular."

"Is there any chance this is a legit op for him?"

"According to our information it's unlikely, but still remotely possible. We didn't want to dig too deep, in case we tripped some kind of diplomatic switch. For now nobody knows we've got him on ice, and we want to keep it that way until Dawson is behind bars and we know one way or the other if Gerard is actually dirty."

"You find out any more about his personal background?"

Macon shook his head. "Still a total enigma. No one knows anything they're willing to admit. And still no pictures of either of them have surfaced. Rafe claims to be American, but there's no record of his existence here. He appeared out of nowhere in Europe fourteen years ago. Which can work to your advantage. His mystique should help you avoid answering any questions, once Dawson's accepted you're for real."

"You'll be substituting my vitals for Rafe's on all the appropriate databases, so Dawson can establish my identity without question?"

"Already done. Including photos. For Sass, as well."

"So, what about Gun?" Sass asked. "Is she some kind of an agent, too?"

Macon shook his head. "No way. She's one shady lady. Graduated from the red-light district of Gothenburg, Sweden, where she was first arrested at age fifteen, to high-priced call girl in Amsterdam, where she was busted for fleecing a member of parliament during a 'date' at age nineteen, to being a suspected drug mule for a Pakistani drug cartel in her midtwenties. Which, by the way, is how she got involved with the Arabs. The drug cartel and the Arabs apparently had some business together that she helped facilitate."

Sass glanced over the file in her hands. "After which, it looks like she slept her way to some pretty impressive contacts in several Middle-Eastern governments. Did Rafe ever work over there?"

"Not in country. But he's had dealings with the London Middle-Eastern community in several of his drug investigations. That's where he and Gun met, according to both their confessions. Details are in the file."

Rio whistled, feeling slightly sick to his stomach. "Why

the hell would an Interpol agent marry a woman with that kind of background?"

Sass snorted. "Must be love."

"And now the poor sucker's working for the enemy. The man's an idiot, letting a woman ruin him like that."

Sass scowled but didn't reply.

"How's your Swedish accent coming along?" Macon asked her after shooting him a warning look.

"Still working on it. The taped interviews and conversations with Rafe are a big help."

"Pick up any useful vocabulary?"

She rolled her eyes. "She calls Rafe *älskling*. Darling. How cute is that. But a lot of the other words she uses aren't in the dictionary…."

Ells-cling, huh? He'd have to remember that one, Rio thought.

There was a knock at the hatch, and Macon went to answer it. Jules Mannheim followed him back down the ladder carrying a small metal briefcase. "See you both made it here in one piece. How'd the sailing lessons go?"

"Think I'll stick to dry land," Sass said.

Mannheim chuckled as he gave her a kiss on the forehead. "That bad, eh?"

"Worse."

Rio had to stifle the urge to call him on the blatant familiarity. He didn't care if Mannheim was her mentor and surrogate uncle, he didn't like Sass's SAC kissing her.

Or any man, for that matter. *He* was her husband.

Damn.

Get a grip, Rio.

This was just a job. Sass wasn't his.

He didn't *want* her to be his, not in any way but one. And

it wasn't jealousy he was feeling. It was just the adrenaline that had started flowing, as it always did at the beginning of a mission, making him react strangely. Maybe it was a good thing. It meant he was really getting into the role.

"Is that the dummy triggering device?" Sass asked, indicating the briefcase Mannheim placed on the coffee table.

"Yep. The briefcase is identical to the one it was in when stolen. We even rekeyed it so the lock is the same." He handed her a small silver key. "Maybe Dawson hasn't moved it to another container and this key will fit, making your job significantly easier."

"Hope springs eternal," she murmured, focusing her full attention on the case, spinning it slowly on the table to view it from all sides.

Rio observed her at work, evaluating her as she evaluated the difficulty of her assignment. He liked what he saw. She was all business, their personal baggage forgotten in the face of her task.

Which was a lot more than he could say for himself.

"Anyway, practice on the briefcase but jettison it before you arrive at Dawson's place. Rio will smuggle the trigger in using this." He produced a high-tech-looking man's shaver. "It goes like this." Flicking the switch to *on,* he twisted and pulled, revealing a space into which he inserted the device. It fit perfectly, like a Chinese puzzle, seamlessly matching the mechanism of the shaver. He held it out to Rio.

He took it and examined it closely. "Impressive. Can I use the shaver?"

Mannheim gave him a withering glare. "Take care of it. That thing's worth more than your life."

He didn't doubt it.

Mannheim then dug in his pocket and brought out what

looked like a pair of sunglasses. "Brought you a fun toy." He handed it to Sass.

"Shades?" She looked up and smiled wryly. "Gee, thanks, boss."

"Those are no ordinary sunglasses," he said. "Put them on and slide the logo on the sidepiece forward."

She did so, and under the lenses her eyes widened. "What just happened? Everything looks funny."

Mannheim produced a penlike object from inside his jacket, aimed it at a bulkhead and clicked it on. Rio expected the red beam of a laser pointer.

Rio saw nothing, but Sass did.

"Wow." She slid the logo back and forth a couple of times. "For detecting invisible motion detector laser matrices. These are way better than my clunky goggles. Awesome!"

"Right in one."

She passed the glasses to Rio to try.

"Cool," he said, peering through them at the invisible beam. "Beats the hell out of the old spray can method, too."

He handed the glasses back to her and she examined them closer. "I'll say. Where did you get them?"

"On the Internet. One of those spy tech places."

Rio leaned back on the sumptuous sofa and drained his beer. Sad state of affairs when the nation's intelligence agencies were buying their equipment from garage-entrepreneur computer geeks—probably still in high school. He made a mental note to find and hire the kid, if Mannheim hadn't already snapped him up. He could use a gadgets man on the team.

"Here are a few other things we thought you could use, Sass." Mannheim produced a small nylon zipper bag. "Just the usual stuff, camouflaged as personal items. Your wire pulley, belay system, climbing gear and even—" he pulled out the last item with a flourish "—the bore scope you've been wanting for your safecracking."

"All right!" She laughed affectionately. "Sheesh, Jules. I'm going to have to start calling you Q."

As Sass looked over her new goodies, Rio got back to his part of the mission. "What did you find on their hard drive?" he asked. "Anything we should know about?"

"There was what we think is an encrypted list of Gerard's contacts," Macon said. "We have one of our agents from NSA working on it. Shouldn't be too hard to break. I doubt if it'll be relevant to your mission, but I'll let you know at the first rendezvous if we find anything interesting."

"Rendezvous?"

"A fishing boat will take up anchor at these coordinates at midnight every night of your mission and stay for three hours." Macon handed him a slip of paper with a set of numbers written on it, which Rio quickly memorized then ripped into tiny shreds.

"That's about a mile east-southeast of Dawson's island," Macon continued. "A one-man inflatable is hidden in the belly of the *Mermaid*'s dingy, with a silent-running motor. Use it to get to us if you need anything. First night is mandatory."

Rio nodded. He'd already noticed the black inflatable during his inspection, along with two wet suits and diving tanks in the hold, and an assortment of weapons and a two-way radio.

"Don't use the radio or your cell phone except as a last resort," Macon warned. "Dawson has extensive electronic countermeasures in place and will detect the slightest outgoing signal. All the rooms in the mansion are also no doubt bugged. The guy is as paranoid as they come, and a certifiable sociopath. He won't hesitate to kill over the slightest suspicion."

This wasn't news to Rio, but it was always good to be reminded. And Sass definitely needed to hear it. She was a loose
cannon, and he didn't want her taking any foolish chances on
this job. They'd need luck to succeed, but at the very least he
wanted them both to come out of this mission alive.

"Dawson will undoubtedly search your luggage when you
get there, and the boat while you're away from it. And it will
probably end up bugged, too."

Rio nodded. "Yeah."

When Macon and Mannheim climbed the ladder to leave,
Sass was still playing with her new toys. Rio walked the
agents topside and saw them off.

"Take care of her, Rio," Mannheim admonished him tightly.

"I will."

"She's going to want to show you up. Don't let her do anything stupid."

He grimaced. "I'll keep her in line."

Mannheim's eyes narrowed. "And I don't need to say—"

"Then don't say it. I'm not interested in being lectured
about a woman I told you from the beginning I didn't want
along on this mission. I'll do my best to keep her alive. That's
all I can promise."

Mannheim didn't like his ultimatum but there was diddly
he could do about it, short of pulling Rio from the job.

Too bad he didn't pull Rio. Or better yet, Sass. Rio needed
all his faculties and concentration to succeed in this op, and
Sass was proving to be a major distraction. Jeez, he'd actually been contemplating seducing her! What the hell was he
thinking?

"Tomorrow's going to be a long day. We'd better get some
sleep," he said stiffly when he was again below decks. "You
go ahead and get ready. I'll clean up here."

She blinked. "That's okay. I'll do it," she returned, jumping up to gather the messy remnants of dinner.

He shrugged. "Whatever."

It wasn't until after he'd showered and brushed his teeth that it hit him he hadn't brought any pajamas. He didn't *own* any pajamas. He always slept in the buff.

Damn.

He was standing in the head doorway with a towel around his waist when Sass walked into the bedroom and halted with a small gasp.

"Sorry! I thought— That is— Is there a problem?"

"I don't suppose you ran into any men's pajamas while you were looking through the dresser?"

Sass shot him an annoyed glance. "Don't tell me, you just *happened* to forget to bring something to sleep in. Why am I not surprised?"

He pressed his mouth into a thin line and marched to his duffel, where he extracted a clean pair of boxer briefs. He winced as she quirked her brow at him.

"Special Agent Hawthorne, I want you to know you have nothing to fear from me," he assured her. "I apologize for my presumptuousness earlier tonight. I was totally out of line and it won't happen again. This job is dangerous enough without personal complications being thrown into the mix."

She looked more annoyed than afraid.

"Get over yourself," she muttered. Grabbing her overnight bag, she hurried into the head.

Brat! Still, this felt much safer than what she'd made him feel earlier. *This* Sass he could deal with.

Letting out a measured breath, he swiftly donned the briefs and slid between the red satin sheets of the far-too-small bed. As he stared fixedly at the ceiling, willing his heart to stop hammering, his consciousness slowly filled with the sound of the shower running, the telltale fragrance of flowery soap and the persistent image of Sass's nude body not ten feet away.

Sweet Jesus give me strength. Brat or no, she was one tempting woman.

This mission was going to be one pure living hell. If the next few days with Dawson didn't end up killing him, he was absolutely sure the nights with Kansas Hawthorne would.

You have to be strong, Sass told herself.

Strong and cool and professional. Getting into a bed that reeked of seduction with a nearly naked man was no big deal. Because it wasn't real. He wasn't her boyfriend, or her potential boyfriend, or even a one-night stand. The man in the bed was *Stewart Rio*, for crying out loud. Stodgy, straight-arrow, by-the-book Rio who never dated other agents.

The image comforted her. Somewhat. Or would have, if it weren't for the too-recent memory of his hard body pressing into hers, the scent of arousal swirling about them, and the sound of his gravelly whisper in her ear asking how badly she wanted to win.

Of course she wanted to win. Badly.

Very badly.

Badly enough to sleep with Stewart Rio?

Yes.

But just sleep.

Nothing more.

She didn't know what had caused his momentary lapse earlier, but he was over it, thank God. Because she didn't need the temptation. He was attractive, but not her cup of tea. Not in the least. And she could just imagine what he'd think of her family tree. The government's number-one thief catcher hanging around with a woman who stole for a living, whose dad was a convicted felon. Yeah, that was real likely.

She'd seen the disgust in his expression when he'd spoken of Rafe, the Interpol agent, marrying Gun, the fallen woman.

She closed her eyes, counted to ten, smoothed her hands down the front of her extra-large sleep shirt, flung open the door and strode into the bedroom.

To her surprise, all was quiet and still. The glow of her nightstand lamp was the only light, just bright enough to throw an exotic red halo over the bed and the man who occupied it.

He was asleep, the thick fringe of his lashes throwing spiky shadows onto his angled cheekbones.

She sent up a prayer of thanks and slipped into the bed, scooting as close to the edge and as far away from him as possible—which unfortunately wasn't far enough. She could still feel the heat radiating off his body. She didn't know what she would have done if he'd been awake. Wanting to talk. Or get even closer.

No.

He didn't want…closer.

And neither did she.

She had to keep reminding herself of that. And when they got to the mansion, she'd have to keep taking a long time getting ready for bed so he'd be out cold before she joined him. Otherwise she'd never be able to fall asleep. She'd stare at the ceiling the whole night, worried that she might accidentally touch him. Or worse, that he might change his mind and…well, tempt her into changing hers.

That would be a disaster. Because of all the men on the

planet, Stewart Rio would be the very worst man to give in to temptation with, for all the reasons she'd just mentally listed.

Slowly, she felt herself relax, enjoying the sensual feel of the cool silky sheets, the soothing, rhythmic rocking of the sailboat and the melodic lap of water against the wooden hull.

She'd just slipped into that peaceful twilight between consciousness and sleep when a deep rumble next to her murmured, "Night, baby."

Sass was not in a good mood when she rolled out of bed the next morning. She had not tossed and turned all night—but only because she'd made herself lie stiff and perfectly still, barely breathing, waiting until Rio fell asleep. Of course, who knew when—or if—that had happened. She *would* get stuck bunking with the one man on earth who didn't snore. Either that, or he'd been playing possum, too.

She was exhausted. Not a good way to start an op.

"Coffee?" he asked, carefully avoiding her eyes when she padded out from the cabin.

"Please," she answered, grateful, if vaguely surprised at his unexpected domesticity.

She inhaled one cup, then poured herself another from the nearly empty pot. She must not be the only caffeine junkie on the boat. This time she sipped more slowly, and noticed the brew was actually pretty tasty. Unusual for a man. Even one armed with a coffeemaker. "This is great. Who taught you to make coffee?"

He paused in his preparation of some kind of eggs, but still didn't look at her. "My dad. Lord pity the fool who spoke to him before he had his morning coffee."

The cobwebs started to clear a bit and she smiled. Clive's coffee stank. "I like him already. What kind of work does he do?"

"He's dead."

She cringed. "I'm sorry." If she'd been less groggy she would have remembered the rumors about his dad being an FBI agent killed in the line of duty. Hadn't Clive said his name was Spencer Rio?

"Don't be. He died a long time ago."

As if that made anything better. She still felt her mother's and sister's horrible deaths as though they'd happened yesterday, even after over twenty years had passed. "Still, it couldn't have been easy on you. How old were you when you lost him?"

She knew she'd made another mistake when he faced her, his gaze sharp as a poisoned dart. Would she never learn to keep her mouth shut?

"He was murdered when I was eighteen, sold out by the two-bit thief who was his informant," he gritted out. "I joined the Bureau so I could find his killer and even the score."

She shivered at the intensity of emotion reflected in his rigid expression and taut muscles. No wonder he hated thieves. "Did you? Find the killer?"

"No."

"What about the informant?"

He turned away again. "No. He disappeared."

She blew on her coffee, absorbing this new dimension to Stewart Rio, which she suspected not many people saw. Now she understood why he was so dedicated to his job. That kind of motivation was an immensely powerful thing.

Sort of like her own. She wagered she had even more hidden motivations than Rio. Ones that steered her life just as surely, but in a different way. And ultimately were the reason she would never settle down. Could never settle down. For fear terrible things would keep happening to those she loved.

Her irrational need for a "normal life," had ended up taking away all those dearest to her... From the time she was born her family had always led a gypsy life—always moving, never staying in one city for more than a year or two. Until her wishes came true and her dad actually bought a house for them. Then—

"My mother and big sister were blown up when I was twelve," she murmured before she realized she'd opened her mouth. Horrified at her unintended confession, she stared fixedly into her coffee cup as his head whipped around.

"Blown up?"

Double-damn. "It was a natural gas accident. We'd just moved into our new house—" the house she'd begged for "—and apparently there was a faulty line or something." She plunked her cup on the counter. "I don't know why I told you that. I'm not trying to one-up your pain. I'm really sorry."

And she was. She'd only wanted to mentally remind herself why getting involved with Rio was complete insanity. From any angle.

Deciding it was far too early for this kind of conversation, she turned to start back to the cabin. Picking out clothes to bring along to Dawson's sounded a lot safer than analyzing the depressing constraints on her love life.

"Food's ready," he said. "Stay and eat."

She eyed the iron skillet in his hand, filled with a fluffy concoction of eggs, cheese, diced vegetables and ham. Her stomach gave an unladylike growl. "Guess we're going to have that morning-after breakfast, after all."

He grunted with a curl to his lip. "Usually I feel a whole lot better the morning after."

She took a deep breath and regrouped. "Nervous about the mission?"

"Tired and cranky."

"Couldn't sleep, eh?"

He shot her a mordant look. "I noticed you didn't do much better."

She lifted her chin. "I slept fine."

"Yeah. Which is why your eyes have enough luggage for Paris and the buttons on your blouse are off by two."

She looked down. And huffed out a breath. "I knew that. I did it on purpose. It's the newest thing. In Paris."

One perfect brow arched, the first amusement she'd seen on his face that actually reached his eyes.

She gave up and let out a resigned chuckle. "Hell, Rio. We're in deep shit, aren't we?"

"Maybe your buddy Jules has a shovel we could borrow," he drawled, dishing up the eggs.

"Yeah, right after I kill him for setting me up. He had to have known this would be incredibly awkward."

"Baby, if anyone was set up, it was me. Sydney knows I'm determined to retire from the Bureau. Throwing you into my bed is no doubt a clever attempt to give me a reason for staying."

She choked on a green pepper, and stared at him, aghast. "That's ridiculous."

"I agree. Nothing could make me stay. Not even great sex."

Her face suddenly got all hot. "Rio—"

He held up a hand. "I know, I know. I think we're both in agreement about that."

"Which is…?" she asked cautiously.

"Physically attracted, but no interest in pursuing any kind of relationship."

Good. That was exactly how she felt. Uncannily so.

So why the sudden churning of disappointment in her stomach?

She ignored it. "Right. So, what are we going to do? Because this isn't working."

"The way I see it," he said, scraping up the last of his breakfast, "we have two choices. One—take sleeping pills."

She gave him a wry half smile. "That could work. And the other?"

He carefully set his fork and knife onto his empty plate. "Two—we go back in the bedroom, take off our clothes and get rid of the tension so we can both concentrate on our jobs."

Chapter 6

For a few seconds the idea was so tempting Sass actually considered accepting Rio's outrageous suggestion. His it's-just-sex pragmatism spoke to the side of her that had grown wary of emotional entanglements.

Then reality set in.

For all its appeal, it's-just-sex wasn't her style—especially with a professional colleague. No matter how hard she'd tried, she just hadn't been able to deal with the kind of slam-bam-thank-you-man encounters so common among her live-for-today colleagues in C-Ops. It made things too messy.

"I appreciate your honesty, Rio. I really do. But I think I'll pass on that."

He nodded, looking the slightest bit disappointed. "Sleeping pills it is, then."

She rose and headed forward to pack. "Thanks for breakfast. Leave the dishes. I'll do them in a minute."

By the time Sass had filled a suitcase, made the bed and cleared the kitchen, the *Mermaid* had cast off and they were cruising toward Dawson's island hideout.

The day was bright and sunny with seagulls dipping and soaring about the mast in cheerful abandon. Sass's stomach felt as if she'd swallowed one of the freewheeling birds.

This was stupid. She never got nervous before an op. Ever.

Then again, she'd never been on an op like this before. She'd always gone in alone, and was in and out of the targeted place well before the adrenaline had stopped pumping.

Rio came up behind her where she stood close to the prow, and to her shock looped his arms loosely around her waist, lacing his fingers over her abdomen. She jumped at the warm contact, her first instinct being to bolt.

"Relax," he murmured, resting his chin against her hair. "Great view, huh?"

She had no idea. She couldn't focus with his body pressing into hers. "I guess."

He was silent for a moment, and she could hear his calm, even breathing, feel the steady beat of his heart against her back. Was the man made of ice?

"You're trembling," he said quietly. "Premission jitters? Or me?"

Even though she felt like an idiot, denial was useless. She gave a weak chuckle. "All of the above."

He grunted softly. "Hit me with the top ten."

She might be a loner, but from her research she knew Rio's management style centered on team building and establishing trust between members. So she didn't balk too much at his probing. For the next few days their very lives would depend on each other; it was better he knew her concerns before going in. *All* of her concerns.

She tried to relax and calm the shakes. "I do extensive advance planning for all my missions. I haven't been able to do that this time. I have no maps, no floor plans for Dawson's mansion, no clue about security, I don't even know where the triggering device is located that I'm supposed to switch out. I've never been undercover. Never been to a terrorist auction, or even met a terrorist. I don't like the responsibility of having a partner. And to be honest, what's happening between us is scaring the crap out of me."

She felt his head bob. "I hear you loud and clear. Guess we'll both have to improvise a bit. On all fronts."

An understatement if ever she'd heard one. "You've put in a lot of work on this case, Rio. Three years' worth. I'm worried I'll blow it for you."

After a slight hesitation, he ventured softly, "And maybe get us killed in the process?"

The man had a preternatural way of cutting to the heart of things.

"Yeah. That, too." Big-time.

His arms tightened around her, but instead of making her panic, the gesture felt somehow reassuring. She allowed herself to lean against him, just for a minute.

"Sass, listen to me carefully. You're the rock star on this mission, the talent. Think of me as your bodyguard. I'm just there to protect you, so you're free to do what you do best."

"But you're supposed to find evidence—"

"Forget that. We'll have all the evidence we need if you can pull off your part. I'm a damn good operative, Sass. I'll do whatever it takes to get us out of there alive. Just concentrate on getting to the trigger and trust me to take care of the rest. Trust me to take care of you."

She didn't quite believe him about his role in all of this—

she knew he was a lot more hands-on than that implied. Didn't quite trust there was anything he could do if Dawson decided to kill them both—she knew Dawson was a vicious thug. But she appreciated his efforts to talk her through her nerves. He was an excellent SAC. No wonder Sydney wanted to keep him around.

"I'll try," she said.

"You'll do fine. Just be yourself."

For several minutes they just stood there on deck together, she absorbing as much of his strength as she could through the contact of their bodies.

Strange how she could almost feel his confidence flowing into her veins, giving her courage to face the treacherous mission ahead.

"How long till we're there?" she asked.

"Less than an hour."

"I'd better go below and change, then." She stepped away from him, feeling suddenly chilly despite the warmth of the day. "Any preference as to hairstyle and color?"

His smile was disarming. "Just how it is."

She made a face. "You—" she poked him in the arm "—are not helping matters."

"No?"

She walked away without comment, for fear of incriminating herself. She couldn't possibly be starting to like the man...could she? It was one thing to respect him. Or even lust after him. But *like* him? Yikes. How had that happened?

Nevertheless, it was with a considerably lighter heart that she came up the ladder a while later, wearing the clothes she'd decided on for their first meeting with Dawson. It was nice to know she was going into this thing with a friend, not the enemy she'd thought of him as before.

A wolf whistle sounded from the cockpit.

She struck a pose, then spun and struck another, facing him. "You like?"

"Damn, woman."

He looked her up and down, from the sleek black pageboy to the fuchsia, cleavage-inducing Vera Wang sundress, to the gold, four-inch-heeled Kate Spade sandals.

"Get those shoes off or you'll break your neck before we even make it to Dawson's place. How are you going to run in those if we have to?"

"I'll take that as a yes," she said, peeling off the most exclusive shoes she'd ever worn and tossing them onto the stern bench. "I figure if we have to run we're already dead. Until that happens, the more attention I attract, the less there will be on inspecting our luggage. I'm a little worried about Jules's gadgets."

"I'd be more worried about falling out of that dress," he muttered.

She grinned at the transparent, masculine battle in his expression—between outrage and drooling. "I'd think you'd like that."

Hadn't she always said men were predictable?

"You're supposed to be my wife! Wives don't wear—"

"You marry a call girl it's probably because you like your women on the trashy side. Right, Rafe?"

Rio's brows lifted into his scalp.

She sauntered up and stood in front of him, her upthrust breasts a whisper away from his torso. "What's the matter, Rio? Can't take the heat?"

Suddenly, his hand shot out and grasped her behind the neck, holding her in an iron grip. He tugged. Just a fraction. Bringing her nipples into kissing contact with the solid plane of his muscled chest. They reacted instantly, hardening and zinging with erotic sensation.

Rio's face was harsh, his stance intimidating; even the color of his eyes had gone from blue to a dark, menacing steel. He'd become a totally different person.

"Be careful, baby," he growled. "Gun might be a coy flirt, but Rafe is a ruthless, dangerous man, willing to do anything to get what he wants. I wouldn't tease a man like that if I were you, or you might end up with more than you bargained for."

She licked her lips, fighting the illogical arousal created by his show of dominance. The boat hit a swell and the movement made his coarse-knit shirt rub across her nipples. Pleasure streaked through her whole body, stabbing at her center. She stifled a moan.

Then just as suddenly, he let her go.

"I better change," he said gruffly. And was gone.

Her face burned. Her body burned.

The line in the sand between them was unmistakable. She wasn't quite sure who had drawn it, but one thing was increasingly clear. If either of them broke down and crossed over it, there'd be no going back.

And if that happened, another thing was for damned certain. She would not recover from the tumultuous encounter anytime soon.

He liked being Rafe.

Rio knew enough about undercover work to know it was time to get out when you started to enjoy playing the bad guy. The next step was to *become* the bad guy. As Rafe Gerard had apparently done.

Rio also knew enough about himself to realize the main

reason he liked being Rafe was because he liked Sass being Gun even more.

Of all the stupid times to try living out a sexual fantasy.

He stood behind the wheel of the *Mermaid,* slowly maneuvering the craft into the berth Dawson's armed guards indicated he'd been assigned in the private mini-marina.

Having put himself firmly into character, he felt rock steady. He was ready for anything Dawson threw at him. But was Sass?

He glanced her way, gratified to see her toss the waiting guards the lines and give the four gun-jockeys a haughty once-over. Her hip was cocked, her attitude as brash as her bright fuchsia dress. Shutting off the engines, he strolled over and threw a casual arm around her shoulder.

"Be ready for anything," he murmured. Then he called to the guards, "We're here to see Dawson."

"Mr. Dawson don't like visitors," the head guy called back. "You got an appointment?"

"He's expecting us. Rafe Gerard and Gun Sundstrom. We're here for the auction."

After a two-sentence conversation into his walkie-talkie, the guard in command motioned them off the boat with the business end of his Uzi. Rio unhooked the rail, stepped across to the dock and held his hand out to help Sass, who'd donned those mouth-drying gold heels again. Four pairs of hawklike eyes watched her long legs make mincemeat of the gap between the boat and the jetty.

An absurd jealousy ripped through Rio. *She was* his *woman.*

To prove it, he yanked her to his chest, grasped her chin and kissed her.

Their first kiss wasn't a long one, but suddenly he felt as though he'd taken a slug to the gut. Her lips were soft, her gasp breathy and her taste like paradise. He jerked her away, searching her face for her reaction. She looked stunned, the gold flecks in her green eyes swimming in a sea of shock. So he pulled her back and kissed her again.

This time he brushed his tongue over her lips, then took the bottom one between his teeth and gave her a quick nip.

"Don't forget, baby, you're *my* wife," he admonished.

She shoved his chest. "Bite me again and I'll be your widow," she snapped in a thick Swedish accent, turned on a toe and started to march down the jetty.

Ignoring the snickering guards, he ambled after her, calling, "Aw, baby, you always say you like it when I bite you."

He heard a distinct "harrumph" as her head tossed. He grinned, and followed her shapely bottom as it swayed sexily toward land.

Two of the guards hurried ahead and had a golf cart waiting for them at the top of an oyster-shell path he presumed led to the mansion. Though much smaller, this island was as heavily overgrown as Seven Moon Island, so it was impossible to tell for sure what lay ahead. They took their seats on the rear bench that faced backward and the cart started with a jolt.

"What about my suitcases?" Sass demanded of the two guards who'd gotten in the front seat.

"We'll send for them later," the driver said.

"After we know you're really who you say you are," the other added in an indifferent tone.

Something in the way he said it made Rio's skin prickle in warning. He put his arm around Sass and pulled her close, in case they had to exit the cart, fast.

They exchanged a look of perfect understanding. She'd sensed it, too. His respect for her skyrocketed.

Sure enough, several hundred yards into the tangled jungle, the cart came to an abrupt halt and the guards jumped out, aiming their machine guns at them. Rio's fingers tightened around Sass's shoulder.

"Get out!" the head honcho ordered. "You're no more Rafe Gerard than I am Tinker Bell."

Rio calmly contemplated the guard from where he sat. "Well, Tink, I hope you have a good supply of fairy dust. 'Cause you'd lose that bet."

Sass crossed her legs and put her hand on his knee, gazing out at the greenery on the side of the path, giving all the appearance of being bored.

The honcho swore roundly. "Get the hell off the cart before I shoot you where you are."

On his knee, Sass's fingers gave two distinct squeezes, then jerked it slightly to the left. In his peripheral vision he saw the undergrowth rustle to the left of the path. So there were two guys waiting to ambush them from that direction. He was beginning to think she was right about the running.

"Yeah, whatever," he drawled, making to stand up.

Giving Sass's shoulder an answering squeeze, he slid his fingers down her arm, moving her hand onto the metal edge of the seat just before he shoved her off and launched himself at the honcho. Before the guards knew what had hit them, he wrenched the Uzi from the honcho's grip, bashed his head with it, swung it around and shot the gun out of the other guy's hands.

The honcho went down like a lead balloon and the other guy howled in pain, blood spurting from his limp arm. Rio whipped a check on Sass, who had crouched behind the cart just as he'd intended. He grabbed the wounded man's gun and tossed it to her.

"Cover me," he ordered, then sprinted into the jungle at the same time the men in the underbrush started firing. Sass's weapon blasted back, giving him time to circle around and silently make his way behind them, all the while listening for her squeezed-off shots to give him their positions. For never having worked together, he and Sass were acting in damn good harmony, almost as though they'd rehearsed this act.

He spotted the two men hidden among a small clutch of palmettos. Using the Uzi as a club again, he snuck up on the guy to the left and whacked him upside the head, flipped it, and rammed the muzzle into the other guy's neck.

"Don't even think about it," he growled.

The man froze, then slowly raised his hands in the air, dropping his weapon.

For guards, these guys were pretty pathetic. Rio couldn't help but think Dawson was testing them as much as he was testing his visitors. Maybe they were new recruits. He had a feeling they wouldn't be around long.

Swiping up the two machine guns from the ground, he prodded the second guard. "Throw him over your shoulder and let's go."

When they got back to the golf cart, he found the honcho handcuffed to the steering wheel and swearing a blue streak, his walkie-talkie smashed on the ground and Sass standing over the wounded man lying next to it. She was still wearing those jump-me heels, one hand on her outthrust hip and the deadly Uzi cradled in the other like Al Capone's best girl.

Damn, was she sexy.

"Put him on the back bench," Rio ordered the captured guard. "And give me your cuffs."

In seconds they were both secured to the cart. He decided to leave the wounded man where he was. Taking the key from the cart's ignition, he stuck it in his pocket and told them,

"Don't feel too bad. You were definitely outnumbered." He turned to Sass. "What do you think, baby? Should we blow this pop stand or go find Dawson and tell him his hospitality sucks?"

She pretended to consider. "Why don't we find Dawson and just blow his head off? Say! We could practice on these guys!"

"Now darlin'." He stripped all the guards of their ankle weapons and stuck two in his waistband. The others he tossed into the shrubbery. "I think your blood sugar is getting low again. Maybe we should find something to eat instead."

She stuck out her bottom lip. "Spoilsport."

Her fake Swedish accent sounded really cute, and her tough-girl act was really turning him on. He had to resist the urge to grab her, lower his mouth to that plump lip and nip it again. Or better yet, suck on it. Maybe later.

He pointed up the road. "I assume the mansion is that way. Shall we?"

She took two steps on the oyster-shell path and stopped. "I can't walk on this stuff. I'll ruin my shoes."

"What?" He rolled his eyes. "Damn, baby, I'll buy you new ones."

"These are Kate Spade shoes," she said, emphasizing the brand name as though that explained everything. He'd never heard of them.

"We need to move," he said a tad impatiently. "Dawson will be expecting the guards to report in soon."

"I'm telling you, I—"

Muttering a succinct swearword, he swiped her up, slung her over his shoulder and started walking.

"R-Rafe!" she squealed, kicking her legs. "Put me down this instant!"

He didn't, not until they were within sight of the mansion. He gave a low whistle at the huge antebellum-style estate house, and dumped her down on her precious Kate Whatevers. When she opened her mouth to give him whatfor, he laid a finger on her lips. "Shhh. Look, Dawson's standing on the roof deck. Can you get us up there without being seen?"

Her tirade thankfully halted before it began as she turned to look where he was pointing. "Piece of cake." She glared at him skeptically as she adjusted the top of her sundress. "That is, if you can climb."

"I can climb anywhere you can," he assured her.

"I guess we'll find out, won't we?"

It was simply incredible.

Rio stood back in amazement as Sass swiftly worked her magic on a first-floor window security alarm with a couple of bobby pins pulled from her bra—at least he assumed that's where they'd come from, since she'd made him turn his back.

"I've already seen everything you've got," he reminded her dryly. "At least in that area."

She snorted. "Maybe in your dreams."

He wasn't about to argue that point. At least not at the moment. They had about thirty seconds to get through that window before the perimeter guards came around the corner again. "How much longer?"

"Done." She slid the window up noiselessly and disappeared through it.

He followed quickly, closed it tight and crouch-ran to where Sass waited behind a huge, ornately carved wooden table and chairs. They'd gained entry into the dining room. Double doors opened to the main hall where he could see a grand stairway ascend to the upper floors.

"This way," she whispered, cracking open a closed door on the opposite wall. "Servants' entrance."

An unadorned hallway revealed the service stairway at the rear of the house.

"Wait here." Before he could stop her, she popped up, banged open the door and clattered noisily down the hall in those dumb high heels. "Oh, dear," she declared, "I seem to be lost. Why, hello there!"

Rio watched in alarm as she tottered past an armed guard and fell against the wall behind him, giggling, drawing his attention away from Rio.

"Gosh, I was looking for the little girls'. Where did I go wrong?"

Swallowing a string of curses, Rio vaulted out from his hiding place and cracked the man over the head with the butt of the Glock he'd relieved one of the guards of. Dawson was going to have to send out for more Tylenol if this kept up. Rio just hoped none of them held a grudge.

Sass was already zipping up the stairs, so Rio sprinted after her. The very top of the stairs choked in and ended at a narrow door that opened to the roof. A small, square window revealed the cammo-clad back of another guard. In front of the man stretched an expansive deck scattered with several sets of outdoor tables and chairs. Miles Dawson sat at one of the tables, calmly sipping a drink.

"Strategy?" she whispered.

"Why change now?" he drawled.

With a quick nod, she tottered through the door and ran smack into the guard's backside. "Oops! Sorry," she called airily in her singsong Swedish accent. "Oh, wow! What a view!" She stretched out her arms and made for the outer railing. "The ocean's *gorgeous!* So blue and— What?"

Rio gritted his teeth as the guard rushed at her, gun raised, stopping just short of grabbing her. The man looked to an astonished Dawson for guidance. The last thing Rio saw before dashing out the door and darting behind a nearby table was Dawson's eyes as they narrowed dangerously. He wasted no time in getting to Dawson's back. With immense satisfaction, Rio jammed the Glock into his spine.

"Hello, Dawson. Surprised to see us?"

Dawson's jaw dropped, a tense beat passed, then he let out a bark of laughter. "Damn, Gerard. How many of my men did you kill getting up here?"

"None yet. But that could easily change. Call off your dogs. *All* of them. Test's over."

Dawson chuckled and gave the guard a quick sign. "Fair enough."

The guard's walkie-talkie squawked as he relayed the order to stand down. Gerard and Sundstrom had passed inspection.

"And by the way," Rio warned softly. "*You're* the one I'll come after if any of your men *ever* points a weapon at my woman again."

The threat didn't faze Dawson. "Ah, the lovely Gunilla." His face broke out in a broad leer as he took inventory of Sass's body and revealing attire. "Even more beautiful than I was told. I don't blame you for being protective, Gerard. But I hope you won't be *too* possessive of her." He bent over her hand in a lingering kiss. "Here, we like to share among friends."

Rio desperately wanted to strangle the man. "Touch more than her hand and I'll feed your guts to the vultures."

Dawson's brow rose a fraction. Rio sensed he was on the brink of pushing the bastard too far. "Unless, of course," he added, lowering the automatic and tucking it back into his waistband, "she says it's okay."

There. That ought to placate him. Sass, on the other hand…
She had a smile plastered in place, but if looks could kill he'd
be burned toast.

"*Älskling,*" she said sweetly, "you know that only happens
when you can't get it up."

Dawson choked on his drink. "I can see we're in for a
lively few days," he said with a gleeful snigger. "I'm so glad.
Terrorists usually bore me to tears."

"We're not terrorists," Sass said mildly. "We're intermediaries. Here to make money, nothing more."

"Clever girl," Dawson said, the words honeyed with ap-
proval. "Politics are so tedious. Don't you agree, my dear?"

"Absolutely. I much prefer shopping."

Dawson's gaze met Rio's in a brief moment of male indul-
gence. Rio wanted to cheer—right after he puked. Sass was
pulling off her role with exactly the right combination of dit-
ziness and sociopathic violence. Unbalanced was good. It allowed for a large margin of error. Now if Rio could just keep
his temper in check, they'd be home free.

"Where are my manners?" Dawson declared, totally
charmed by Sass's Gunilla. He indicated the wrought iron
glass-topped table where he'd been sitting. "Come join me,
please. Patrick!" he barked at the guard. "Ring the kitchen and
have lunch sent up. With champagne. Lots of it." He gave Sass
a predatory smile. "We must celebrate the beginning of what
I hope will be a very close friendship."

Rio clamped his jaw shut. Like any sane woman would be
attracted to him. With his middle-aged paunch and receding
hairline, the only things Dawson had going for him were fear
and a large bank account.

"Oh," Dawson added to the guard, "and I want to see those
useless guards up here, now."

The really strange thing was, Rio didn't usually have a temper. In fact, he couldn't remember the last time his blood had boiled over anything at all, with the sole exception of his father's murder. Not until Sass Hawthorne had come rappelling into his life, he thought with a jab of annoyance.

"Rafe? *Älskling?*" Sass took his arm and nestled up against his side, all warm and cuddly. "Are you angry with me? You know I didn't mean it," she cooed softly. To his shock, she put her hand to his cheek, sliding her fingers into his hair, then went up on tiptoes and gently kissed his lips.

Puppy-dog eyes, she'd said of Gun looking at Rafe in the photo. That was exactly how Sass was looking at him now.

Rio's heart did a crazy twist in his chest. Without thinking, he tugged her close and kissed her back.

This time there was no fear, no agenda, no ulterior motive. Just pure sweet emotion flowing between a man and a woman.

And that's when Rio knew he was in deep trouble.

Because this woman, this infuriating female thief, moved him as no other woman ever had. And he'd do just about anything to have her under him, naked.

But what really scared him was what she might do once he got her there. To his focus. To his future.

Hell, and most of all, to his heart.

Chapter 7

"I have to confirm your identities you understand," Dawson told them a few minutes later as he put down the phone after speaking briefly with one of his minions about running a check on them. He smiled pleasantly.

Sass smiled back and tried not to appear as nervous as she felt. She prayed Macon and Mannheim had done their jobs securing their covers.

"Only to be expected," Rio said dismissively. "I'd be worried if you didn't."

Just then the stairway door opened. The four guards from the marina and the one from downstairs trooped through it. One limped badly, three had streaks of blood dripping down their faces from the head bashing Rio had given them and a fifth was cradling his wounded arm in the other. They all appeared terrified.

Dawson glared down his nose at them and his lips curled

in obvious fury. "You call yourselves guards!" he yelled. "You let a woman overpower you! A *woman!*"

Sass bristled but didn't speak. Gone was the pleasant smile. He looked as if he were about to kill someone.

He jumped to his feet. "I should shoot the worthless lot of you!"

"Please, Mr. D—" one of the men began.

"Shut up! Nobody said you could talk!" Dawson suddenly reached over and grabbed the Uzi from the roof guard's hand. "Which one of you was in charge down there?"

No one stepped forward.

"Which one?"

"I was," the guy who'd been the leader at the marina said, his eyes vibrating with fright.

"Not any more." Dawson growled, and raised the Uzi.

In a flash, Rio's hand clamped onto Dawson's arm.

Their host turned on him, his teeth bared viciously. "What the hell are you doing?"

"Not in front of my wife," Rio said calmly but firmly, still gripping Dawson's arm.

Sass held her breath, her heart stopping in her chest. Her pulse took off into hyperspace as the two men locked eyes.

Suddenly, Dawson gave a hoot of laughter and tossed the Uzi back to the roof guard. "You are something else, Gerard. Not in front of my wife," he mimicked, laughed again heartily, then slashed a hand in the air. "Take them away, Sergeant! And the next time they screw up, shoot them all."

Sass wanted to let out the breath she was holding but wasn't sure she dared. *This man was a psycho.* The sick game of intimidation he'd played with them upon arrival was bad enough. But he would have killed that guard without blinking if Rio hadn't interfered.

Holy crap.

What had she gotten herself into?

Lunch arrived promptly, and she wondered uneasily what would happen to the chef if it wasn't to Dawson's liking.

As the food was served, Dawson got a phone call that their identities had checked out. Thank goodness. One less thing to be worried about.

It crossed her mind that perhaps Rio's bold actions and their unorthodox arrival might have made Dawson more wary and therefore they'd be watched extra carefully, but that didn't appear to be the case. Despite his anger with the guards, with Sass and Rio he didn't hide his admiration. That they'd managed to make it all the way to the roof without being stopped had impressed him and he made no secret of it.

He flirted with Sass shamelessly. She swallowed her distaste and let him. But she didn't flirt back. The man made her skin crawl.

Rio watched her like a predator, registering every move as Dawson fawned over her through the interminable luncheon. She was more than grateful, knowing he was there, ready to step in and put a stop to anything he didn't like.

Her father's description of Dawson sifted through her mind as they ate—*dangerous and unpredictable...and a pervert.* The first two he'd already proven. And she was starting to believe that last part, too.

She got the sinking feeling that winning this auction may not be all about the dollar amounts they offered.

"Liza will show you to your room," Dawson told them when they finally all got up from the table.

Liza, a voluptuous redhead clad in a skimpy French-maid outfit, gave Rio a come-hither smile and indicated he should follow her. Sass figured she better tag along. This time *he* might need rescuing.

"Will our luggage be there?" Sass asked Liza as they started down the main staircase. She hazarded a glance at Rio. To her surprise, he was studying the artwork on the walls, not the woman's swinging hips.

"After your bags are inspected they will be brought up," Liza answered.

Sass pretended to be offended. *"Inspected? Doesn't he trust us?"*

"Mr. Dawson trusts no one," the maid replied. "But you must really have impressed him. He put you in the best room on the third floor."

Great. Sass should be happy they'd been so well accepted by Dawson. But the expression on Liza's face when she opened the door only heightened Sass's sense of unease. The maid's gaze slithered over first her, then Rio, as though in anticipation of…of what? Nothing good, she was sure.

But she temporarily forgot her apprehensions when they stepped into the bedroom. "Unbelievable," she murmured. "It's gorgeous."

Truthfully, it was beyond gorgeous. Gleaming antiques, sumptuous fabrics and elegant accessories graced every inch of the room, which was dominated by a huge, elaborately carved four-poster bed sitting smack in the center.

Before she could react, Rio came up behind her and ran his hands up and down her body.

"Why don't we try it out?" he murmured suggestively, urging her toward the bed.

She jumped. "Rafe!" She let out a nervous giggle, batting at his hands. After fending off Dawson through lunch, this was the last thing she needed.

Rio nibbled on her neck, and barely whispered, "Don't forget, the room's probably bugged." His hands crept to her breasts.

She spun from his grasp. But made herself smile and waggle her finger at him. "You are a very bad boy."

He caught her, pulling her flat against his chest. "You know it, baby." He gave her a quick kiss, then swatted her butt and let her go, to her immense relief. She knew they had to pretend to be husband and wife, but she'd hoped to ease into it a bit slower.

"So, where is everybody?" he asked Liza. "We're not the first bidders to arrive are we?"

"No, you're the last," she informed them. "Everyone is waiting for you at the pool."

"The pool, eh?" Rio slid his sultry Rafe-gaze over Sass. "I trust you packed your bikini."

Warmth bloomed in her midsection at his half-lidded regard. Lord, the way he looked at her. As if he wanted to eat her up.

And the bathing suit she'd had to bring wasn't going to help matters any. But she'd had no choice. There hadn't been a single one-piece among Gun's things.

However, just because she'd brought it didn't mean she actually had to wear it. Yet, anyway.

She tapped the end of his nose. "*Älskling,* you know I prefer swimming in the ocean."

He gave her a lazy smile. "Who said anything about swimming?"

There was a knock on the door and Liza went to answer it. "Your suitcases are here."

After depositing their bags on the floor of the humungous closet, the young man who'd brought them led the way down to the pool, where the other guests were gathered.

Sass barely had time to register the tropical-themed pool— complete with palm trees, stone waterfall and lagoon-disguised hot tub—before they were greeted with a smattering of sardonic applause from five men lounging on teak pool furniture next to it.

"Here come the hotshots now," said the closest one, who had the coal-black hair, features and accent of a Middle-Easterner.

Sass thought the gathering looked more like a photo shoot for *Town & Country* than a group of terrorists. There wasn't a scruffy or unkempt man in the bunch. So much for stereotypes. But the eyes that ruthlessly inspected her as she and Rio approached were cold, calculating and totally devoid of friendliness. That much fit.

"I see now why you were so easily able to distract the guards," said a Japanese man nursing a brandy, staring openly at her breasts. There was a murmur of agreement from the others, as though her skimpy attire could be the only reason for her success.

She gave him a cutting look. "Of course. Men are such fools," she returned, leaving it open to interpretation whether she meant the guards or present company.

The man slammed down his drink and was about to leap to his feet when Rio clapped a hand on his shoulder. "Don't even think about it, pal," he said with dead calm.

Under her breath, Sass counted to ten, thankful for Rio's mitigating influence. She was so not cut out for this undercover stuff. She wasn't sure what she wanted more—to turn tail and run, or to kill the chauvinistic bastards now and be done with it.

Dawson, whom she hadn't noticed standing in the shadows of the cabana bar, snickered. "Now, now. Let's not come to blows just yet." He walked into the sunlight. "May I present your competition in my little auction?" Starting with the Middle-Eastern man, he introduced them in a circle. "This is Selim, Hetsuro, Mikaelov, Joaquin and Betty." Sass did a double take on Betty, and realized he might actually be a she. It was hard to tell under that butch haircut. "Everyone, this is Gunilla and Rafe. They work as a team."

"A married team." Rio's tone was soft but impossible to misread.

No one got up or offered a handshake. A good thing. She had no desire to touch the slimeballs.

Rio chose an empty chaise, sat back and patted the space in the V between his thighs. "Have a seat, baby."

He no doubt sensed her unease and wanted her within grabbing distance, she thought wryly. For once she didn't mind. She was all over the map right now, and she remembered how reassuring his touch had felt earlier. She needed that again.

She plopped down in front of him, crossed her ankles and sighed when his arms came around her to guide her back against his chest. She was beginning to like this position. A lot.

He was so strong, so sure. How did he do it?

Closing her eyes, she felt his calm, quiet self-assurance surround her like a force field, protecting her from the evil hovering around them. It seeped into her, banishing her nervousness and bolstering her own self-confidence.

Despite the potent chemistry between them, she understood that the reason for his embrace wasn't personal. Somehow, he instinctively got that holding her helped her cope. He was being a good leader, helping his team adjust to the rigors of a particularly tough assignment. So they could succeed together.

His motives didn't matter; it was working.

When she opened her eyes again, she discovered the men

were deep into a discussion of Spanish versus Portuguese port. At first she was confused by the bland and innocuous topic of conversation. But naturally politics would be the last thing these men would discuss. Too volatile.

The sound of female laughter from inside the house brought the conversation to an abrupt halt. The French doors opened and the same young man who'd brought up their suitcases escorted a bevy of bikini-clad women out onto the pool deck.

"Ah! Ellis has brought dessert," Dawson said with a lecherous grin. "Get the ladies something to drink, Ellis," he ordered, then beckoned the giggling young women to approach.

They gathered around him, each bestowing a long, wet kiss on their host. Sass had to keep her mouth tightly closed for fear her jaw would get splinters from the deck at the way his hands freely roamed their near-naked bodies as he returned each woman's eager kiss. They had to be hookers.

Gun had also been a hooker, Sass reminded herself. At age fifteen. Today, at age twenty-nine, this kind of behavior would be less than a blip on Gun's jaded radar. Still, the last thing Sass wanted was to watch whatever was coming next in Dawson's little planned entertainment.

Luckily, there couldn't be a better time to get to work.

Feigning boredom, she stretched and got to her feet. "It appears I'm overdressed," she said with casual disinterest. "Think I'll go upstairs and change. Maybe take a swim."

Rio caught her hand and tugged her back. He kissed her, whispering under his breath, "Be careful."

The kiss wasn't for her, but the onlookers, and to camouflage his words. She knew that. But…the memory of his first kiss still hovered on her lips. It had been so good….

So she kissed him back. Taking her time about it. She held his face in her hands and used her tongue, lingering over his mouth so long, enjoying his taste and his heated response so much, she almost forgot that this was only part of their cover. When she lifted, his eyes looked slightly glazed.

She knew exactly how he felt. Wow. The man could really kiss.

She licked her lips and was treated to one last dose of him. *So good…* Just one more—

No. *Time to go, Kansas.* She pulled in a steadying breath and straightened, looking him bravely in the eye.

"Don't you touch any of those girls, Rafe Gerard," she admonished as a parting shot, and strode off to do her job.

While she could still remember what it was.

Inside day work was not Sass's forte. B and E was her thing. Give her a good old-fashioned night burglary anytime over traversing halls filled with thinking, alert people who could guess what you were up to at any second. Electronics she could handle. People were always a crap shoot.

On the other hand, you had to deal with what you had.

She flashed a smile at Ellis when he opened the French door for her. "Remember how to get to your room?" he asked, returning her smile broadly.

"Um…" She couldn't miss the invitation in his gaze. Hmm. Maybe she could use this. "Well, now that you mention it, I might get lost."

She batted her lashes. From the corner of her eye, she saw Rio frown as he watched their conversation. She winked at him and followed Ellis into the house.

"How 'bout a tour?" she asked as he led her toward the grand staircase. "I'd love to see the rest of the mansion. Is it old?" No time like the present to start her visual inventory.

Ellis shrugged. "No idea. But I guess I can show you around if you like."

She trailed after him as he showed her the entire first floor: the luxurious living room, giant dining room, expansive great room with a fireplace the size of a small house and every stereophonic and video gadget known to man, and gourmet kitchen bustling with white-clad staff preparing their next meal.

She lifted her nose. "Smells great." She made note of an open door leading to a walk-in pantry and the utility room beyond it.

"Mr. Dawson brings his own people wherever he goes," Ellis explained. "Including his personal chef."

"That must be nice. Do you travel with him?"

There was also a door with a dead bolt on it she suspected led to the garage.

Ellis nodded. "Seven staff members and six bodyguards have been with Mr. Dawson for some years now. Others are hired on a temporary basis."

If they were lucky and lived through the job interview, she thought.

She didn't ask, but Ellis looked as if he was about eighteen. She shuddered to think how he'd come to work for Dawson "some" years ago. "You've lived in a lot of places, I guess."

"I enjoy moving around," he said smoothly.

"Hope he pays you a lot."

Ellis just gave her an enigmatic smile.

By now they'd moved to the second floor. "There are four bedrooms in the west wing," he said, gesturing to the left. "Mr. Dawson's personal offices are in the east wing, and are off-limits to everyone except his personal bodyguards."

"Even you?" she asked, flirtatiously running her finger

down the front of his tight, white muscle shirt. She had to admit, for a uniform it was pretty nice worn with his white linen drawstring pants. She briefly wondered how Rio would look in an outfit like that.

Ellis gave her another of those nonsmiles, bringing her back to reality. There was a kind of hollow quality to it. The kid was obviously experienced far beyond his years. Like Gun. For some reason, the thought saddened her. But she couldn't afford to get sentimental. The guy had to know who was paying his salary.

"Do you think he'd mind if I took just a little peek inside his office?" she whispered conspiratorially.

She had no doubt Ellis knew exactly what she was doing. It didn't matter. She figured it was expected that the bidders would try anything to get a leg up on the competition, including sneaking into Dawson's office, if they could, to get a look at whatever might pertain to the auction.

He gave her a grin. "I suppose that would be okay," he said, surprising her. He knocked on the double door leading into the east wing. As the guard on the other side opened it, Ellis pointed up to a corner of the ceiling. "I'm sure you've noticed the cameras everywhere. Just so you know, there isn't a single inch inside the mansion that's not covered by video surveillance—other than the bathrooms, of course." His grin didn't falter as he motioned her in. "In case you were thinking of doing any midnight excursions."

She grinned back. "Midnight excursions? Why, whatever do you mean?"

They shared a chuckle over the outrageous idea that any of the bidders might actually succeed with something like that. Including her.

She loved it. An overconfident enemy was her best friend. And she had expected the cameras. Dawson would be pretty stupid not to have a full array of monitoring equipment. And he was far from stupid.

There were four guards posted in the east wing hall. One in front of each of the doors that opened onto it, including the one through which they'd entered.

"Just showing Miss Gunilla around," Ellis said loudly enough for all to hear. The guards stood their ground but nodded, the first moving aside when Ellis opened the first door for her to look inside.

It was Dawson's office. Divided into a desk area and a conference area, it took up the entire back half of the wing. To her disappointment, there was nothing to see but furniture. The surface of every piece was pristinely bare and polished to a soft glow, reflecting the vacant space above. Even Dawson's computer had been hidden away.

Ah, well. That just meant more fun later.

"Motion detectors and laser sensors, of course," Ellis said. "Wireless entry alarms on the windows."

"Very impressive." Not. It was all pretty standard stuff. Wireless alarms? Not terribly secure. Of course, Ellis could be deliberately not mentioning the more creative countermeasures. Or maybe he didn't even know about them. If Dawson was as paranoid as everyone said, that would make sense.

On the other hand, as often as he moved around, installing extensive security in each new place would be a real pain, and expensive as hell. Easier by far to employ lots of guards. Which meant less work for her, but more unpredictability.

The next room he showed her was filled with color video monitors. There had to be a couple dozen of them, some with stationary views, some moving, showing every possible door, hallway and public room in the house, and outside, as well.

So this was where all those cameras fed. Probably also on a wireless network. But…where were the bedrooms? Hadn't Ellis said all the rooms had cameras?

Two guards sat watching the screens. They seemed particularly interested in the ones that showed the pool area.

Ellis made a *tsk-tsk* noise, and said, "Looks like the gentlemen are having a good time."

Sass kept her face carefully neutral as she glanced at the monitor. The hookers were all naked now, hanging all over Dawson and the five other terrorists, who were in various stages of undress, engaged in a variety of unsavory activities. She swallowed her nausea and searched the screens for any sign of Rio. He was nowhere in sight.

"Where is that husband of mine?" she mused aloud, taking a count of the women. All five present and accounted for.

What was Rio up to?

"I expect he's looking for you," Ellis said. "We can skip Dawson's bedroom if you like, and go straight up to yours."

"No," she said. "I'm curious to see how Dawson lives." She gave Ellis a conspiratorial smile. Praying her suspicion wasn't right.

"All right." He led the way, and this time Sass couldn't help the gasp that came out when Ellis revealed what was inside the last door.

Dawson's room was like a torture chamber. The iron bed looked like something from the Inquisition rather than a place to sleep. Chains and restraints hung from the black iron canopy; whips, handcuffs and things she didn't even want to know the use for were displayed along the walls and on low tables all around the room.

But what made her stomach really clench was when she spotted another row of monitors lined up opposite Dawson's bed. Sure enough there were ten of them: the same number as bedrooms in the mansion. And each monitor showed the same subject.

A bed.

Each bed was different. To her horror, she recognized one of them.

It was *her* bed. Hers and Rio's.

"Where the hell is she?" Rio demanded of the empty bedroom as he paced back and forth.

He'd wanted to follow Sass upstairs anyway, but when Dawson's call girls had started in on him, he'd quickly excused himself. They were all passably pretty, but the thought of touching any of them held zero appeal. Especially with Sass waiting for him up in their bedroom.

But she wasn't here.

Where had that kid taken her?

Or maybe, Rio chided himself, she was actually doing what they'd come here to do. Breaking into Dawson's office.

Damn, he really had to get control of his raging hormones. They were messing up his ability to think.

Just then, the door burst open and she rushed in. When she saw him, her steps faltered. "Oh!" The blood drained from her face. "R-Rafe!"

The muscle-bound kid was standing behind her, an indecipherable look on his face.

"Yeah," Rio said slowly, trying not to let his imagination steamroller over him. "You want me to leave?"

"No!" She bit her lip. "No, of course not. Why would you ask that?" She turned, and said to the kid, "Thanks for the tour, Ellis. We'll see you later."

"Sure thing, Miss Gunilla."

After she closed the door, she gave Rio the strangest look he'd ever seen. "Ellis gave me a tour of the mansion."

"Oh? See anything interesting?"

"I did." She took a few steps into the room and folded her arms under her breasts, making them push up and nearly out of her dress. She twisted around to gaze up at the wall. "You'll never guess."

He forced his gaze away from her breasts and tried to spot what she was looking at, but couldn't see anything except paintings—other than wallpaper and crown molding. "Tell me."

She glanced back at him, her eyes filled with an emotion he couldn't place.

What the hell was going on?

"I saw monitors."

Huge surprise there. "And this is news how?"

"Well, there's a camera not only in the hallways, but in every bedroom," she said with a low laugh that in no way matched the nervousness flaring in her eyes. She walked over to the bed and flopped down on it, spreading her arms in a voguish gesture. "The camera is aimed at the bed. Dawson likes to watch his guests. According to Ellis, he insists on it."

His gaze roamed over her body. She looked like a sex kitten stretched out across—

"*What? He… He watches…?*"

Rio stared at her as the meaning slowly sank in. He turned to examine the wall again, but still didn't see anything that resembled a camera. "Well, too bad," he muttered. "I'm not into exhibitionism. I'll cover the lens. When I find it."

Her head gave a shake and she sat up. "He'll just send someone in to fix it. Any guest who doesn't play along is escorted off the estate immediately."

"You mean, they're not allowed to participate in the auction?"

She nodded and climbed off the bed, coming toward him. "The camera is on permanently, but it's also on a motion sensor that trips a DVR when anything in the room moves."

"A DVR? He *tapes* everything, too?"

"Mmm-hmm. Everything." She put her arms around his neck. "It's recording us now."

He could feel the tremor in her limbs, but her outward body language betrayed none of the consternation he knew damn well she must be feeling. Hell, he was feeling it, too. He wanted her crazy bad, but not in front of an audience. And she didn't want to have sex with him at all.

But if what she said was true, if they didn't make love with each other—and in front of a camera to boot—this whole operation would be over before it started.

Before he realized what she intended, she put her lips to his. They quivered.

He swore silently and kissed her gently, his mind searching frantically for a solution. He found none. Other than—

He swore again, aloud. "We'll leave. I don't care what's at stake."

"No." She shook her head firmly. "We can't go. This is too important."

"There'll be other jobs," he insisted. "This one isn't worth our privacy. It's outrageous—"

"Our clients will be furious if we leave before the auction. Besides—" She backed up a step and her chin rose a fraction. "I used to do this sort of thing for a living, remember? Being watched won't bother me." She lifted a shoulder in a brave show of fake nonchalance.

Rio fought hard not to react to her blithe portrayal of the worldly Gunilla. She couldn't possibly mean it, of course. She may be a thief, but she definitely wasn't a whore or anything close to one. She wasn't even into fooling around. Her acting abilities were starting to astound him.

"Really?" he murmured. He held her eyes for a long, assessing moment. Just how far was she willing to take this little masquerade of husband and wife?

"Hell, it might even be a little fun," she said. Daring him. Tempting him.

He squelched his body's instinctive leap of arousal and his mind's just-as-instinctive censorious response and asked himself the more important question.

How would Rafe Gerard react to all of this?

Yeah, that was a no-brainer.

"So you think it might be fun, huh?"

"Why not?"

Why not, indeed? Hell, if she didn't mind an audience, why should be?

He strolled to the dresser and pulled out her bikini from the top drawer. "In that case…." He tossed her the scraps of fabric. "Let's get the show started."

Her eyes snapped to his. "What do you mean?"

"I mean put that on." He dropped onto the end of the bed, sprawled back and propped up on his elbows. "But first, I want you to strip for me."

Chapter 8

Sass's seductive expression morphed to panic. Rio pretended not to notice.

She was the one who'd suggested they take this path, not him. He would have abandoned their damned mission right then and there. He'd already said they should leave. This whole thing went *way* beyond the call of anyone's duty.

But she was arguing to stay. He had to know if she was serious.

Because, he was game if she was. He'd be a fool to insist on aborting the op rather than have sex with a gorgeous woman who was already driving his libido nuts. Okay, he'd be an honorable fool…. But hadn't he just decided to shake up his stodgy image?

The real risk was, what if she changed her mind right at the critical point? That could prove awkward, or worse. He'd be glad to leave right now but he didn't want her to blow their cover later by panicking and turning her husband down on camera. He had to know.

Giving her a little taste of what was to come should serve as a wake-up call, before it was too late.

He regarded her evenly. "Yes? No? What's it going to be?"

At least where she stood, only her backside would show on camera. He'd give her that modicum of modesty.

He watched as she licked her lips several times, then glanced down at the bikini dangling from her fingers. He saw the exact second she decided to give him what he wanted.

He couldn't believe it.

Unwilling excitement rushed through his body. He was hard in an instant.

He shouldn't be turned on by this. God knew he hadn't forgotten the camera watching them, or the dangerous situation. But he couldn't help his body's instinctive reaction to the idea of Sass Hawthorne taking off her clothes, regardless of what his head was telling him.

He also understood with raw certainty that he'd been dying to get her naked from the first moment he'd met her a year ago. Suddenly he didn't care that she was a thief. All that interdepartmental enemy stuff had just masked his real desire to get to know the provocative woman who'd bested him and captured his imagination as no other woman ever had.

It was her idea, he reminded himself.

This was his chance. He might never get another.

His inner Rafe slipped out all too easily.

"Come on, baby," he urged, his voice growing husky with guilty anticipation. "Strip for me."

Her eyes were warm pools of murky emotion and uncertainty, plainly aware there was more going on here than catering to their host's perversions. Her cheeks and breasts flushed bright rose. Under the clingy fabric of her dress he saw her nipples swirl to tight points.

Hesitantly, she reached behind her back for the zipper, fumbling with the tab.

"Let me help," he murmured. He sat up, circled his hands around her and tugged the zipper all the way to the end.

She stood wedged between his thighs so he could feel the tremors in her body when she slowly began to lower the dress from her shoulders. He could smell Gun's perfume, sultry and exotic, and under it the intriguing musk of Sass's own woman's scent. He had a powerful urge to follow the alluring trail of it with his nose and lips and let it draw him to her secret places, to explore and find the origin of her intoxicating, unique fragrance.

The dress slipped over her arms and down to her waist, exposing her luscious breasts. So perfect… Round and full, spilling out of the lacy black bra that held them up at eye level as he sat on the bed.

His throat went dry. *What was he supposed to be doing again?* He couldn't remember. All he could think about was putting his mouth on her lush breasts and taking his fill.

To hell with it. With a groan, he wrapped his arms around her and pulled her close, burying his face in her soft exposed flesh.

He unhooked her bra.

He heard her weak inhale as his tongue slowly licked up the deep divide of her cleavage. She tasted sweet and arousing and blissfully succulent. Her heart thundered as he slipped the satin straps from her shoulders and her bra slid off completely.

"Oh, baby," he murmured, taking her in his hands, cupping her, filling his palms with her, lifting her to meet the brush of his eager thumbs. He dragged his stubbled jaw over her sensitive flesh. She cried out softly, and drilled her fingers through his hair, bringing his lips to within a fraction of the pebbled tip of one blushing breast.

He shouldn't.

If he tasted her, it would be impossible to stop. He'd want to tumble her on the bed and rip off those lacy panties and drive into her until she cried out again—this time his name.

Except it wouldn't be his name, it would be another man's. It had to be.

Her fingers pressed against his scalp, urging him closer, so his lips kissed the sweet crown of her nipple. With another groan, he opened his mouth and surrounded it, sucking it in and swirling his tongue around the hard point, once, twice, before switching to the other and repeating the agonizing ritual.

Then he pulled away before he lost all control.

Her hands were buried in his hair and her breath was coming in ragged pants; her breasts glistened with his saliva and thrummed to the tympani of her heartbeat—and his. He felt the pulse of it deep in his groin, where it throbbed with the combined force of his rampant arousal. *He wanted her. So badly he shook with it.*

He looked up and their gazes met. Dark and luminous, her eyes begged him....

To what? Stop? Or to keep going?

Suddenly he couldn't stand the thought of anyone watching her but him. With a curse, he got to his feet and stepped behind her, so his own body shielded hers from the prying lens of the camera.

He crushed her back against his chest, kissing her neck with all the intensity of his desire.

"He can't see you now," he whispered.

She trembled in his hands.

He slid off her panties.

She was completely naked, except for her wobbly gold shoes, black pageboy wig and his wedding band.

He forgot why they were there. He forgot his name. He forgot everything except his overwhelming need to claim this woman as his.

He held her tight, gliding his hands over her warm, naked flesh, trembling as badly as she was. And whispered in her ear exactly what his body wanted to do to hers. With hers. In hers.

He slipped his fingers between her thighs and she made a mewling sound in her throat. But her legs opened, just enough to let him in farther.

"So wet," he murmured, "so hot."

He was just conscious enough to be shocked by what he was doing. And more shocked that she was letting him. Encouraging him. That she wanted him to touch her. There.

"For you," she whispered. "Just you."

He slid his middle finger into the depths of her womanhood, swirling, probing, making her squirm in his arms.

Making her pant.

Making her moan.

Making her come apart with a sudden gasp and a shuddering, quivering, inarticulate cry.

It wasn't his name.

But it wasn't another man's, either.

His body screaming for release, he turned her and held her, bracing his feet apart to support her boneless weight. And soothed her when a different kind of trembling sifted through her limbs.

"Shhh, it's okay," he murmured, and lifted her chin for a kiss. Her eyes gazed back at him, open and vulnerable, and when he whispered, "Do you have any idea how beautiful you are right now?" they suddenly filled.

He kissed her again and held her close, trying to spare her from his raging erection. Wondering what the hell he should do now. Tears were the last thing he'd expected. "You all right, sweetheart?"

She nodded but wouldn't meet his eyes.

Her chin was still in his hand so he tilted her face up again. "Baby, I was the luckiest man in the world the day you became my wife," he said, and watched as her embarrassment turned to something…less definable. "I'll do anything for you. If you want to leave this place, just say the word. We'll go right now."

Her eyes closed and her head gave a small shake. "No." She shook her head again, more steadily, and opened her eyes. "Hell, no."

And just like that she was Gun again. She pressed up against his body and reached for him, making him back away with a choked-out groan.

"Baby, you don't want to be doing that."

The backs of her fingers brushed lightly up his painful arousal, and he saw stars.

"Yes, I do."

Her hands felt so good on him, her naked curves so pliant against his, so incredibly feminine, and she was so obviously willing—he was that close to giving in to temptation and pushing her onto the bed, making her wrap those incredible legs around him, ramming into her and—

He took a deep breath. A *really* deep breath. And set her away. *No way in hell.*

Jeez, Louise. And he'd thought to teach *her* a lesson. There was one somewhere in here for him, too, about getting so tangled up in your cover you forgot about your mission.

"Later," he said, and swiped up her abandoned bikini from

the end of the bed—right after removing her hand from him. "That will still be there tonight, believe me. Meanwhile, maybe we should get downstairs with the others."

Awkwardly, he tied the bikini top strings around her neck and back. He'd done plenty of *un*dressing, but had never actually dressed a woman before. The top ended up a little loose, but personally, he liked the look. The bottoms were easier. Except for the part where he had to touch her so close to where he so desperately wanted to be.

She didn't protest, but cooperated with languid limbs and a shy, just-satisfied smile on her lips that did nothing to tame his arousal. Especially when he thought about how he'd put it there.

Which he *wasn't* going to think about. Not now.

The bikini was brow-raisingly tiny but Sass didn't even blink. When he finished tying it, she twined her arms around his neck and gave him a long, resolve-melting kiss.

Dawson. He had to think about Dawson and the trigger—

She gave him one last brush. "Okay, later then, *älskling*."

He blew out a breath and prayed he lived that long.

"Come on. Let's go downstairs."

"Aren't you going to change?" she asked, not moving.

He stopped halfway to the door and checked his shirt and mercifully roomy linen pants. "Why?"

"I thought we could go to the beach. You'll need swimming trunks."

The look she gave him held the edge of a dare.

She wanted him to change into *swimming trunks?*

His face heated. The rest of his body didn't need heating. It was already hot enough to incinerate.

"You brought some, right?" she asked.

"Yeah. I did."

"Well?" Gun tipped her head. And smiled.

It was tit for tat, eh? A little bit of this for a little bit of that? Definitely a dare.

Hell, this was one she'd lose. He'd been in enough locker rooms not to be shy of other men looking at his butt. Not remotely.

Wordlessly, he went to the dresser, got his trunks out of the top drawer and tossed them to her. "Hold these for me."

Then he turned his back to the camera and proceeded to strip out of his clothes. Every last stitch. And when he stood before her wearing nothing but a half smile, proud and tall and long and thick, she did nothing but stare, her mouth open in a perfect O of…well, shock, he supposed.

"Baby, why don't you hand me those trunks?"

Her mouth snapped closed, then her tongue peeked out and swiped over her lower lip. "Why don't we go skinny-dipping instead?"

His half smile faltered. This woman would be the death of him yet. "Sure. But I don't aim to walk through the living room in my birthday suit."

"Too bad." She passed him the trunks with a wink. "I'll find some towels."

He yanked on the flimsy shorts and raked a hand through his hair.

This was *so* not working it was ridiculous. Rather, his plan was working far too well. The having-sex-with-Sass part, anyway. The doing-their-job part was failing miserably.

He had to fix his appalling lack of concentration quick, or they'd never accomplish what they came for.

The problem with that was, only one thing came to mind that would help his flagging concentration. Getting her under him and himself inside her as soon as possible. If he could do that, if he could just relieve this overwhelming physical need for her, he might be able to focus again. *On the mission.*

But it had to be somewhere private. He didn't want their lovemaking to be recorded for anyone else's skewed pleasure. He also had to know she was coming to him of her own free will, not because she felt forced into it.

The beach sounded private....

And it was her suggestion.

Perhaps she was feeling the same crazy desire as he was.

They both knew this was only part of their cover. That if they made love it meant nothing between them personally. That it was merely the adrenaline, the suggestiveness of the situation and their unusually potent chemistry that was coming out as this intense sexual need.

At least he prayed it was that. Because if these feelings he was having for her were real, he was in a heap of trouble.

Nah. Impossible. Sass was the opposite of what he wanted in a woman for the long term. He wanted soft and her edges were hard. He wanted pliant and she had a stubborn streak a mile wide. He wanted domesticated and she lived for danger and excitement.

No. He was only craving her for the here and now. He was sure of it.

Which was just fine. That worked so much better.

He strode to his duffel and dug around for the box of protection he'd brought with him in a temporary fit of optimism that she might change her mind after their talk on the boat. Not that he'd really believed it, of course. But he prided himself on being prepared for anything. By-the-book did have its advantages.

He popped one of the square packets into the hidden pocket of his swimming trunks. Then he popped in another for good measure.

"Ready?" she asked, watching him from the doorway.

"Oh, yeah."

Ready, willing and able.

He just hoped the beach was good and deserted.

And that he wasn't making the biggest mistake of his life.

Sass's blood was screaming through her veins with more speed than it had ever done scaling a skyscraper or cracking a safe full of classified documents. And it wasn't because of the job she was on.

It was all because of Rio.

What he'd just done to her.

What he was planning on doing to her.

She didn't know whether to be mortified or excited beyond belief. She was both.

She told herself to be cool, calm. Not to make a big deal out of this.

But the way he'd touched her…lit her instantly on fire…made the whole world disappear with his slow hand…she'd never experienced anything like it. No man had ever made her feel that way before. Like a tab of C-4 ready to detonate. And she'd detonated all right. She could still feel the aftershocks.

She'd been brain-dead and helpless for want of him, the camera completely forgotten.

She wondered why he'd held back….

His body was incredible. He'd known exactly what he was doing when he'd stripped naked for her. Lord, he'd been…huge. He'd wanted to show her what he offered, how much he wanted her. And yet, he hadn't taken her….

Could it be he was actually trying to protect her modesty under these impossible circumstances? That would be just like

Rio, she realized with a tug at her heart. He'd done what he had to, to preserve the mission, but he'd shielded her completely from exposure. He'd wanted to do more, but his unflagging sense of honor wouldn't let him. An incredible man.

He was walking in front of her now, jogging down the stairs to the first floor as they went to find the others. She couldn't help admiring his broad, bare back and tight butt, only enhanced by the supple blue swimming trunks that highlighted every luscious outline as he moved.

What would it be like to have his strong shoulders pinning her down beneath him in the soft sand, his muscled chest pressing into her, robbing her of breath, his lean hips moving between her thighs as he scythed in and out of her...?

She almost tripped, and grabbed the banister.

Stop it! Stop it this instant! she ordered herself.

That wasn't going to happen. For good reason, he'd put a halt to the madness in the bedroom, and now she'd thankfully come to her senses, too. Rio might hope they were going out to the beach to finish what they'd started, but he'd be taking that trip solo while she broke into Dawson's office.

As much as she might wish otherwise, having sex with Rio was still as bad an idea as it ever was. She didn't know how they'd get around that camera in the bedroom, but somehow they'd find a way. People got headaches, didn't they?

An unbidden stab of regret sliced through her. He would undoubtedly be an awesome lover.

But no. She had to stop thinking about Stewart Rio and start thinking how best to breach Dawson's office and find the triggering device. That's what she was here for. Not to drool over some man.

Back to business.

They met Dawson coming out of the forbidden east wing.

Their host was alone, looking a bit disheveled and as though he'd been drinking. She figured he'd been indulging in his favorite voyeuristic hobby, taking advantage of the presence of the call girls he'd so thoughtfully provided his male guests. Had he also watched her and Rio? Even as she hoped so for the sake of her plan, the thought made her ill.

"Going for a swim?" Dawson said with a leer at her barely there turquoise bikini. He chuckled suggestively. "Lovely day for a little skinny-dipping."

Her stomach turned over. But she was back to being Gun now, so she buried her distaste and winked back at him. "Isn't it, though?"

"We thought we'd go to the beach," Rio said, sliding his arm around her.

"Oh, I'm afraid that's impossible," Dawson quickly replied, making Sass halt on the stairs. "No one is allowed off the grounds once they're here."

"Why not?" she asked, her plan crumbling. "I don't like swimming pools. I prefer the ocean."

Dawson chuckled again. "I'm sure you do. But you must understand, I'm forced to keep an eye on all my guests, to prevent anyone from putting the auction in jeopardy."

"By swimming?" she asked with real annoyance. Damn. Nothing on this mission was going right.

Rio's hand slid down her hip and around her abdomen. "We could go back to our room," he suggested, an odd smokiness to his voice.

Far too tempting.

Frustration whipped through her. That he could so easily distract her. That he was just making things harder. That he was actually making her think about doing it.

She reached up and nipped his jaw between her teeth, then licked away the sting. "Later, darling. I want a swim now."

She started down the stairs in her teeny-tiny bikini, dragging the end of her towel behind her, hoping she didn't trip and land on her face. She could feel Rio's stunned gaze on her, hear the scratch as he rubbed his jaw.

That nip had shocked him. Okay, it had shocked her, too. Totally out of character. *Her* character.

But she was Gun now. And as much as she hated to admit it, Sass liked being a bad girl for once. Sure, she was really one of the good guys, working for the FBI. But she was a *thief.* Bad was in her blood. And playing Gun was bringing all sorts of things up from the hidden depths of her personality. Pulse-kicking, heart-pounding, stomach-zinging things Sass had only felt before when practicing her risky trade. Never with a man.

But then, she'd never met a man like Stewart Rio before. Dudley Do-Right on the outside, Dirty Harry on the inside. It was a lethally sexy combination. One that had already thrown her into terrifyingly unknown territory and was threatening to blow her known world to smithereens without even trying.

Especially if she were forced to have sex with him tonight.

Slinging her beach bag over her shoulder, she did a perfect runway turn at the bottom of the stairs, and looked up at him, doing her best to hide the confusion running rampant through her. "You coming, or what?"

He paused for a heartbeat, then said, "Baby, you can count on it," and sauntered down after her.

She had to lock her knees to keep them from dissolving. She understood exactly what he was saying.

And thought about tonight.

With a shiver, she told herself not to panic. She could do

this. Whatever was required. Even if they had to play to the camera in order to stay in the game.

There had to be a lot worse things than sacrificing her body to a devastatingly handsome man she had no doubt would sacrifice his very life to protect her.

There was just one thing worrying her. If she did, how on earth would she protect her heart in the process? Or would she end up sacrificing that to him, as well...?

None of the other guests were around, so Sass and Rio lounged by the pool with Dawson as she tried to come up with a new plan for getting into his office.

"Call me Miles," he said with snakelike charm.

Ellis brought her a strawberry daiquiri and Rio a beer.

"So, Miles, how is this auction going to work?" Rio asked.

Dawson steepled his fingers. "I'll explain all that at dinner when everyone is present. Let's talk of other things, shall we?"

Sass thought she detected a hint of impatience in Rio's pursed lips, but he covered it well as he sipped his beer and tried again. "Okay, then, how long have you lived here on the island?"

She didn't listen to Dawson drone on about all the places he'd lived and people he'd met. She had just a short time to figure out how she could sneak into the office. And the first thing she had to do was get away from—

"You should put on some sunblock." She jerked back from her thoughts to see Rio studying her. "You know I don't like it when you freckle. Put some on."

"All right," she said, disregarding his imperious tone, and reached for her bag to get the SPF 30. She wondered where this was coming from. He hadn't once mentioned sunblock on the boat.

Acutely aware of both men's eyes on her, she smoothed the lotion on. Gun wouldn't have hesitated to give them what they wanted, so she better not, either. Starting with her feet and working up, she slowly stroked the cool liquid onto her body, prolonging the process, pretending enjoyment, lingering on her thighs and the slopes of her breasts until she was more heated from embarrassment than from the sun.

When she was finally finished with her front, Rio held out his hand. "Come over here," he ordered huskily. "I'll do your back."

She hesitated. She didn't want to go within spitting distance of the man, let alone have him touch her again—her body was still tingling from the last time. Unfortunately, Dawson was watching and she didn't have a choice. So she perched on the edge of Rio's chaise and passed him the lotion. Bracing herself for the impact.

His fingers were strong and slippery on her skin, his voice low in her ear. "We'll give him a show, then I'll distract him for you."

She almost sighed with relief. Thank goodness they were thinking the same way. This was all just a performance!

He lifted her onto his lap, pulling her into a kiss.

As his mouth moved over hers, she squirmed, trying to avoid contact with the obvious ridge of his arousal—okay, maybe part of the performance was real—but he just groaned softly and pressed her hip hard up against it, deepening the kiss even further.

She tried not to get caught up in the kiss, in the feel of him all around her, honestly she did, but it was useless. He felt too good.

Her resistance melted. Oh, yes, she thought, sinking into

his embrace, there'd be much worse things than giving herself to this man.

Suddenly, he broke it off and growled, "Baby, I want you to do me. Now."

She blinked. "You... What?" Surely, he didn't—

"Here." He thrust the lotion bottle into her hand. "I'm burning up."

So was she, but—

Oh.

She desperately needed a fan. Or a new brain. The heat had addled the old one.

She took the bottle and he reclined back on the lounge with a knowing smile. With sudden dismay she realized she'd have to touch *him* now. All over.

Every corded muscle.

Every enticing plane of solid flesh.

Every tantalizing inch.

Ho boy.

It was no use to steel herself against the magnetism of his firm male body. She knew that the first second her fingers touched his skin. So she just decided to enjoy the moment.

Her hands glided with slick pleasure over his broad expanse of shoulders, reveled in the springy hair on his arms and chest and were oh-so-tempted to follow the dark V of curls that arrowed down from his navel to disappear into the waistband of his trunks.

She saw him there, the blunt, rounded tip of him, lurking just below the rim of the taut fabric. His eyes dared her.

She couldn't. Wouldn't.

Shouldn't.

"What's the matter, baby? Shy?"

He leaned forward and brushed his lips over her mouth, extending his tongue to touch hers when she hesitantly opened to him. Taking her jaw in his large hand, he held her immobile as his tongue licked and swirled around hers, not letting their lips meet. It was a sizzlingly sensual, intimate act that sent a cascade of desire down her spine.

When she opened her eyes, his sultry gaze was intent on her. Ripe with invitation.

God help her, she wanted to say yes.

"Do my back before I take you right here," Rio said, his voice rough with restraint.

"Don't stop on my account," came Dawson's quiet encouragement, startling them both out of the moment.

Rio's expression froze for a nanosecond, then he lazily sat up and turned his back to her. "I can wait," he said. "Hurry up, baby. I want a swim."

She let out a measured breath and spread lotion over his back as quickly as she could. How did he always do it to her— make her lose her sense of direction every time they got close? She really needed to work on that. Somehow.

As soon as she finished up he grabbed her hand and pulled her toward the pool.

"Rafe, no!" she protested, seeing where he was headed. She tugged against his hold. "I don't want—"

"I do."

He jumped into the water, with her in tow. Sputtering to the surface, she swatted at him. "Look what you've done! You've ruined my wig, you big oaf!" It floated in the water like a piece of flotsam on the waves as she struggled against his grip.

He just laughed. "Good. I hate when you wear those ugly things anyway." He took her around the waist and plucked at the pins holding up her real hair. Bobby pins flew every which way as he yanked them out and the arrangement toppled. "There, that's much better."

She touched the sweaty, clumped mass and scowled. "Damn it, Rafe, now I look like a scarecrow!"

He drew her close. "Baby, you always look beautiful. Come here," he said, and kissed her, drowning any further protests.

She'd lost count of how many times he'd kissed her since this morning. He seemed to do it at every possible opportunity. She knew it was just part of their cover, but...damn. It was nice.

However, kissing Rio wasn't going to get her into Dawson's office.

"Let go of me, you sex maniac," she said, and pushed at his chest. "Now I have to go up and wash my hair."

"Nah, allow me," he said with a grin, and dunked them both under the water again. "There, see?"

She coughed and spit out water—at him—then jerked herself free. "Jeezus, Rafe! Sometimes you can be such a little boy."

"Not so little," he returned, his grin widening.

"Oh, honestly." She stalked out of the pool and swiped up a towel. "I'm going to the room to shower and change. If you value your life you won't try to follow me."

With that, she marched into the house and slammed the French door behind her to the sound of his chuckles. She held her breath for several seconds, praying Dawson wouldn't send Ellis after her. He didn't.

Their ruse had worked! She was all alone in the vast living room. Throughout the whole first floor the only sound was the soft hum of the air-conditioning.

Swiftly, silently, she flew up the stairs to their room. Once inside she strolled to the dresser, chafing with impatience from having to appear casual. That camera watching her every move was a real pain.

Closing the bathroom door, she took a deep breath and checked carefully for signs of a camera in here, too. Ellis had said there were none in the bathrooms, but she couldn't trust that. But apparently he'd been telling the truth. All she found was a sound bug. With a sigh of relief she donned clingy green bike shorts and an even clingier green bandeau, then pulled a featherlight catsuit over them, this time a tan one for daytime. After turning on the shower, she fetched her toiletries bag and retrieved the equipment she'd need: the carabiners, pulley-line and belay hidden in the hair impliments, her tools from the manicure kit, the toothbrush bore scope and her infrared sunglasses. Then she unlocked the triggering device from its nest in Rio's shaver and wrapped it in a velvet jewelry bag before carefully placing it at the bottom of the fanny pack she used for jobs.

The bathroom window alarm was child's play for a professional, no doubt part of the original mansion security. Good. That meant Dawson really hadn't upgraded everything, relying instead on his cameras and trusted guards for his front line of defense.

In less than a minute she'd bypassed the alarm and slid through the window.

Her pulse kicked up. Quickly, she tossed the miniature grappling hook onto the roof so it latched onto a protruding pipe vent. Donning her gloves she glanced around. No guards in sight. With a couple of hand-over-hands she hoisted herself up the wire to the roof and flattened herself against it, checking again for guards. So far so good.

She scampered over the steep peak of the roof and down the other side to a spot right above her target, as far away as possible from the roof deck where she knew a guard was posted at the rail.

This was where it got tricky. Guards patrolled the grounds, especially the house perimeter, frequently. She had to rappel right past a third-floor window to get to the second-floor office. And she didn't know what extra measures had been installed on the office windows themselves. Any one of which could get her caught.

No time for second thoughts.

She slid down the wire. The third-floor window's curtains were closed. She silently went past it to her target.

Bracing her feet against the office windowsill, she searched for wires, beams, any clue to the security.

That's when she saw the camera inside.

Pointed straight at her.

Chapter 9

"Your wife is a real hellcat," Dawson remarked as Sass disappeared through the French doors in a huff that looked so real Rio cringed.

He sipped his beer with a frozen smile. "She's a handful all right."

The surprising part was he'd actually started to enjoy it— never knowing what to expect from her next. Something which usually annoyed him to no end. Now he looked forward to every volatile minute in her company. Why? He'd always liked things solid and predictable. He preferred his women sweet and tractable. And spitfire Sass was anything but.

No, that wasn't true. Earlier in his arms she'd been sweeter than honey and willing to follow his lead anywhere he took her.

A wave of slow-burning guilt lapped at his conscience. And look where he'd led her....

"I'm amazed your bosses allowed the marriage."

"My bosses?" He turned to the man he hadn't thought he could hate more than he already did, and snapped back to the conversation at hand. *Focus*.

Dawson meant Interpol. So he knew about Gerard's real job. Rio shifted in his teakwood chaise, painstakingly banking his guilt and growing anger. "Are you kidding? They couldn't believe their good luck. Figured she'd be an invaluable source of information."

"And is she?" His host looked only mildly interested, but Rio knew it was far from an idle question.

"A veritable font. She's been a lot of places I could never go." Dawson frowned.

"Don't worry, she knows exactly where her loyalties lie," Rio drawled, practically choking on his next words. "Besides, I never betray my friends and associates. Bad for business. And you know I'm all about the business."

"I'm glad to hear that," Dawson responded. But he still looked dubious.

Rio carefully set the hook. "In fact, a man in my position could be a real asset to a man in your position. Rivals could be arrested. Enemies eliminated. All nice and legal."

The other man's frown eased. *Bingo*. "Ah. I see how that might be useful. So tell me, how would one take advantage of such an arrangement?"

Rio shrugged. "First, I'd have to trust you. And I gotta say, Miles, so far you haven't given me much reason to."

That earned a wan smile. "And second?"

"Second, you'd have to make it worth my while. *Really* worth my while."

Dawson laughed. "Now you're speaking my language."

Rio tipped back his beer and drained it. That had gone well.

Dawson had taken his bait. Hopefully the gambit would lead to some good intel. The more he could get out of Dawson about his business, the greater Rio's contribution to the outcome of the operation. Actual names were the most valuable commodity of all. If he could get a few new leads on other terrorists whose sick agendas Dawson aided, the mission would be considered a rousing success. And Rio could retire from the Bureau in a blaze of glory.

And maybe then he could forget about the woman who was turning him inside out.

Damn her hide! He'd been on dozens of undercover stings and ops, and had never before felt an iota of guilt over anything he'd had to do to get the bad guys. *Never.* Until now.

But this was different. What he'd done to her should have been between the two of them, alone. Not done to feed some sicko's fantasies. Regardless of the reason. He didn't care that she'd seemed to be okay with what happened, or even that it had been her idea. It didn't matter that he'd hidden her from view.

No matter how much he wanted her, he just shouldn't have.

After a glance at the French door, Dawson checked his watch. Rio battled back a surge of anxiety.

Was he already wondering about Sass's whereabouts? She hadn't been gone that long, but Dawson's paranoia and short fuse were not to be trifled with.

Abruptly, Rio got to his feet. "Don't suppose you have a workout room?" He flexed his rigid arm muscles. "I'm feeling a bit stiff."

"On the third floor."

"Great."

"Maybe I'll join you. I don't use it nearly enough."

Probably never, judging from the marshmallow look of his body. "Sure." Dawson tagging along would keep him in his sights. No doubt Dawson was thinking the same thing about him.

Dawson led the way into the house and up the stairs, pausing at a set of double doors. "I just need to get some shorts. Come on in."

Rio followed him into a hall filled with guards. This must be the private wing Sass had told him about.

"Would you like to see my office? I understand Ellis already gave your wife the tour."

Rio's neck hair rose thinking that Sass could be behind one of these doors at this very moment, a whim away from discovery.

He turned his back so Dawson wouldn't spot his sudden tension. "She told me about the monitors. I'd rather see those."

"Yes, I saw your conversation," Dawson said, swinging open a door at the end of the hall. "And what came after. Your wife's a hot little number. Next time I want to actually see her."

Fury flashed through Rio. The bastard!

"Don't count on it," Rio said coldly, forcing himself to appear calm. "I don't share my woman with anybody."

"Yes, I noticed your reticence. Very gentlemanly."

Before Rio could reply, they stepped into the room. His brows shot up, fury merging with incredulity. The place was a BDSM fantasyland, filled with stuff he'd only seen in the backs of certain unsavory magazines. And some he had no clue what they were.

"If you see anything you'd like to borrow, just say the word," Dawson informed him with a gleam of unnatural interest in his eye.

"I'll keep that in mind," he choked out.

Then he spotted the monitors lined up on the wall. Every

one of the ten screens showed a different bed, full-on. Five were occupied by his fellow guests and the call girls.

Another, familiar bed held only a wet bikini tossed on it.

He clenched his fists at his sides to keep from doing something really, really stupid. He hoped to hell the gym had a punching bag.

"Ready?" Dawson, who'd donned shorts and a T-shirt, asked as though nothing around him were the least bit unusual. "Or would you rather stay here a while?"

Not. "Let's go."

Rio followed him up to the third floor.

Dawson paused in front of their bedroom. "Don't you want to change, too?"

"Suppose I should."

Rio fervently hoped Sass had remembered to leave the shower running while she was gone. "Baby?" he called, walking in. "It's me and Miles."

There was no answer, but his shoulders notched down somewhat at the sound of spraying water coming from the bathroom.

"Women and their showers, eh?" Dawson commiserated. "It's been what, half an hour?"

Suddenly the water shut off and a second later the bathroom door flung open. Sass walked in and halted in surprise. "Oh!"

She was dripping wet but thankfully held a large towel in front of her.

Rio moved immediately to shield her. "Sorry, darlin'. I need some workout clothes. Miles and I thought we'd pump a little iron."

Sass recovered quickly, wrapping the towel around her with a smile. "Good. That'll give me a chance to relax and do some reading." She indicated a novel on the nightstand with a Swedish title. "Now you boys shoo. And take your time." She raised up on her toes to give him a peck, then she disappeared back into the bathroom.

He grabbed his gym shorts from a drawer. "Just a sec," he told Dawson, and went after her. "Talk to me," he whispered after turning on the sink faucet, searching her face and body for any sign of injury. His breath eased out when he saw nothing.

"He's got cameras on all the windows. I have to find the network router and hack a loop into the code so I can move around without being seen."

As she'd done in their recent competition. He stripped out of his damp swimming trunks. "Location?"

"Best guess, the attic above the east wing."

"Can you get there?"

"I'll find a way."

He pulled on his gym shorts. "How long do you need?"

"Buy me half an hour."

He gave a curt nod and turned off the faucet. As he opened the bathroom door he grasped her face in his hand and gave her a short, intense kiss. "Don't leave the room," he told her loudly in Rafe's arrogant voice of command. "I want you here when I get back."

As he and Dawson walked down the hall together, he sternly told himself to put her out of his mind. Concentrate on his own job. This was a golden opportunity to get information out of Dawson. Sass would be all right. She was a pro, a thief. This was what she did. It was unnecessary to worry about her.

Too bad he was worried. Big-time, judging by the roiling knot in his stomach.

And too bad he was thinking of her less and less as a thief, and more and more as a woman.

A woman he was beginning to care about. A lot.

Hell. *His* woman.

Like it or not, he may as well admit the truth.

Sass Hawthorne had gotten under his skin and wasn't leaving anytime soon.

And *that's* what worried him more than anything.

Sass couldn't believe her luck having Rio and Dawson walk into the room at exactly the best possible moment. If they'd planned it that way it couldn't have gone better. Now she had the extra time she needed to finish this phase of her work without Dawson wondering where she was. It was almost scary how much she and Rio were in sync, just naturally, without trying.

Though she had to admit, he hadn't looked himself just now. He'd looked about to blow a gasket, or…something.

But there was no time to analyze it now. She had to get a move on.

This morning on the roof deck, Sass had noticed a hatch opening on one of the exterior walls of a dormer. She'd thought at the time it might be a way into the attic. Now she hoped she was right.

She decided to use the back stairs rather than scale the wall. Easier to explain if she got caught by the guard that was posted up there. Lightning fast she slipped back into her bike shorts and bandeau, along with black Keds, then loaded her equipment and catsuit into her fanny pack and topped it with suntan lotion and a scarf.

Before leaving the room, she had one more thing to do. She casually climbed onto the bed, arranged herself with the Swedish novel lying on her stomach and pretended to fall asleep. She held the pose for a full minute, then swiped up her things and stepped out into the hall.

She reached the roof door without running into anyone. Peering through the small, glass square, she saw that the same cammo-clad guard was posted on the deck as earlier, but now he was standing at the railing, scanning the woods and the grounds below.

Carefully, she tried the door.

Locked.

She picked it and gingerly turned the knob, then silently slipped through the narrow gap.

She hardly dared breathe as she noiselessly crept across the deck toward the hatch, eyes flicking between the padlocked latch and the guard's back.

Plastered against the dormer hatch, it took her three harrowing tries to pop the padlock. Her heart nearly stopped when it sprang open with an audible *snick*.

She snapped her gaze to the guard. He didn't react.

Her pulse started again.

She gave the hinges a quick dab of lubricant and eased open the hatch, then squeezed through it, silently closing it up again, snug and tight. And prayed the open latch wouldn't give her away.

In the two seconds of illumination climbing in, she picked her spot on a plywood platform to crouch for a few moments, letting her eyes adjust to the near-total darkness. The only light came from the far side of the attic, sunlight pulsing through the slowly rotating blades of a vent fan.

Pulling Mannheim's infrared glasses from her fanny pack, she slid them on and switched on her flashlight, inspecting the attic space.

It was huge. And even emptier than Dawson's office.

She resisted the urge to swear aloud. Could she be wrong about the location of the camera router? Maybe it was hidden somewhere in Dawson's office, or in the utility room off the kitchen.

No. There it was! Far across the dark void she spotted a small, telltale antenna barely visible as it emerged from the loose, blown-in insulation between two joists.

She frowned in annoyance. That type of insulation clung to everything it touched, and itched like crazy on your skin. But she had no choice but to crawl along the joists on her hands and knees, because if she put a foot down in the wrong place she'd go right through the thin Sheetrock ceiling of a bedroom below.

She was sorely tempted to just try networking into the router with her wireless. But undoubtedly that would set off all sorts of alarms on the main monitors and she'd be nabbed within minutes. No, she had to do this one the old-fashioned way.

She pulled her catsuit over her clothes and zipped it all the way up. Then she slid the switch on her glasses to infrared vision.

Whoa. Very sneaky. The attic was crisscrossed with invisible beams.

But nothing she couldn't get through. It took her six minutes to reach the router. And another seven to hack into the software via a hard terminal and her mini-keyboard. Quickly, she programmed a freeze-frame into the cameras watching Dawson's office windows—after first erasing the seconds when she'd crawled out of the bathroom window and then rappelled down the wall from the roof earlier. She did the same thing for the cameras in the third-floor hall and back stairway. She thanked her lucky stars for Dawson's afternoon entertainment which had distracted the guards at the monitors from spotting her during those few seconds of exposure on each.

Speaking of entertainment… Next she rewound the DVR

and programmed a loop into Dawson's private perv-cam in her and Rio's bedroom so it would show her on the bed sleeping for the half hour she'd be gone. Lastly, she programmed a second loop into it, to take effect later tonight. They'd have to time things exactly right, but this should allow them the hour or so of time they needed to sneak off to their rendezvous with Mannheim on the water at midnight. That took another three minutes.

For a long second her fingers suspended over the keyboard. She desperately wanted to erase from the DVR the minutes she'd spent with Rio in their bedroom, too. Rewind it to before he'd touched her. And blown open her whole world along with everything she'd always wanted or believed.

But if she erased those fateful minutes, and Dawson went to watch them again, he'd know the program had been tampered with.

As much as she hated to, she left them intact.

Finished, she gathered her things, crawled back to the platform and peeled out of her catsuit, taking care to roll it inside out before pouching it. She eased out of the hatch, locked it back up and made it down the stairs to her bedroom in nine more minutes.

With eight minutes to spare, she stowed her gear back in her toiletries kit, rinsed the insulation out of her catsuit, crawled onto the bed and lay back with a sigh.

She'd just arranged the Swedish novel on her stomach and closed her eyes when Rio walked in.

Rio had never been so glad to see anyone in his life as when he came into their room and found Sass had made it back from her second-story sojourn, safe and sound.

His heart gave a lurch of joy and relief.

She opened her eyes and smiled. *"Älskling."*

"Hey, baby. Miss me?"

"Like crazy." She even looked as though she meant it. Her foray must have been a success. Thank God.

"Good. I'm going to grab a shower."

Her smile turned slumberous and she stretched out on the bed. "Why don't I join you?"

He halted, a sudden, painful desire to hold her warring in his mind with his new resolve not to. "But you just cleaned up."

She tilted her head seductively. "Who said anything about cleaning up?"

He swallowed, doing his best to convince his libido that this was just a ploy. Her way of getting past the camera and into the bathroom with him so they could have a little private tête à tête about how her sortie had gone. Not—

God help her if she really did mean—

"Baby, you know you don't need an invitation," he said, heart thumping.

He went in and turned on the shower, stripped and stepped under the spray. Then he took his time soaping up head to toe. With his eyes closed. Hoping she wouldn't come in. Praying she would.

"Would you like me to do your back?"

Letting out a long, measured breath, he rinsed the soap from his face and shook out his hair, then slowly turned to look at her through the clear glass enclosure. Frustrated desire backed up inside him clear to his throat, burning like acid with the need to say yes.

He'd been hard since they got on that plane yesterday, and was getting harder by the second. He made no move to hide it.

"Darlin', there's nothing I'd like more. But if you come in

here," he warned her steadily, "you better be naked. And you better want me."

The way her gaze was caressing his nude body made him want to reach out and yank her in regardless of what she answered. Regardless of how disastrous a mistake he knew it would be.

There was only so much a man could take.

She licked her lips. He ordered himself to be more patient than he'd ever been before.

The bathroom was bugged, but there were no cameras. He'd checked. So they weren't forced into anything they didn't want to do. Not in here.

They both knew that.

He wanted her so badly he couldn't see straight. She'd felt so unbelievably good in his arms earlier, had responded to his touch so willingly, so beautifully, so sensually, he was dancing on the edge of madness waiting to feel that again. To feel her again. This time, from the inside out.

But only if she wanted him, too. For real. Not to appease their unpredictable host, not to save the op. Suddenly that was more important than anything else. More important than the camera. Than Dawson. More important than their whole mission.

He needed to know she wanted him as much as he wanted her.

But she still hadn't moved. He figured that was his answer.

Blinding disappointment hurtled through his limbs and spun to a dead halt at the center of his chest.

No, more than disappointment. Bewilderment—at the unexpected pain of her rejection.

She wasn't for him, he reminded himself as he swiped up the shampoo and turned away, unable to bear her silent rebuff any longer.

She was difficult. Independent. A danger junkie. *She was a thief.* Not anyone he wanted in his life after this mission was over.

Getting more involved with her would be a huge mistake. This way was best. This way he wouldn't risk falling for Sass just because he'd made love to her in a weak moment.

A moment when he'd thought maybe he was all wrong about the kind of woman he wanted in his life.

He froze as he heard the distinct *click* of the shower door open and close behind him. Felt her presence there in the cubicle. So close.

Desperate indecision swirled through his gut.

This was such a mistake.

Her hand slid lightly up his soap-slick back and he ground his teeth, wanting to turn and shout at her, "No! I've got my life figured out and you're not part of it!"

He whirled, but the words caught in his throat.

This was one mistake he wanted so badly he could taste it.

She was still dressed. Her silky green shorts and tube top slowly turned black from the shower spray. Her hair was already wet, water running in rivulets down her face and shoulders, disappearing into her cleavage and dripping off her chin and nose. Her hand came to rest on his chest.

"I thought I told you to take your clothes off if you came in here," he gritted out, angry because he had no idea what she expected him to do. Why could she *never* do as she was told?

Her other hand reached over to the soap holder and two small packets rolled from her fingers onto the ceramic shelf.

Their eyes locked.

"I like it better when you take them off for me," she murmured, invitation rife in Gun's breathy voice.

Fear and a dizzyingly powerful punch of arousal slammed into him.

Damn the fear.

Damn the mistake.

Damn Stewart Rio and his damned honor.

He became Rafe.

And reached for her. Pushed her back against the shower wall. Dug his fingers into the flesh of her sides and hooked his thumbs into the upper edge of her top. With a growl he yanked it mercilessly down.

Her lush breasts sprang free, falling into his waiting palms.

He stepped into her, pressing his body against hers as he cupped and squeezed her with his hands, trapping her pebbled nipples between his fingers.

With a moan she caught him behind the neck and brought his face to hers, whispered, "Don't stop," and captured his lips in a blazing kiss. He groaned at her fervor, grinding his hips into hers, opened to the paradise of her tongue and lips as they wantonly explored his mouth.

He ripped her top farther down, taking the shorts with it over her hips, pushing the unwanted garments to the shower floor, stripping her bare as he was.

He kissed her and she kissed him back and he kissed her some more, and then he felt her hands leave his neck and trail down his body.

"No," he hissed, and grabbed for her wrists, jerking them above her head.

Her eyes widened. She squirmed against his grip. He held tighter. Her tentative struggles inflamed him further. He was one thick, throbbing, massive bundle of unfettered need. If she so much as touched him he'd go off like a rocket.

He'd never been like this before, never felt like this before. So completely out of control.

He covered her mouth with his and drank of her. Tasted her

sweet, compelling flavor. Shifted her wrists into one iron fist and touched her body. Everywhere. Wedged his knee between her legs and spread them. Sent his fingers into her hot, honeyed heaven.

She moaned and writhed and panted, tugging at his grip, undulating to the rhythm of his strokes as he fed her fire with his tongue and his fingers. *Suckle and sweep. Suckle and sweep.*

Her body began to quake. She gave a breathy gasp.

And suddenly he couldn't take it any longer. He dropped her wrists and reached down to grab under her knee, wrapping her leg around him. Then he fisted his erection, guided it to her center and plunged into her.

She cried out and clutched him around the neck.

"Don't move," he ordered between clenched teeth.

She stuttered out a moan. "O-ohh!"

"Not a muscle," he hissed. "Not unless you want to get pregnant."

With a mewl her gaze darted to the soap dish. "We forgot—"

Rio liked how she said "we." Most women would blame him.

But Kansas Hawthorne wasn't most women. To his misery, he was learning that more with each minute in her company.

However, this time the blame *was* on him. All of it.

"No," Rafe said, daring to push farther into her. Loving how her wet heat enveloped him. "I didn't forget."

"But—"

Water cascaded down on them, steam swirled around their bodies like a fog of forgetfulness—who they were, where they were, what they were doing there, all obscured by the sultry miasma surrounding them.

"Look at me, baby," he said, and her questioning gaze lifted to his. "I needed to feel you like this first. Without any barriers."

She sucked in a breath as his thumb found the hard pearl of her need.

"Trust me?" he whispered.

Emotions he couldn't even begin to fathom flitted through her desperate green eyes. He felt himself between her legs, inside her. Large, hungry, pulsing to the rhythm of their thundering heartbeats. He smelled her desire. Heard her tiny hiccup of sucked-in breath.

Saw her hesitate. Felt his heart clench. Then watched her nod.

"Want me?" he asked.

He knew the answer. She'd made that clear by coming to him. He would never have taken her this far if he'd had the slightest doubt.

But he needed to hear it. Spoken aloud.

Her arms tightened around him. "Yes," she whispered.

This time there was no hesitation. At least he'd earned that much.

He didn't need more, he told himself. This was all he wanted. *All he wanted.*

He circled her nub of sensation and her head tipped back, eyes drifting closed.

"I told you to look at me," he ordered, voice gritty with restrained need. "I want you to know who you're with."

Her fingers clutched at his hair as she looked back at him. "I know who I'm with—" She didn't say his name, but he could see she wanted to. Only barely stopped herself in time.

But which one?

It didn't matter. Two names. One man.

His chest filled with pride and an overwhelming sense of possessiveness. She was his! All his.

Only his.

He swirled his thumb over and back, around and around.

"Come on, baby," he urged low and rough, capturing her eyes, gazing deep into them, "Show me you want me right where I am. Show me I'm your only man."

Her sharp, moaning breaths hitched and her body started to shudder. Her leg slid from his hip, so he held it, supporting her weight as he brought her to climax.

He watched as she fought to keep her gaze on his through it all, as her body clenched and flew apart from his touch and his words. And he fought his own desperate battle not to join her.

Her hot, tight inner muscles milked at him, tempting him almost beyond reason to let go and throw caution to the wind. To follow her into the pleasure and damn the consequences.

Almost.

Her expression turned languid and she looked up at him with such utter devotion and trust, he had to clench every muscle in his body to stop the floodgates.

She wrapped her arms around his neck and pulled his lips to hers. Then she sighed, long and breathy, ending in a single whispered word, barely audible.

"Rio."

Chapter 10

Sass had feared all along it would happen.

And now it had.

His name on her lips, his body joined with hers, the powerful feeling of belonging. They all meant one thing.

She'd fallen for Stewart Rio. Hard.

She sighed and leaned back against the shower wall; she couldn't help smiling up at him.

He didn't smile back.

Instead, he jerked out of her with a curse. She gasped in shock as he grasped her arms and held himself away from her for a long, tense moment, glowering down at her.

Frantically she played back the last few seconds. She was sure she hadn't spoken it aloud—that stuff about falling for him. She knew how he felt about her. He wanted her body, but only temporarily. He'd repeatedly said she wasn't his type of woman. She accepted that. In fact, it was a damn good thing.

The water shut off. In the sudden silence she heard a rustle and a snap, and in one move her legs were wrapped around his waist and he was inside her again. His strong arms held her as he drove in deep enough to make her cry out in a bolt of unexpected pleasure.

"*Nhhh!*"

His mouth covered hers in a bruising kiss, his tongue thrusting in concert with the steady pumping of his hips. Need seared through her for this man who was claiming her as no man had ever done before. Brutally, forcefully, giving her no quarter.

The way she had waited to be claimed all her life.

She surrendered to it, and reveled in his possession, in his hunger for her, in every groan and grunt of pleasure she gave him. He swept her up in his passion and she drowned in it, in his fervent kisses and his heavy thrusts, in his body's mastery over her.

It would hurt so badly when he left her, but right now she didn't care. He felt too good.

His breathing was labored, his groans long and rumbling. He held her tight. "Come on, baby, stay with me now."

Her excitement peaked as he hilted into her with three last, overpowering plunges. She hurtled over the brink to the sound of his roared-out release.

And knew there was no going back. Not now. Not ever.

He pulled her close as they stood there in the shower on shaky legs, recovering their breath and their wits.

"You okay?" he asked between gulps of air.

She nodded. "Yeah."

And she was. She'd never felt better in her life.

"I'm sorry," he panted out. "I didn't mean to…"

Her heart missed a beat, fearing the worst. Did he already regret making love to her? "Mean to what?" she asked.

He adjusted his hold on her, loosening it. And pulled in several more deep lungfuls. "To take you like that. I'm sorry. I lost control."

From his expression she could tell he wanted to say more but he just shook his head, glancing around the bathroom. Reminding her that even if there was no camera, it was bugged and this private encounter was likely being listened to. He scowled as if he wanted to find the bug and smash it.

At least she hoped that was why he was scowling.

She trailed her fingers through the hair at his temples and smiled, saying lightly, "*Älskling*, you know I like it when you lose control. It's how I know you love me." She gave a sigh of pleasure. "I always lose control with you."

She kissed his momentarily stunned lips.

After a pause he nuzzled her and murmured, "Does that mean you love me, too?"

"From the first moment I saw you," she whispered, knowing that was closer to the mark than she ever wanted to admit. An immediate, hopeless schoolgirl crush on the enemy, one that had compelled her reckless strategy in their second competition. To attract his attention in the most basic way.

Stupid, stupid, stupid.

She knew it was completely impossible, anything between her and Special Agent Stewart Rio, other than a brief undercover affair. Even if he wanted to get involved with her on a longer basis—which he didn't—she could never allow herself to weave any hopes or dreams around him.

She wouldn't settle down. Couldn't settle down. Ever. With anyone. The first time she'd tried, her mother and sister had died. The next time, when she'd begged her father to go straight and live a normal life, he'd ended up in prison.

She was a jinx. A normal family life just wasn't in the cards for her. There was no way in hell she'd put anyone else close to her in jeopardy. No way.

But when Rio smiled down at her and said, "Same for me, baby, from the very first second," all those warnings flew from her mind. Her heart took wing, soaring in the warmth of that smile, never thinking of the danger it carried—to be swept off course, or even hurtled into oblivion.

Then he took a deep breath, kissed her, swatted her on the butt, and said, "Let's get dressed. It's almost time for supper."

She blinked as he stepped out of the enclosure and grabbed a towel.

So much for romance, she thought with a sigh.

On the other hand, she should be grateful for the man's unromantic attitude. If he'd been tender, or the least bit lovey-dovey after they made love, she'd be done for. Tenderness was the one thing that would lay her out completely.

"Good," she said with a bright smile, accepting the towel he offered her. "I'm starving."

He leaned down for a final kiss, and murmured, "Yeah, you'll need your strength for tonight."

She tried to ignore the secret thrill that irrationally spun up her spine. He only meant for their midnight rendezvous with Mannheim, she was sure. Nothing more.

He was not already thinking about the next time they'd make love, she told herself.

Unfortunately, she was.

Supper with Dawson and the other auction bidders was about as strained as anything Sass had lived through to tell about. Sleazy conversation about how the others had spent the afternoon, along with the predatory looks they sent her and uncouth suggestions they gave Rio regarding her, made Sass's hackles rise to the point where he wrapped his arm around her shoulder at the table and squeezed her tight. As a signal not to let loose whatever sharp-tongued set-down she was composing in her head, no doubt.

They both knew she had to get through the next couple of hours without drawing attention to herself—other than as a non-threatening bimbo—so her absence wouldn't be noted when she slipped out later.

In the bathroom they'd quickly made plans by writing with their fingers on the fogged up mirror as they dressed. Dawson had hinted at some sort of entertainment this evening, so Sass would steal away then and break into his office to locate the trigger. Meanwhile Rio would try to schmooze more info out of Dawson and the others about their terrorist activities, as much as he could. Not an easy task.

Especially if she alienated them all with a cutting reaction to their low-brow conversation.

"Miles, you said you'd tell us how the auction will work tomorrow?" Rio reminded him, transparently deflecting the topic into safer territory while she cooled down.

She took a long sip of her wine. Once again he'd recognized her agitation and saved her from blowing it at a sensitive point in their operation. Her respect for him went up another few notches. Not that it wasn't already higher than for just about any other professional she'd dealt with. Even Jules was beginning to pale by comparison.

Of course, she was probably a bit biased by this point.

Though it didn't involve her directly, she made herself listen to Dawson describe what would happen the next morning.

"It's very simple, really," he explained expansively. "Secret, written bids for possession of the nuclear trigger will be turned in by each of you after breakfast. I'll read through them and announce the winning dollar amount. Anyone who wishes may drop out and leave the island at that point. But any bidder who feels they'd like to top the high bid may do so. Everyone will have a chance. At that time the bidding will be closed and the winner will be given the triggering device. My advice to you is to bid high early. You'll only get two shots at it."

Sass kept her mouth firmly shut, determined to stay out of trouble and simply be Rio's arm candy for the duration of the meal.

This part—the auction—was Rio's deal. He was the one with the expertise on what the device was worth on the terrorist market. She had no clue. It was his task to place a bid high enough to be credible but low enough not to win, for their plan to work.

Slowly Sass tuned out the buzz of voices and relaxed against Rio's strong shoulder, enjoying his arm around her and the steady beat of his heart beneath her hand on his chest.

She inhaled, loving how he smelled. Clean and fresh, and all male.

Unable to help herself, she turned her face into the crook of his neck and gave him a kiss there, delighting in the fact that she could express such open affection toward a man without any unwanted consequences. Because Sass was only acting in character. Gun was crazy in love with Rafe. It was so nice to pretend, if only for a few minutes, that Sass was crazy in love with Rio, too, and he with her.

Something she'd never be able to experience in real life, so she intended to take advantage of this once-in-a-lifetime opportunity to see what it might be like to be in love like that.

And worry later about the pain of having to let her lover go when all this was over.

In response to her kiss his fingers brushed lightly over her bare shoulder and trailed down her arm to latch onto her waist. She shivered at his slow, deliberate touch. She had worn a skintight, strapless cocktail dress in bright jade-green, which went stunningly with the sleek, Irish-red, shoulder-length wig and teetering, backless Barbie mules she'd picked out for the evening. An outfit designed to be shed in less than three seconds when she needed to get into her catsuit quickly, later on.

His fingers reminded her it could also be swiftly shed for other reasons....

She closed her eyes and fought off the instant desire that shuddered through her.

Honestly, she didn't know what had come over her—this intense reaction for a man whom just a week ago she'd considered her enemy. Now all she could think about was making love to him again. How had her feelings changed so suddenly, so completely? It was nuts.

Not that they'd exactly made love in the shower.... It had been more like mindless, whirlwind sex.

Amazing mindless whirlwind sex. Totally amazing.

Who was she kidding? There had been way more to it than that. She'd felt it swirling around them, arcing between them. Something deeper and more compelling than mindless sex could ever be. At least for her.

And that's where the danger lay. The danger—and the appeal.

The appeal of throwing herself completely into Stewart Rio for the next day or two and experiencing every last emotion she possibly could with him. Their affair would end as soon as the mission was over. So he wouldn't be at risk.

The danger was all hers.

What would the following days bring?

There was only one thing she was sure of. If she did fall

in love with him, she was headed for a heartache. A *huge* heartache.

Stewart Rio was everything she'd ever wanted in a man, and more.

And she couldn't have him.

"That was you?" Rio asked the terrorist Joaquin, donning an appropriately impressed expression. He put his arm around Sass, who'd snuggled up to him on a couch in the great room where everyone had gathered after supper. Rio made another mental note to deliver to Macon at their rendezvous. He couldn't believe the way his fellow guests were running off at the mouth. "I heard about that bombing in Lima. Can't believe you got away with it," he said, encouraging the man to further indiscretion.

Joaquin grinned broadly. "Our *federales* are idiots—the ones who aren't bought and paid for."

Rio gave a silent snort. The idiot was Joaquin. He'd gotten drunk or maybe stoned and was bragging about his vicious activities with the Sindero Blanco, a fascist terrorist outfit in Peru, to anyone who'd listen.

Of course, Joaquin wasn't alone in his indiscretion. At Dawson's behest, Ellis had laid out a remarkable array of mind-bending substances—everything from a fully stocked liquor bar to a variety of drugs and hallucinogens, to platefuls of gooey chocolate brownies and other sticky treats. Selim, Hetsuro, Mikaelov and Betty were also freely indulging. And as a result all of the auction bidders were wagging their tongues.

Except Rio himself. He stuck to a slowly nursed beer and kept silent except for the occasional confession-encouraging remark.

Sass was on her third umbrella drink, which Ellis fixed with an affectionate flourish. If Rio hadn't seen her slip the kid a C-note earlier not to put alcohol in her drinks, he'd think she was as sloshed as the others.

The other men snickered mercilessly at the bright pink, whipped-cream-topped concoction.

"For such tough woman you drink girly drink," Mikaelov said derisively. "You try good Russian vodka. Make girl into man!" He poured a glass from the bottle before him and sloshed it over to Sass.

She wrinkled her nose. "No thanks, think I'll stick to being girly."

Selim gave her a cold smile. "She can take down a guard with her bare hands but she is afraid of a little alcohol. Or perhaps you are afraid you will get drunk?"

Rio knew they were attempting to re-establish the pecking order. She'd intimidated them with their impressive entrance this morning, and the chauvinist terrorists didn't care for that. They wanted her on the bottom rung beneath all the men, where they believed a woman belonged. They were just warming up at dinner, and now they'd be relentless. He kept silent, knowing it was better for their plans if she were marginalized. Then no one would suspect she was the real talent on the team and he was the window dressing. He just hoped she didn't lose it first.

Sass made a face. "Why should I be afraid of getting drunk? I like getting drunk."

"A little too much," Rio interjected sternly, and picked up the vodka, intending to down it himself so she wouldn't have to.

In a flash she snatched the glass from his hand. "Says who?" she retorted. "I'll drink what I want." With that she threw back the vodka, grimacing as it went down. "Pig swill," she muttered.

He grasped her jaw and jerked her face to his. "Behave," he snapped. "Or I'll be forced to punish you."

Her chin rose a fraction and she harrumphed. "Promises, promises."

While he fought a smile she wrenched from his grasp. Petulantly, she flopped back against the couch, swiped up her tall pink glass, hiccoughed once and pretended not to sway against him. Well, pretended to pretend.

Again she was astonishing the hell out of him with her focus and her acting abilities. He knew she wasn't drunk, a fact confirmed by her steady muscle control and the occasional sharpness of her gaze. But she was doing a hell of a good impression.

Already she'd "accidentally" let slip one of Rafe's more creative exploits, drawn from the files they'd read on the way down. Afterward, she'd put her fingers to her mouth and glanced at him in consternation, as though she'd violated his instructions not to reveal any information about his work. The juice of the mysteriously taciturn Rafe Gerard had instantly skyrocketed, judging by the subtle respect he'd been shown by the group ever since.

"I take it Mr. Gerard is skilled at doling out punishment?" Dawson asked Sass with a disgusting gleam in his eye.

She gave their host a knowing smile. "Oh, yes. A master at it. Why, you should have seen him…do you remember that neo-Nazi punk who was picked up by the police in Belgium and found beaten—"

"Gun!" he said sharply, cutting off her recitation of yet another report from Gerard's file. "I'm sure our friends have a hundred similar stories they could tell. They're not interested in mine."

She bit her bottom lip and kissed his jaw, gliding her fingers inside his black evening tuxedo to stroke his chest. "Sorry, *älskling*. I know you didn't want me to say anything. I'm just so proud of my man, I can't help bragging."

She smiled up at him with a mixture of seductiveness and adoration. Like Gun. Hell, she was playing Gun's part better than even Gun could herself.

Rio was finding it very difficult to maintain Rafe's cool, macho facade. He wanted nothing more than to grab Sass's neat, curvy body in that tight little-nothing dress, pull her onto his lap and French-kiss her lush, pouty mouth to within an inch of her life, then drag her upstairs and do the same to the rest of her body.

Mercy.

This sweet-dirty bad girl Sass was the embodiment of every red-blooded man's secret fantasies.

And she was all his.

For tonight anyway.

But before he could do anything about it, she had to finish up her work for the night. Which meant he had to be patient.

For the next hour or so he endeavored to concentrate all his attention on the bits of information the terrorists were letting drop rather than on Sass's delectable body shifting and pressing up against his. Or her lips on his neck or her soft sighs in his ear. It wasn't easy.

But somehow he managed because by the time Dawson announced the evening's entertainment he'd squirreled away a whole lot of leads for Macon's anti-terrorist unit to investigate.

The entertainment, as he might have suspected, was strippers. A step tamer than the hookers, at least, but still not his thing. Not that he didn't like naked women. In fact, he loved naked women. He just happened to prefer it to be a woman he knew and wanted, and to get her that way himself.

Someone like Sass. Now if she was up there on stage, that would be—

"Oh, *herregud*," Sass said, laying her singsong accent on thickly, "not this again. You boys enjoy the show. I'm going to freshen up."

"Why don't you join the ladies in the spotlight?" Dawson suggested with an exaggerated wink. "I'm sure you dance better than all of them."

She stuck up her chin. "Of course I do," she said, but spoiled the effect by stumbling slightly against the couch.

Rio made himself look incensed. "You've had too much to drink, Gunilla. You're embarrassing me."

She was instantly contrite. "I'm sorry, darling. I didn't mean—" She tried to lower herself in front of him but he prevented her.

"Go upstairs," he snapped out. "Make yourself some coffee. I want you back here in an hour. *Sober!* Do you hear me?"

"Ja, älskling," she whispered, and tottered off looking as if she were about to burst into tears.

"You were a little hard on your wife," Dawson remarked, watching her hurry out to the stairs. "Don't you think?"

Rio turned a glare on him. "Not that it's any of your damned business, but no. She's a great lay but she lacks discipline. I have to keep a tight rein on her. For all our sakes," he said pointedly.

The five terrorists nodded approvingly. Well, four of them. The one called Betty just looked bored. "Sex isn't worth that much hassle," Betty said. "I'd get rid of her. Permanently."

Rio stared for a moment, again wondering if Betty was a man or a woman. Not that it mattered. "I'll take it under advisement," he said, then turned his attention to the strippers who strutted in from the patio. And sat, relegated to the couch, watching as they started their bumps and grinds.

While his woman put her life in danger.

And all he could do was smile through clamped teeth and count the seconds she was gone.

Sass made it upstairs, out and over the roof to the point above Dawson's office window in record time. She'd done it before, so she concentrated on spotting the guards in the darkness, keeping her eyes and ears open to anything that might give her away.

The moon hadn't risen yet, so it was a bit more difficult to navigate, but she preferred it that way. Less chance of being seen. And she knew if she was caught she was a dead woman.

This afternoon she'd noted that Dawson's office window had the same security system as the one she'd disabled in her own bathroom, so all she really had to worry about was timing her descent and entrance to avoid the guards passing below on their five-minute patrol circuit.

Lying open and exposed on the roof, she kept absolutely still, listening to the approaching bootfalls of the two guards as they rounded the southwest corner of the mansion. She held her breath, praying they wouldn't shine their flashlights upward. They didn't. They continued by her and disappeared around the northwest corner.

Go!

Instantly she skimmed down the wire, planting her knees on the sill of her target window. With a wink at the camera she'd disabled earlier, she whipped out her tools and made short work of the alarm system. Using her glass cutter, she scored and tapped out the entire rectangle of glass between the mullions directly above the window lock and reached in to unlatch it. It slid open without a sound.

The delicate glass pane she held with an ordinary suction-

cup kitchen hook—no reason to get high-tech when an every-
day item worked just as well and caused a lot less suspicion—which she gingerly hung from the inside windowsill for
the moment.

Flipping her IR glasses, she surveyed the invisible beams
crisscrossing the room, choosing her path through the matrix
guarding the window very carefully. She smiled. She was
thinner than the intruder they'd planned for. One beam should
do it.

From her fanny pack she pulled two small, round mirrors.
The mirrors were mounted on long, flexible goosenecks with
adjustable clips at the end, which she snapped onto the inside
edge of the windowsill, careful to avoid the hanging glass
pane. With a precise, well-trained hand she positioned the first
mirror, neatly bisecting her chosen infrared beam and reflecting it back to its source at both ends. She repeated the process with the second mirror, resulting in a gap in the beam
between them of about two feet, through which she carefully
crept. Reaching back, she slid the window closed.

Recalling the configuration of the beams behind her, she
slowly turned and got her bearings. Inside the room there
were only five or six beams; most of them were concentrated
at the windows and door. With one exception. There was another matrix protecting a large, colorful painting of Rainbow
Row in Charleston mounted on the wall behind the conference table.

Bingo.

She'd found Dawson's safe.

Chapter 11

Patience, Rio.

For the hundredth time since Sass left, he resisted the urge to check his watch. Hell, she'd only been gone half an hour.

Instead, Rio watched Betty as he—she?—glanced at the clock for the umpteenth time in the past ten minutes.

Now, why would he be doing that? Rio's danger radar sounded its alarm loud and clear.

Betty covertly glanced around the room noting everyone's position. His eyes sought out Dawson as he leaned against the bar in back, idly watching the strippers perform.

Something was definitely up.

Please, not now, Rio prayed. Not with Sass in the wind and him unable to protect her.

While the other men loudly cheered a buxom brunette's gyrations, he rose from his seat as casually as he could and strolled back to the bar, empty bottle in hand.

The last thing Rio needed was anything happening to Dawson. If he had to, he'd save the bastard's life. He was too valuable as a source of information to lose at this point in the game.

"Another beer, Mr. Rio?" Ellis asked with a smile. "Or
maybe something a little stronger this time?"

"Actually nothing, thanks." He turned to prop his elbows
back on the mahogany surface. "Tell me, Dawson," he said
in a low voice. "Got any firepower behind the bar?"

Dawson glanced at him sharply. "Why?"

"Betty's acting strange. I've got a bad feeling."

Dawson's jaw set. "Don't worry. Nobody gets past my—"

At that exact second there was a huge crash and the French
doors exploded inward, setting off high-pitched alarms. Three
men in black combat gear charged through the flying glass
and wood, machine guns in hand. Cursing, Rio grabbed Dawson and catapulted them both over the top of the bar, landing
on Ellis. The strippers were screaming, the terrorists swearing and the intruder commandos shouting orders at the top of
their lungs over the piercing alarm.

"Everyone down on the floor! Hands behind your heads!"

Both Ellis and Dawson lunged for a stash of guns hidden
behind the bar. Rio stretched out his hand for one, but Dawson hesitated.

"Damn it, I just saved your miserable life!" Rio ground out
above the din. "Give me a goddamn gun!"

There was a machine gun blast and the alarm abruptly
ceased.

"Don't move!" came the barked order from the other side
of their tenuous wooden shield. *"Or you're all dead!"*

Reluctantly, Dawson tossed Rio an Uzi and a Glock. "How
many men did you count?" he whispered. It had to be a
double-cross, trying to win the auction before it started.

"Just three." Rio checked the Uzi's clip and flipped off the safety, then stuck the Glock in his waistband. "How many bodyguards upstairs?"

"I said don't move!"

"Six inside. Seven more outs—"

His words were cut off by another blast of bullets and a death cry from one of the terrorists. The strippers screamed even louder.

"Assume they're dead," Rio said. If he and Sass could get by the outside guards, these guys would have made mincemeat of them.

"Get these damn women out of here."

Rio and Dawson exchanged a look when they both recognized the voice starting to give orders. *Betty.* So he'd been right.

"Next time I'll listen to you," Dawson whispered.

"If we live that long. Where the hell are your bodyguards?"

And where was Sass? Rio was on the verge of panic imagining her walking into the middle of this. Or worse, being caught in the act upstairs. Obviously, these men were after the trigger, also.

On cue, above their heads came the sound of wild gunfire and heavy boots running down a hardwood floor. *The east wing.* Rio's blood froze in his veins.

"Goddamn it, enough of this crap," he muttered, wanting to shout and take off at a run, but forcing himself to stay and be calm. "I've got to get to Gun."

"Let's take care of these bozos first," Dawson said.

Rio nodded. Using hand signals, he indicated Dawson left, Ellis right. He'd cover center. One…two…three!

As one unit, they came out firing and caught the intruders by surprise. In the split second it took the commandos to swing around, they were all dead.

Betty stood motionless, a shocked, comical expression on his face, holding a gun on what was left of his competition. For a short moment nothing happened. Then Dawson pulled his trigger and Betty went down in a shower of blood.

"That'll teach him to mess with my auction," Dawson said calmly.

Suddenly there was a commotion on the stairs. The three of them spun, weapons zeroing in on the noise. Rio's heart stalled.

Sass!

Two commandos held her between them, each with a machine gun trained at her head. They entered the room dragging her along. Whimpering, she struggled against their hold, but in a feminine, ineffective manner. *Thank God.* If she was playing bimbo they couldn't have caught her in action.

The commandos took in the scene, showing brief surprise that Betty and their compadres were dead. But they recovered quickly.

One commando yanked Sass in front of him, let his machine gun drop on its strap and pressed a long, vicious knife to her neck.

"Put down your weapons or sexy gets her throat slit."

None of them moved. Rio's pulse thundered. *The bastard was so dead.*

"All right, fine." Dead Meat pressed the blade slightly and a thin line of red appeared on Sass's throat.

Rio's mind screamed and he had to physically restrain himself from moving a muscle, when a trail of blood reached the edge of her green dress. *She was still alive; still alive.* Going off half-cocked was exactly what they wanted.

She struggled harder and wailed desperately, "Omigod! Baby, do something!" But her eyes were dead calm. *Good girl.*

Dawson snorted. "I don't give a damn what you do to her, you're not getting the triggering device."

Lightning fast, Rio switched the machine gun to his left hand, jammed it at Dawson's head, whipped out the Glock and trained it at the goon holding Sass. "Shut up, Dawson. Kill her and you're next," he growled at Dead Meat. "Feeling lucky?"

During the time it took Meat to say, "As a matter of fact—" Sass silently mouthed *one...two...*

Rio readied himself. On *three* she snapped her head to the left, exposing the commando. Rio took the shot. Ellis blasted the other guy.

After the sickening, hollow thunk of bullets piercing flesh came the dull thuds of the bodies hitting the Berber carpet.

Standing in an island of blood and dripping with splatter, Sass took a slow, deep breath and gingerly righted her head. "Guess I should have asked about your last weapons qual rating before I tried that stunt."

Rio lowered the Glock. His hand was shaking. "Yeah. That probably would have been smart." He didn't think he could move.

"So, what was it?"

"Top of my class."

"Good to know." She reached up and tried to wipe drops of blood from her cheek but they just smeared. Her hand was shaking, too.

"You two are one hell of a team," Dawson said with what appeared to be genuine admiration. "Whatever Interpol is paying you, I'll double it. Hell, I'll triple it."

Rio finally got himself unparalyzed and held out his arms. Sass ran into them, hugging him fiercely as he held her, her spattered body trembling like an out-of-tune outboard. Or was that him?

"No, thanks," he said to Dawson. "Not our idea of a good time."

"There are two more," Sass mumbled against his chest.

"What?" He pulled back a bit and held her cheek in his palm. Thanking God it wasn't her blood that streaked the pale skin or soaked her dress and matted wig.

"Upstairs. I saw four intruders. They used some kind of gas to knock out the guards."

"The idiots!" Dawson exploded. "That's what they have gas masks for!"

Rio grasped her by the shoulders, instantly realizing the implications. "The other two. Where are they now?"

"Dawson's office," she said. "They must be after the trigger."

That's when it hit him. "Did you...?" he whispered urgently.

"Yes. But—"

Suddenly, there was a sharp, deafening boom right above their heads. The whole house rocked from the impact. The upstairs alarms started to shriek.

Dawson swore virulently and grabbed up his machine gun. "Over my dead body. Let's go!" he called, already making for the stairs, Ellis on his heels.

"Will you be all right here?" Rio asked Sass, with a glance at the three surviving terrorists who were staring wide-eyed at the ceiling and all talking at once.

"You're kidding, right?" She ripped the bloody wig from her head, tossed it aside and grabbed the Glock from his waistband. "I'm going with you."

He didn't like it, but there was no time to argue, so he gave a grim nod and they hurried after Dawson and Ellis.

At the double doors to the east wing Dawson grabbed the handle and twisted. "Locked."

"Keys?" When Dawson shook his head, Rio shot out the lock.

"Where are the gas masks?" he called to Dawson over the wail of the alarm.

"Security room. I'll go for them."

They went in SWAT style, one covering the other.

The unconscious bodies of the guards lay strewn along the edges of the hall, but there was no sign of any commandos. Rio's eyes stung a little from the residual gas, but nothing serious. Holding their breath, Rio and Sass checked pulses while Dawson hurried into the security room. At once the alarms cut off. He emerged and tossed them each a mask.

"They alive?" Dawson asked after slipping his mask on, and Rio nodded. Dawson's expression was lethal. "Not for long." He raised his machine gun and aimed it at the first guard's head.

Rio put his hand on the barrel. "Let's take them by surprise." He jerked his chin at the office door as Sass worked her magic on the lock with a bobby pin from her hair. She nodded.

Ellis gave them both a considering look.

Dawson relented and they did another entry maneuver. Inside the office the four of them halted in unison and scanned the space. No intruders.

One side of the room was a shambles, furniture and paintings in shreds and splinters.

The wall safe hung open on one hinge.

Empty.

Sass stared speechless at the gaping hole where just fifteen minutes earlier she'd cracked the safe and switched the real trigger for the dummy. A war of emotions surged through her, starting with, thank God she hadn't come ten minutes later, and ending with, what the hell would happen to their mission now?

"Messy but effective," Ellis muttered, bringing her out of her stupor.

"I'll kill them! Every one of those incompetent guards is going to eat my gun," Dawson growled.

A shiver traveled up Sass's spine.

"And leave the island completely defenseless?" Rio pointed out.

Dawson snorted derisively. "Like it wasn't before. I should have shot them all when I had the chance."

"At the very least you'll need someone to deal with all the bodies," she said, noting that one of the guards had regained consciousness, stumbled to the door and was listening.

Still shivering, she looked him in the eye. He knew exactly who had just saved his life. Ellis gave her a quiet look of admiration.

Dawson noticed the guard, too. "Rouse the others and get after those commandos," he barked. "Find them and get that trigger back, or die trying! Leave a couple men to take care of the mess downstairs," he added.

The guard nodded numbly and staggered away.

Rio's worried gaze met hers. "You okay, baby?"

She nodded and gave him a weak smile, but for some reason she couldn't get her shivers under control. "What happens now?" she asked. "I guess we go home, huh? Since the auction's off."

"My men might catch up to them," Dawson said.

Rio shook his head. "Not going to happen. This was too well planned. If we'd had Betty to question, maybe…"

Dawson slashed a hand in an impatient gesture. "Doesn't matter. There'll be other auctions. In fact, I want you two to stick around for a few days. I'm expecting another shipment and your client will have first dibs. As a thank-you for what you did today."

"No thanks are necessary," Rio said.

"What kind of a shipment?" Sass asked, her heart sinking. The last thing she wanted was to stay a single minute longer in this lunatic asylum with this awful monster.

"Let's just say it's something your client will be very, very interested in," he said, giving Ellis a sidelong glance. "Far more flexible than a nuclear trigger."

Rio, damn his hide, nodded. "We'll have to contact the buyer, of course, just to be sure."

"Of course. You can use my phone. It's secure." Dawson glanced around the room. "If I can find it in the rubble."

Rio smiled coolly. "Thanks anyway. We have our own channels."

Sass was having a hard time staying on her feet. She leaned her back against the wall, rubbing the goose bumps on her arms.

Dawson shrugged. "Whatever you want. Ellis, get my computer up and running. I need to find out who did this. They're going to regret the day they were born."

Ellis gave a humorless smile as he swept debris off the desk and laid his machine gun on it. "Another convenient car accident?"

Dawson's eyes went cold and black. "Maybe a gas explosion. We haven't done one of those in a long time."

A gas explosion? The words echoed in Sass's mind in sickening reminder.

Suddenly she couldn't breathe. She wanted to cry out in protest. The sound built up in her lungs but couldn't squeeze past the huge, aching lump in her throat.

"A natural gas explosion?" she managed to croak. "You can do that? Make one happen on purpose?"

"Yeah. You know. At their house you open the oven and turn the gas on, then set the heating thermostat a few degrees higher. Gas builds up in the house and when the thermostat sparks as it kicks on, bang! Problem eliminated. Don't tell me you've never heard of that?"

She gazed at him in absolute, utter horror. *Omigod!* Hot tears backed up behind her lids. Why *didn't* she know? Why had no one told her? "I had no idea."

She'd barely gotten the words out when Rio put his arm around her and turned her toward the door.

"Come on, baby. Let's get you cleaned up. See you later, Dawson."

Jules! It was his doing. He'd protected her from that precious, awful bit of knowledge by pulling her out of the week long explosives training at Quantico for a job so she wouldn't find out. Why had he done that?

Dawson waved them off as he took a seat in front of the computer table Ellis had swung out from an antique armoire, amazingly undamaged.

Ellis gave her a worried frown. "I'll send Liza up with some tea, Miss Gunilla."

Rio closed the office door when they went out, propped her against the hall wall across from the security room and said, "Wait here. Don't move." Then he disappeared into the room where all the monitors were still lit up.

Her mind slowly going blank, she watched as one by one he yanked the cords right out of the backs of the monitors, sound recorders and DVRs until all the screens were black, all the red power lights blinked off and the cords were a tangle on the floor. In a haze she saw him grab a bottle of water that stood next to the console and pour the liquid over it, dousing all the keys, switches and buttons thoroughly. The console popped and sputtered as the electronics short-circuited, and silence fell over the room. As a final measure he swiped up all the headphones scattered around and one by one ripped the thin wires from the earpieces. No one would be listening or watching anything for a good long time.

"There. That ought to do it," he muttered with a grimace.

She watched wordlessly, a zombie. Feeling leaden and angry and helpless and devastated all at the same time.

They'd said it was an accident. The gas explosion that had killed her mother and sister. Something wrong with the line leading into their new house. Nobody had ever, not once, mentioned the possibility it could have been deliberate. Murder.

"They said it was an accident," she whispered, and Rio pulled her into his arms, urging her out toward the staircase.

"I know, baby. I know. And it probably *was* an accident. Dawson's an animal. A vicious criminal. But there's no reason anyone would have had to deliberately kill your mom and sister."

She stopped on the stairs and searched his face. "But there is. My dad was a thief," she said. "Is a thief. I'm sure he had enemies. He's in jail now, but back then... Maybe—"

Shock stamped itself on Rio's face. Genuine, thorough, total shock. His arms dropped from around her to his sides. "Your father's a thief? In jail?"

The abrupt arctic chill coming from him fueled her sudden uncontrolled shivering. She rubbed her arms harder, trying to get back the comforting warmth of his embrace that had been there just a second ago. *Oh, God.*

"Yeah. For the past twelve years." She shuddered out a painful sigh, knowing exactly what was coming next. Knowing there was nothing she could do to stop it.

This was where the man gave her a look as if she were from outer space and carried the plague, too. He wouldn't touch her again. Then he'd find some excuse, any excuse, to leave her, never to darken her door again.

Which could prove awkward under the present circumstances with Rio.

Still, she could use some alone time right now. To work through things in her pain-numbed mind. Deal with this terrible new possibility about the explosion that had changed her young life. Come to grips with nearly dying herself, here today. Try to make sense of this feeling of utter abandonment and betrayal by the man who was now staring at her with a new, ugly wariness in his beautiful blue eyes. Eyes that had once looked upon her with—

No. She wasn't doing this. She had to pull herself together.

"Why don't you go downstairs and check on things?" she suggested, drawing herself up to be strong but failing miserably. She only shook harder. What was wrong with her?

"Forget it. I'm going up with you," he said, and replaced his arm around her, practically pushing her up the remaining stairs.

"You really don't have to."

His arm tightened almost painfully. "Yes. I really do."

"Rio, if you're—"

His finger pressed across her lips, silencing her. "Don't talk."

When they got to their room, he closed the door behind them, and to her surprise, marched her straight into the bathroom.

"Get undressed," he told her gruffly, opened the shower door, turned on the water, then backed out and did the same for the faucets in the oversize Jacuzzi bathtub. When she still hadn't moved, he ground his jaw and reached for her. "I hope you don't mind, I'm throwing this out," he said, and started peeling off her clingy strapless dress. The jade one she'd imagined him peeling slowly down her body as he covered her with kisses… "It's soaked in blood."

Her body jerked at the horrible contrast in images. Suddenly, she couldn't stop the tears that had pooled in her eyes from leaking over her lashes. She was shaking so hard now she stumbled.

Rio cursed under his breath and ripped the dress off her completely. He practically carried her into the shower. "Come on, baby, help me rinse you off."

She stared at the drain, watching the bright red water slowly turn pink, then clear, as he rubbed his hands over her skin. Counting the bobby pins he plucked from her hair as they hit the ceramic tile. *One, two, three, four... Three, two, one...boom!*

"*No!*" she whimpered.

"All right, into the tub! *Now*. You're getting shocky."

He lifted her into the warm, steaming water, and she was grateful for his strength since she seemed to have lost every bit of hers. Her whole body felt like melting jelly. He held her until she'd settled, resting her head on the back edge of the bathtub.

"Can you sit by yourself?" he asked. "Darlin' you've got to try, now. Just for a minute."

She nodded and he let her go. She slipped into the water, slowly sliding farther and farther down, welcoming the comforting cocoon of warmth, until she was completely under. She couldn't raise herself but it didn't matter. It felt so good to be surrounded—

"Damn it!"

She felt herself being tugged up, out of the blissful abyss. She could breathe again, she idly noted, as a large, hard body slid in next to her and gathered her into a pair of corded, muscular arms. She sighed and curled into him, not objecting too strenuously when he lifted her feet onto the opposite edge of the tub.

"Stay with me, baby," he ordered—a bit desperately she thought—and the air was filled with the most exquisite scent of flowers. Roses and lilacs and jasmine. *Like her mother had planted out in the front garden, the weekend before*—

The certainty hit her, like an explosion coming out of nowhere. She didn't know how she knew. But suddenly the fog cleared and she knew what they'd all tried to hide from her.

"Someone killed her," she said in a broken little whisper, feeling the hot trail of tears on her cheeks. "Someone killed my mama."

Chapter 12

"Load it up with sugar," Rio instructed Liza the maid, who'd brought the tea Ellis had promised. "Lots of it—and leave the pot."

Rio was still in the tub with Sass, but had added some sweet-smelling bubble bath in hopes the scent would help rouse her, so they were mostly covered in suds.

"What's wrong with her?" the maid asked, handing him the cup and saucer. "She sick?"

"Shock. The intruders roughed her up a bit. Thanks. Close the door on your way out, will you?"

"Sure you don't need help?"

"I can handle it."

Liza swished out in her provocative uniform, closing the door, and Rio lifted the cup to Sass's lips. "Drink. It'll make you feel better."

Her color was coming back after fifteen minutes of soaking in the hot water with her feet up. Her strength was making a stab at returning, too. At least she didn't still look like she'd pass out any second. And to be honest, he'd needed the time to gather himself, as well. He'd killed men in the line of duty before, but it was never an easy thing. And her news on top of that had shaken him even more. It was good he had her to focus on.

"Why are you being so nice to me?" she asked, her voice alarmingly thin and weak.

"Why wouldn't I be nice to you?" he asked with a frown. He'd been shaken, but not put off. "You're my—"

"I'm a thief," she whispered, cutting him off. "I just told you my father's a thief, too. You hate thieves."

He tipped the cup to her lips again, letting her sip, giving himself a moment to assemble. She was right. He did hate thieves. But…

"I don't hate you, Sass," he said. "I never have." And as screwy as it sounded, it was the truth. He'd thought of her as annoying, as his adversary, sometimes even his enemy—definitely as a pain in the butt—but he'd never hated her for being a thief. In fact, he'd had to keep reminding himself that's what she was. Strange.

He kissed her forehead. "Never."

Her eyes, deep forest-green with dark smudges below, sought his. "Your face said otherwise, when I told you about my father."

He gave her another sip and sighed. "I'll admit, you broadsided me with that one. Why isn't it in your file?"

A corner of her lips twisted as she swallowed. "Jules. He wanted to spare me the embarrassment of my background. He even helped me change my name. That information is in my Bureau security file but only accessible as Need to Know. You're sure you don't hate me?"

Grateful he'd knocked out the entire surveillance console so they could talk freely, he set the cup down on the edge of the tub and took her face in his hands. "Sass, you're my partner, a damn good one, and you've become my lover, as well. I wouldn't be much of a man if I let something like this affect my feelings for you, now, would I?"

She licked her lips, lowered her eyes. "But your father…"

He let out a measured breath. "Yeah. That's a tough one. When my father was murdered in Chicago, I swore revenge on every thief in the universe. But I was young. It's kept me focused in my job, but eighteen years gives a man perspective. I got over my need for blanket revenge a long time ago." Pretty much.

She was silent for a moment, then whispered hoarsely, "Chicago?"

"Yeah. Why?"

"That's where our house was. The one that—" She swallowed. "Just north of the city. In Evanston."

"Oh, baby." He held her close as she fought to keep the pain at bay. "Go on, darlin', let it out. I'm right here."

To his relief, she did, clinging to him as the quiet sobs racked her depleted body. He didn't try to shush her, didn't give her meaningless assurances. Simply let her cry it out. She'd probably never had the chance before, forced to grow up early with no mother and a father in prison. How old was she when he went away? No wonder she'd turned to Jules Mannheim as a father figure. Too bad Rio hadn't known her then. They could have helped each other through their traumas, like now.

Suddenly some things about Kansas Hawthorne made a lot more sense to him. Her disinclination to get close to people, her uncanny skill at breaking and entering, her determination to maintain the best record at the Bureau, her sheer single-mindedness. He'd wondered about all of that, even as he'd admired her for it.

But now…now it just made him angry. Angry that her life had been twisted away from normalcy by her thief father. Thieves were an anathema, poisoning everything they touched!

But Sass was a thief, too. Would she be poison, as well, if he got involved with her? If he asked her to be with him? To belong to him? He looked down at the shiny gold band around his finger. Some women would say the same of him. He'd just killed a man, hadn't he? Maybe they were more alike than he'd like to admit.

She'd been quiet for a while, but now she stirred in his arms. "Sorry." She covered her eyes with her hand. "Jeez. That's never happened to me before. I'm sor—"

"Shhh," he said, gathering her to him. "It's okay. You've had a rough day. You almost died. And heard some terrible things. You're entitled."

"Some tough FBI agent," she muttered. "What a baby."

"I don't even want to hear it. You're great at what you do, Sass. You've had no undercover training, yet managed to achieve everything you were sent in to do and more, and under incredibly dangerous circumstances. You just had too much thrown at you at once today. I've seen strong men crack over far less."

Her fingers flattened against his chest, smoothing over his skin. "Thanks," she whispered. "I could never have gotten through any of this without you."

He exhaled, relaxing now that she was reviving. "Sure you could," he assured her, and kissed her on the temple. Enjoying how her hand trailed back and forth through the rough hair on his chest.

Growing more aware by the second of their nakedness, the lushness of her curves pressing into him, the softness of her skin… Of his own body's reaction to his awareness.

Hell. He'd be a real jerk to take advantage of her vulnerability now.

But he couldn't resist just a taste.

"We're good together," he murmured, and leaned over to cover her lips with his. "Real good."

He kissed her gently, softly, tasting her, the *real* her, for the first time. She tasted sweet and fragile and beautiful and unguarded and all those things he fancied he'd been looking for in the woman of his dreams.

Could it be that *she* was the woman of his dreams?

Her arms slipped around his neck and she opened to him, letting him take the lead, set the pace.

He held back, needing to show her he wasn't always that caveman from the shower this afternoon. That he could be sensitive and caring, too. Not just out to take what he could get.

Too soon he lifted his lips, missing her already. "Water's getting cold. We should get out."

She gazed up at him, the uncertainty and vulnerability once again welling in her eyes, breaking his heart.

"You don't need this right now," he said quietly. "You have to get your strength back."

She gave him a little nod and disentangled her arms from around him. "Yeah."

He could almost hear what she was thinking. She was dead wrong.

"Sass," he said, and captured her gaze. Grasping her thigh, he rolled so he was lying on top of her between her legs. He grabbed the short end of the tub. And entered her. She gasped softly and clutched his shoulders as he battled once again not to lose it. He pushed in all the way, as far as he could go, and held himself there inside her for an endless moment looking deep into her eyes.

Then he kissed her and pulled out.

Rising from the tub, he lifted her in his arms and carried her to the shower where he carefully rinsed the bubble bath from her hair and skin.

He gave her another kiss. "You know I want you, right?"

She nodded. This time with somewhat more conviction.

"Not here, though, in this place. When we make love, I want to do it right. Okay?"

"Okay," she whispered.

"Good. Let's dress and get out to the *Mermaid*. Call Macon and alert him to the situation. And get our instructions."

She took the towel he handed her. "Think he'll pull us out?" she asked.

Her tone worried him. She still looked and sounded as if she could crumble. He wanted nothing more than to put her to bed and feed her a big bowl of chicken noodle soup and rock her in his arms until she was totally back to her feisty, pain-in-the-rear old self. Not necessarily in that order, either.

But that was a man's thinking. He didn't have the luxury of thinking like a man, or of her as a woman. He had to think like an SAC. They were still deep in-mission. They seemed to be on Dawson's good side for the moment, but even so, one slip could still get them killed.

"I doubt Macon'll want us to leave the island," he said. "Not with another shipment coming in so soon. Who knows what that could lead to." He watched her face tense up. "But if you want out, just say so. I'll pull the plug, no problem. We're done with what we came to do."

She visibly gathered herself. Her spine straightened, her mouth formed a determined line. "No. I'm fine."

She wasn't fine, and they both knew it. After what had happened, no one would blame her for choosing to cut and run, least of all him. Hell, he wanted to whisk her away from here himself, out of danger. Protect her from the likes of Dawson, not throw her to the wolves.

"Rio, I'm fine," she repeated, and he wondered if she was trying to convince him or herself.

It didn't matter. If she said she wanted to stay, they would stay. This was a mission, he reminded himself, and they were both professionals. Personal considerations had no place in the picture.

"Okay," he said. "Let's see if we can get out of this house."

Sass followed Rio down the central staircase clutching her overnight bag to her chest. She'd only packed the things she didn't dare leave at the mansion. Rio had done the same, and was toting a small duffel over his shoulder.

When they got to the second-floor landing, she told him, "Wait. I have to get something." There was one thing she definitely needed before they could leave.

He paused with a frown as she ducked behind one of the large potted palms grouped in the corner of the roomy gallery that led to the east wing. Holding her breath, she reached deep into the narrow space between the inner and outer ceramic pots. And extracted her catsuit, Keds, fanny pack of equipment and the velvet jewelry bag containing the nuclear trigger. The real one. Thank God it was still there.

"What the hell…?" Rio exclaimed under his breath, peeking at her behind the palm.

"I was finishing up in Dawson's office when the commandos stormed the mansion. I made it out, but this was the only place available to hide my things before I was caught," she explained.

"It was that close?" Rio drilled a hand through his hair. "Damn, woman."

She zipped up her overnight bag. "Tell me about it."

She gave him a wry smile. One day she might even be able to talk about it without her knees shaking. In about a hundred years. For now she was grateful to be able to walk out of there alive.

They continued down to the living room, where they found two of Dawson's remaining guards removing bodies while the house staff cleaned up the mess.

"We're going to check on our boat," Rio announced. "Tell Dawson that's where we'll be."

Ellis straightened, looking worried. "He wants you to stay."

"We are staying. Just not at the mansion."

"It won't be safe at the marina. We can't spare any of the guards."

"We'll take our chances. Have his other guests left?"

"Two have, the last one is packing now. Crazy. It's well past dark."

"Good riddance, I say." Rio grimaced. "Send a message if Dawson needs us for anything. But preferably not before morning," he added.

Nodding, Ellis tossed him a key for a golf cart parked out front, and they made their way to the dock where the *Mermaid* was tied up.

"Looks like the boats were spared," Sass said with relief. "Think the commandos bugged them?"

"Doesn't much matter. They're dead, the ones with the dummy trigger are long gone and Dawson's monitoring equipment is totally demolished. But we should probably check, in case some of our departing friends got creative."

They unlocked the *Mermaid*'s hatch and climbed down into the salon. She'd never been so glad to be anywhere in her entire life. What a difference a day made.

She dumped her bag onto the sofa and Rio did the same. After a thorough inspection they'd found three bugs and disposed of them. "There. Now we're sure." As Rio walked past, she snagged him around the middle in a fierce hug.

"Hey, what's that all about?" he asked with a smile, looping his arms around her, too.

"Don't mind me," she said, feeling slightly awkward and embarrassed. "Just needed to feel you close for a minute."

She was acutely aware that this was the first time she'd ever reached for him. Until now, it had always been him reaching for her.

"Why would I mind?" he said gently. "Sass, listen—"

She lifted her face and kissed him, to cut off his words. She didn't want to hear them. No doubt he intended to let her down easy, reminding her that what they had was only part of their cover. That he loved to make love with her, but that was as far as it would ever go.

She knew that. He'd said it often enough.

So why did the thought depress her so thoroughly?

She must be experiencing some weird kind of Stockholm syndrome. Why else would she be feeling like she was falling in love with Rio? That she was actually wishing he wanted more than an undercover fling? Something more permanent?

Talk about insanity under pressure.

She tore her lips from his and took a step back, releasing him. "Sorry. I, um…"

"Baby, any time you want to kiss and hug me, you just go right ahead."

She gave a nervous chuckle, smoothing her hands down her short skirt. "Yeah?"

"Oh, yeah."

"Even when we're back in Washington?"

She slapped her hand over her mouth. The words had just leaped out. She hadn't meant—

"Even then," he said mildly.

He regarded her evenly for what seemed like an hour. She didn't dare speak, terrified of what might come out. *Total insanity.*

"You know I plan to retire," he said, one eyebrow rising.

She nodded.

"Very soon."

She nodded again.

"I'll be moving down South," he said. "In fact, probably somewhere around here."

Finally she managed to break out of her verbal paralysis. "I know. Don't worry. I'm not asking to run away with you. I know we're just…temporary."

"Sass—"

She put her fingers to his lips. "It's okay. You've never led me on about that. I'm okay with it. Really. In fact, it's better this way. I'm not the settling-down kind. Not at all. I love my job and would never leave it."

He frowned. "You're sure?"

"Absolutely. I just wanted to—" *Taste you. Feel you. Fall in love with the most amazing man I've ever met.* "—to see what was under those stiff button-down shirts. Find out if you were as sexy as I thought you might be."

His jaw worked. "And?"

"You're more. Way more. I can't wait to—" Abruptly, she turned away. *Too much information.* "Anyway. How long will it take your retirement papers to go through?"

"Pretty quickly, I imagine. But I'll stick around long enough to see Dawson in jail."

Her heart felt suddenly hollow. "So, a few days?"

"A few weeks probably."

"Ah."

She bit her lower lip and sat down on the sofa next to her bag, fiddling with the straps to give herself something to hang on to. This was ridiculous. She needed to snap out of it. She was scaring herself. She'd known the man—*really* known him—less than seventy-two hours.

Besides, even if she fell totally in love with him, she could do nothing about it. Nothing. For his protection.

"What do we do now?" she asked, leaning her head back on the butter-soft leather sofa. "Do we dare call Macon?"

"We got all the bugs. I think we're safe for now." He went and fetched his cell phone from the strongbox where they'd secured some of their things before leaving the *Mermaid*.

She closed her eyes and listened as he dialed and spoke to Macon, quickly giving him a complete status report. As Rio talked, she felt the sofa dip. Her bag vanished and was replaced by his solid warmth next to her. His arm came around her shoulder and her body sighed in relief as she allowed herself to be drawn close to his side.

She'd always been so strong. So independent. She didn't understand this sudden weakness within her. This need to feel him close, to simply surrender to his care and protection, and let him take care of everything. This was so not like her. She didn't do helpless female.

But there was just something about Rio that made her want to curl up in his lap and never leave.

She must still be in some serious shock.

"So, you want me to meet you?" Rio was saying into the phone. The circle of his arm tightened and she opened her eyes to see him check his watch. "About an hour. Okay. Same co-ordinates? Right. I'll bring it."

He flipped the phone closed and tossed it aside.

"He wants the triggering device," she guessed.

"Yep. I'll take the inflatable—"

She straightened. "No way. I'm coming with you."

"No reason to."

"I'm not staying here by myself. Not a chance."

"Baby, you'll be fine. Besides, it only fits one person."

"Then we'll have to get cozy."

He pushed out a breath but gave her an amused smile. "You must be feeling better. You're starting to be a pain in the butt again."

She punched his arm. "Look who's talking."

He grabbed her and she yelped as he dragged her down on the sofa, under him. Laughing, she beat her fists ineffectually against his firm biceps. "What do you think you're doing, mister?"

"Teaching you who's boss here." He grasped her by the knees and spread them, fitting himself between her thighs.

Excitement thrummed through her whole body. "Is that so." She squirmed, cradling him deeper, wrapping her legs around his. The hard, thick ridge of his arousal pushed up against her center, hot, insistent.

"Yeah. I'm the agent in charge, and you're the unruly subordinate."

"Unruly, huh?"

"Wild and disobedient."

She undulated up against him. He groaned softly and his lids went to a sultry half-mast as he gazed down at her, desire oozing from their depths.

Oh, but, he was sexy.

"Am I that bad, Special Agent Rio?"

Her body hummed with need, her pulse hammering everywhere he touched her. His warm breath fanned over her cheeks, fast, shallow, rough. His masculine scent, seductively familiar, surrounded her, called to her to be his.

"No, Special Agent Hawthorne, you're that good."

He licked at her mouth and she opened for him, letting him tease and probe her with his tongue.

"What will you do with me?" she whispered.

"I'll tell you what I want to do with you," he murmured hot and low.

She lifted her heavy lids, taking in his hungry gaze. Shivering with anticipation. She wanted him as she'd never wanted anything in her life.

"First I want to open one of Rafe's $300 bottles of wine. And then I want to—" He leaned down and whispered the words in her ear. His mouth then covered hers and drank of her. She trembled with need.

"Rio," she whispered. "Why don't you just skip the first part…."

She felt his lips bow into a smile. "So naughty."

His hand slipped up her skirt and past her panties. And he touched her. Her breath caught, hard. "This isn't fair."

"Who said anything about fair?"

His eyes danced like demons as his fingers stroked over her, around her. She bucked. They pushed into her. She moaned.

His thumb sought her trigger. "Come on, baby, show me how naughty you are."

"Don't stop. Please!"

He didn't. Not until she gave him everything she had to give. Until he'd brought her quaking and shuddering to ecstasy. Until his name left her lips like a prayer for a future they could never have.

She squeezed her eyes shut. Felt her panties being slipped off, heard a zip and a rustle, and then he was inside her.

She gave a sob of relief and wrapped her arms around him, holding him close as he started to move.

"Look at me, baby," he whispered.

He watched her and kissed her and thrust into her, and she clung to him, never wanting to let him go. They were both so ready, it didn't take long for them to reach the scorching, panting, blissful edge of climax.

They hung there together for a searing moment, then he grasped her face in his strong firm hand.

"You're mine," he growled, and they both hurtled over the brink of oblivion.

Chapter 13

"There's not enough room. You're too big," Sass said with a frustrated moue.

Rio grinned, in a teasing mood after an amazing hour of making love. "Funny, no one's ever complained about *that* before."

Sass fisted her hands on her hips, but he could see she was fighting a smile. "Egomaniac."

"Sex maniac."

"Neanderthal."

"Wimpy baby."

Her mouth dropped open and her eyes widened in mock outrage.

"Just shut up and get in the raft," Rio said, his grin widening. "Jeez, we're going to be late meeting Macon as it is. And I'm going to let *you* explain why."

She huffed, grumbling, "It's not a raft, it's a damn floating cereal bowl," but nevertheless stepped off the wooden dock into the square foot of space in front of him in the black inflatable raft. He guided her to sit down between his legs and pulled her back tight to his chest.

"There's no room for my legs," she protested, trying to fold them in front of her.

"Hang your feet over the edge."

"Good grief," she muttered, but did as he'd suggested. "I'll get soaked."

"You'll get soaked anyway. That's why we wore wet suits." He turned and yanked the motor's cord, making it sputter to life. As he guided the tiny craft out into the waves, he leaned forward. "Which, by the way, you look awfully sexy in. Reminds me a little of your catsuit...."

She twisted around and made a face. "Don't try to distract me, Rio. It won't work."

He waggled his brows. "Is that a dare?"

"Oh, honestly."

She turned forward again, but he felt her body snuggle back into him. Damn, she felt good, even through two layers of wet suit.

As for him, he'd never felt so content in his life. It was incredible what a good glass of wine and an even better lay could do for a man's outlook on life.

He hooked his arm around Sass's middle and rested his chin on the top of her head, steering out toward the vast expanse of the blue ocean.

Too bad those weren't the source of his contentedness. His life would be a whole lot simpler if they were.

Sure, the wine and the sex had been great. But the real reason he was feeling so fine was because of the woman he'd shared them with.

Sass Hawthorne.

Sass made everything seem…just right.

How the hell had that happened?

More importantly, what was he going to do about it?

They hadn't spoken of the future. Hadn't spoken at all, really. Not about them. Other than her reminder that they were just temporary.

True, he'd told her, "You're mine," as they'd made love, and her eyes had misted with surrender. But earlier when she'd asked, "What about Washington?" she hadn't let him answer.

Would his reply have been the same then as it would be now? The ring on his finger glinted in the moonlight.

You're mine.

Damn, he wanted her!

Now. Tomorrow. In Washington. When he moved down South.

You're mine.

He wanted her to be with him everywhere. For always.

"Do you have any idea where we're going?" she asked, her voice soft and dreamy, her hair streaming in the night breeze over his face and neck, the cool sea spray clinging to his love-warmed skin.

He inhaled deeply, smelling the salt and the wind and the unique scent of the woman he'd so quickly come to love. "Hope so," he whispered. "I sure as hell hope so."

"Ahoy, there! Come aboard," Macon called when they approached the sleek motorboat that was waiting for them at the rendezvous point out in the middle of nothing but miles of black water. "We'd almost given up on you."

Rio grasped Sass around the waist and rose to his feet with her in tow. He figured her legs would be pretty useless after being out of circulation for so long.

"Sorry about that," she said, taking Macon's hand for a boost. "We got a little delayed."

Jules Mannheim sat in the captain's chair of the dimly lit motorboat, looking ominous as a thundercloud in the near darkness. "Nothing serious, I trust."

"Nothing that concerns you," Rio said, making the color rise in Mannheim's face. *Tough.*

Rio hoisted himself onto the slick white deck and dropped down onto the stern bench next to Sass as she was pulling the velvet pouch containing the trigger out of their waterproof seabag.

She passed it to Macon. "Sure glad to be rid of this thing."

Macon quickly freed it from its protective nest and inspected it thoroughly under a light before saying with some relief, "Thank God. I'm truly impressed, Special Agent Hawthorne. Well done."

"She's a real pro," Rio agreed. He casually draped his arm across the edge of the bench behind her. Mannheim frowned and speared him with a dagger look, but he met the man's gaze head-on. After a moment Mannheim looked away.

"What about you, Rio?" Macon said, taking a seat, too. "Get anything we can use?"

Rio nodded. "Plenty. Were you able to plant homing devices on the other terrorists' vessels before they left tonight?"

"Yep. We borrowed a couple of Navy SEALs. Now the Coast Guard is tracking them 24/7," Macon said, pulling a small voice recorder from his windbreaker pocket.

"Good. That'll make the information I've gathered that much more useful. Be sure to have them check the *Mermaid* before we weigh anchor."

Macon nodded and clicked on the recorder. "Shoot."

Rio painstakingly relayed every last detail he'd been able

to glean from his various chats with Dawson and the terrorists. Both Macon and Mannheim listened with rapt attention.

"Excellent. We'll have this typed up and you can fill in anything else you remember when you get back to Washington."

"I guess that means you want us to stay?" Sass said coolly. She'd hardly looked at her SAC since arriving. Rio imagined she had a thing or two to ask him about, but was waiting for more privacy.

"That's an affirmative."

"Are you okay with that, Sass?" Mannheim said, concern in his voice. "If you want out—"

"No. I'm fine." She smiled up at Rio. "My partner's taking good care of me."

Mannheim pulled in a deep breath. "Glad to hear it."

"Because something's come to our attention that we'd like you to investigate," Macon said.

"Oh?" Rio asked.

"Top priority. Show him the file, Jules."

After a short hesitation, Mannheim reached behind his seat for a briefcase and extracted a folder from it. He darted a quick, grim look at Sass before handing it to Rio.

"In our interrogation of Rafe Gerard and Gunilla Sundstrom," Macon said, "we learned that Dawson keeps a diary. A meticulous record of all his dealings. It may go back for years. If we can get hold of it, we can lock him up and throw away the key."

Rio whistled as he glanced through the report. "Any idea what this diary looks like? The intruders emptied Dawson's safe, you know."

"Gerard seemed to think it's electronic. A file on Dawson's computer."

"Well hidden and heavily encrypted, I presume," Sass said

with a sigh. "You know I'm not that great at computers, other than security systems."

"Not a problem," Rio said. "I am."

She darted him a skeptical look. "Really?"

"My team deals with all kinds of theft, electronic included. Remember that big-time hacker ANSIR caught a while back?" She nodded. "Well, I traded him a few years of jail time to teach me his secrets." He turned back to Macon. "If the diary's in Dawson's computer, I'll find it."

"I guess that means I'll have to break you into his office," she said, beetling her brows. "Jeez, Rio. How'm I supposed to do that?"

"With the cameras down and number of guards drastically reduced it shouldn't be too big a problem."

"Easy for you to say."

"Teach me to pick a lock, then, and I'll get myself in."

"In, what, six hours? Yeah, right."

He shrugged. "I'm a quick study." He met her eyes with a lazy grin.

"Not that quick. Okay, fine. I'll find a way."

"We're counting on it," Macon said.

"Don't stop to read the diary," Mannheim warned. "Just make a copy and get the hell out of there as fast as you can. Forget about anything else once you have it."

"Even the new shipment Dawson's expecting?"

"Yes. When we have the diary secured we can move in immediately and hopefully stop whatever it is from changing hands," Macon said.

"Any idea what's contained in this shipment?" Mannheim asked.

Rio shook his head. "Not a clue. Dawson's not been in a particularly chatty mood tonight."

Macon passed him a slip of paper. "Well, we'll go with the shipment as plan B, in case you can't locate the diary. Here's a phone number you can use to contact your 'client' when you find out the details. It's untraceable."

"We should have a couple of code phrases set up," Rio suggested.

"Right. If I say 'Whatever it takes,' it means you should go ahead with the buy. The money will be set up and waiting. 'Not interested' means just concentrate on the diary."

"Got it."

"And, as always, if I ask if you're all right and you say 'We're fine,' I'll send in the SWAT team immediately for an extraction."

"Good," Rio said.

"As for this shipment, I'm not sure what we can do with such short notice other than this." Macon handed him a tiny plastic box.

Rio popped it open. Inside, nested in a bed of foam was a miniscule black dot. "A tracking device, I presume?"

Macon nodded. "Set to start transmitting forty-eight hours from now. Hopefully that gives you a long enough window."

"To get out of there alive before his detection gear is up and running again, you mean?" Rio said wryly, snapping the box shut.

"Something like that. Plant it on whatever the shipment is, if you have a chance. But concentrate most of your efforts on the diary."

"Will do." Rio rose to his feet. "Anything else? Otherwise, we better get out of here in case he comes looking for us."

Macon and Mannheim helped them both back into the inflatable.

"For godssakes be careful," Mannheim said, directing the

words at Sass with a worried look. "If there's any sign of trouble get out of there pronto, understand?"

"Don't worry. We'll be careful." She still wasn't looking at her SAC.

"And Sass…?" Mannheim continued to clutch her hand, even though she was standing in the raft and Rio had her.

"What is it?" she asked, shaking off Rio's impatient attempt to get her to sit down.

Mannheim's jaw worked, then he abruptly shook his head and pulled his hand away. "Nothing. Just be very careful."

"Come on, Sass. We gotta go," Rio urged.

Mannheim sent him a thinly veiled glower. "If she gets hurt, don't come back alive, Special Agent Rio. I want you to find that diary and get out of there. Period. Don't stop to check it, and don't take any chances."

"I never take chances," he responded, holding his temper in check by a thread. Nobody *ever* accused him of being careless or making bad decisions. And that was the only reason he didn't flatten the guy where he stood. But Rio knew this wasn't about his competence. Mannheim's concern was for Sass.

Still, as he steered the inflatable back toward the island, Rio felt a distinct tingle of warning on the back of his neck.

Something didn't feel right.

What the hell *did* Mannheim know that he wasn't telling?

Sass regarded Rio's back as he stood at the stove putting together a post-midnight meal which he insisted they both needed after everything that had happened today. He'd tossed her out of the galley and insisted on preparing the food by himself.

"You're being awfully quiet. Is something wrong?"

He'd been unusually uncommunicative ever since they got back from the rendezvous.

"If it was about what Mannhein said..." She prayed that was it, and not something to do with their out-of-control relationship: second thoughts about her, despite their amazing lovemaking.

He turned, spatula in hand, and gave her a smile. Not a great one, but it was progress. "No. It's not that. I was just—" He sighed. "You know Mannheim better than I do. Did you find his behavior tonight a bit odd? Jumpy maybe?"

She blinked. Whatever she'd expected, this wasn't it. She had an ax to grind with Jules, but it was personal, not business. "Jumpy?"

"He's worried about you. Overly so. Even more than on the day he sent us here."

"You think so?" During their brief meeting she hadn't noticed anything other than Jules's usual overprotective surrogate-father instincts coming out in full force.

"It's almost as if he knows something's going to happen to us."

Her jaw dropped. "Like what?" she asked incredulously. "Jules would never send us—well, me, anyway—back in if he knew our lives would be at any higher risk than they already were."

Rio folded his arms across his broad chest, distracting her momentarily. "Then how do you explain that 'if she's hurt don't come back alive' comment?"

He looked so delicious standing there in his jeans and no shirt, pointing his spatula at her for emphasis, that for a second she almost forgot his question.

But hell, the answer was obvious. Whatever he'd done was to protect her. She knew that.

"He's afraid *you'll* hurt me. Not Dawson." She looked down at the carpet and poked her big toe into the luxurious pile. "As in, you'll break my heart."

Rio didn't speak for so long she thought he might have gone back to cooking. She didn't dare look up. Lest he see the truth in her eyes. That it was too late. Her heart was already breaking. Because too soon she'd have to let him go.

"What if *you* break *my* heart?" he finally murmured.

"What?" she asked, stunned. "Don't be ridic—" Her words caught in her throat when she saw his expression. "You're serious?"

"Why not?"

"Let me count the reasons."

He turned his back and did something with the pan on the stove. "Yeah?"

"Rio, you're the one who keeps saying our relationship is just part of our cover, nothing more."

"Maybe I've changed my mind. Besides, you said it last."

He had her there. "All right, then there's the thing about you hating thieves."

"You're not a thief. You're an FBI agent."

"You've repeatedly insisted I'm not your type."

"What if I was wrong?"

"I also remember you saying nothing could keep you in Washington, not even great sex."

"Okay. That much is true."

"Well, then."

"You could come with me."

Surely, he was kidding. "To where? Podunk, South Carolina?"

He shrugged. "Why not?"

She girded herself against believing he really meant it. This wasn't his brain talking, this came from somewhere farther south.

She said, "Because nothing could make me leave my job, not even great sex."

He glanced back at her with a sardonic half smile. "There you go. See? It'll be you breaking my heart."

She took a step toward him, then made herself stop. Her mind was in chaos. What was this all about? Surely, he didn't mean— He couldn't possibly mean—

"I don't understand," she said, battling to maintain her equilibrium. "I never thought—"

"Never mind. Let it go, Sass," he said, and abruptly turned back toward the stove.

Everything inside her wanted to run to him, to fling herself into his arms. But before she could move, she slammed the gates of her heart against the possibility.

"You didn't choose me, Rio. You got stuck with me. Let's be honest, the mission, our intimacy, it was all forced on you against your will," she said.

"Yeah, yeah. Kicking and screaming," he drawled. Setting the pan aside, he switched off the burner and faced her. "Well, Sass, if it's about choosing, then what do you think of this— I did choose you. Over a year ago." He took a step toward her. "And you chose me, too. Or you wouldn't have hidden that disc in your catsuit the other night—" he took another step "—so I'd have to unzip it—" and another "—and touch your naked breasts." He was right in front of her now, so close she could feel the heat rolling off his body, bringing with it the potent scent of desire. "I could have taken you then, taken anything I wanted, and we both know it."

She swallowed heavily. It was true. She'd wanted him so badly she'd have gladly thrown that stupid competition to have him. If he'd closed the infinitesimal gap and put his mouth to her breasts that night, as he so easily could have, she'd have been lost. Would have ended up naked on that grass with him rocking between her thighs. She could see that so clearly now.

"Why didn't you?" she whispered.

His body brushed hers. "Because my team would have found us. I was going to invite you to a consolation dinner the next evening. To seduce you."

She lifted her face to his, loving the smell of his spicy aftershave, the scrape of his beard against her cheek. "No you weren't. And even if you had, I wouldn't have accepted. You were the enemy."

"I was your *rival,* Sass, *never* your enemy. And now I'm your husband. So tell me, wife, will you obey your husband's one burning wish?"

His lips grazed hers. Teasing. Tempting. "And what might that be, husband?"

His eyes darkened, filling with an emotion that made her tremble all the way to her toes. "Let's give this thing a chance," he whispered. "Maybe I'll convince you you'll like Podunk, South Carolina."

Her heart stood absolutely still. For a single, precious moment she actually believed in the possibility.

Then reality crashed over her.

Her vision blurred. "Oh, Rio, you don't know how much I wish I could. You're everything I've ever—"

She spun away from him. She knew she couldn't have him. Had always known that. None of this made any difference. "I'm sorry," she said. "I can't."

"Why not?" he demanded, anger rising in his voice. "And don't even try to say all this was just sex to you. I know damn well that there's so much more going on here."

"Of course it's not. I— You don't understand."

"So make me understand."

"It's because…" She shuddered out a breath. "Because if I say yes, terrible things will happen. They *always* happen. And I can't stop them!"

As she'd known he would, he dismissed her deepest fears. "Oh, please. Like what? We'll fall in love and live happily ever after?" His voice vibrated with frustration.

"You just don't get it, do you?" she said, desperately.

His jaw set and he stared at her hard. "Apparently not."

"Do you have any idea the things I've gone through? Do you honestly think I haven't been there before? Feeling happy? Safe? *Hopeful?* But something always happens. *Always*. Say we get together, Rio. Say we do everything you just said. And then…and then," she cried, "you'll die! Or go to jail. Or Dawson or some other criminal will get to you and do some horrible thing to you. I'll be left alone to pick up the pieces of my heart. *Again*."

"You can't be serious."

She burst into tears.

The anger left his face, swept away by surprise and compassion. His arms opened to her. "Come here."

He hugged her close, rocking her whole body with his.

"I'm sorry." She fought to control her stupid weeping.

"Shhh," he said. "It's okay."

She waited for him to say he understood, that he'd let her go and find someone else. She prayed to hear those words. And dreaded them more than anything she'd ever had to bear.

But he didn't. He said, "Baby, that's plain crazy talk. And

even if it weren't, you know I can take care of myself. I've had the best law enforcement training in the country. We both have."

She lifted her gaze to his, never so frightened in her life. "But—"

His thumb rubbed over her bottom lip. "However, I will respect your wishes. We'll let it go."

She squeezed her eyelids shut in relief. In agony. "Thank you," she whispered.

"For now."

Her eyes sprang open. "Rio—"

"Baby, trust me. I'm just as uncertain about this—about *everything*—as you are. Who knows what tomorrow has in store? I know that as well as you."

She nodded. Not a complete concession, but at least it would buy her time to explain her reasons better.

"But I'm telling you right now, I won't let you go because of these insane, groundless fears."

"They're not—"

"Sass, this isn't the time to decide anything. We'll talk about it again in Washington, okay?" He wiped the tears from her eyes.

"I'm not changing my mind," she warned him softly.

Her past wasn't going away, and neither was the fact that the kind of life she wanted didn't include the plans Rio had made. Her job was the only safe, stable thing she had. Love was never safe.

No matter now much she wished things could be different.

Chapter 14

Rio had never seen Sass looking so fragile.

As they ate the light meal of stir-fried chicken and vegetables he'd prepared, he became more and more convinced that Sass shared his unanticipated emotions regarding their sudden relationship.

He didn't know quite how to deal with it. Or her off-kilter reaction to their growing feelings for one another.

All he knew was he wanted her. Wanted her in his bed, in his life, for always. And he'd do just about anything to get her there.

But how could a man fight the blind, irrational fear that had taken hold within her, caused by all the heartbreak in her life? How could he convince her the future didn't have to be like the past? That her cycle of bad luck was not her fault, not remotely, and could so easily be broken if she just believed in him?

Her barely held-together expression across the galley table told him everything he needed to know. She wanted him with

the same longing as he wanted her. She was just too frightened to acknowledge it.

And that gave him all the strength he needed to persuade her.

"Leave them," he said as she rose to clear the dishes when
they'd finished.

Her mouth parted as he got to his feet and grasped her
hand. "What are you doing?" she asked, the panic clear in
her voice.

"Come on." He gave her a disarming smile. "I feel like
dancing."

"Like…what? Now?"

He winked. "What better time than now?" It had been an
exhausting and emotional day. They both needed to wind
down before they could sleep. Keeping her firmly in hand
he walked to the stereo, popped a few CDs in the multislot-
ted player and led her up the ladder topside. By the time
he'd pulled her into his arms, strains of Stevie Ray Vaughan
were floating up through the open hatch, earthy, hot and
bluesy.

"I had no idea you were such a romantic," Sass murmured
as she fitted her curves against him, curled her fingers around
his palm and followed his lead as he swayed to the sultry
rhythms. Above them the stars twinkled, and below the water
gently lapped at the sides of the boat. In the distance, the frogs
croaked in a small chorus.

"Darling, there are a lot of things you don't know about me."

Like how single-minded he was. And persistent. And how
he always got what he wanted.

Always.

"Such as?"

"Such as how much I want to kiss you right now."

He brought their laced hands under her chin and tipped it

up with his knuckles, putting his lips to hers. She moaned softly as their tongues met and danced languorously to the beat of their hearts.

"You're doing this deliberately, aren't you?" she whispered when he lifted for a new angle.

"What's that?" He sucked on her bottom lip, dizzy with the taste of her.

"Trying to tempt me. To seduce me."

He drew his tongue around the edge of hers. "No, just dancing."

"Liar." But she didn't pull back as he covered her mouth again and took his time exploring the wet heat of her. Enjoying the sweet scent of her perfume and her desire.

The music brought them closer. The moon hung on the horizon and the *Mermaid* rocked gently under their feet as they moved together to the soulful cry of the electric guitar.

It was the craziest thing. Everything was totally up in the air—the outcome of the operation, Rio's career, his relationship with Sass, his retirement, hell, the whole damn rest of his life.... But he'd never been so at peace. As if he'd finally landed right where he was supposed to be: holding Sass, kissing her, looking forward to more. Much more.

And it wasn't just sex he was thinking of. Right at the moment that might top his list, but what was really on his mind was...coming home. Home to a place with a nice, cozy feel and a good woman to warm the innermost reaches of him. A woman like Sass.

How could she believe it would be dangerous?

He wanted to leave the danger far behind. To build a safe, secure nest for the both of them to retreat to from the cares and worries and stresses of the world. Somewhere they could create something wonderful together. Something satisfying.

Something he could look back on at age ninety-nine and say, yeah, life was good. No regrets.

He gave a mental sigh. Now if he could only convince *her* of that.

The CD player clicked over to an old Eric Clapton album. One thing he had to say for Rafe Gerard, the guy had great taste in oldies.

Rio slid his hand down to cup Sass's bottom and sang softly along, telling her she looked wonderful tonight.

"You *are* trying to tempt me," she murmured, green eyes sparkling up at him like a thousand emeralds.

He nibbled at her earlobe. "Is it working?"

"All too well."

He felt her arm tighten around him and her face nuzzle into his neck, followed by a bleak sigh.

Damn. "But…?" he prompted.

She looked up at him, eyes filled with regret. "I already told you. I won't change my mind. I can't."

Anger returned to him, fast and sure, swamping him with fury at the unfairness of her edict. Why did *he* always have to pay for the sins of others? He took her face in his hands. "Sass—"

"Please, Rio. Don't ask me."

He dropped his hands and seized her arms. He wanted to shake some sense into the woman. "Damn it, Sass! What you went through has nothing to do with me. With us. I am not letting you do this. No way."

She made a mewl of protest as he pulled her none too gently toward the ladder, lifted her down and dragged her toward the stateroom.

She tried to tug away, but there was no chance in hell that was happening.

"Wait! What are you doing?"

"Taking you to bed. Properly, this time."

"Oh, God. Rio, please. No. It'll just—"

He whirled to face her. "Tell me you don't want me, baby. Tell me you don't love me, and I won't touch you, I swear I won't." He scowled down at her. "Go on, tell me."

Her lips parted, but her denial never came out.

"I thought so."

He swept her up in his arms and marched her into the tiny cabin, then dropped her on the berth and lowered himself onto her.

Her eyes were wide, her tousled hair and frightened face pale as moonbeams against the bright scarlet of the sheets. But she offered no resistance as he determinedly stripped off her clothes, then did the same with his own.

He gave a growl of satisfaction as he settled between her smooth, quaking thighs.

She was so exquisitely beautiful. So in need of his protection. So trusting.

So his.

"Surrender to me, Sass. Give yourself over," he murmured.

"I want to," she whispered. "So much."

"I'm willing to take whatever risk I must to have you. Let me make this decision."

"It wouldn't be fair. To you." Desperation colored her tone.

He thrust into her, into the hot, wet center of his universe. She cried out, and he plunged deep, as deep as he could go.

He ground his jaw against the need to go deeper yet, so deep he disappeared within her.

"How do you feel when I'm inside you?" he demanded, his voice low and harsh as footsteps on gravel.

She swallowed heavily. "Complete," she whispered.

He pulled out. It took every ounce of willpower he had.

He growled from the frustration, his body screaming with the need to return to her. To be one with her. To plant his seed in her and make her his, inexorably.

"And now?" he asked. "Without me?"

A look of anguish enveloped her face. "Hollow," she murmured. "Like I'm missing a part of myself."

It was his turn to swallow. She gazed up at him so miserably it took all his strength not to do something monumentally stupid. He rolled off her, clutching the sheet in a death grip for a long moment before reaching for the box on the nightstand. With shaking hands he sheathed himself.

"Please. Make love to me," she whispered when he returned to her.

"Nothing could stop me," he quietly assured, and joined his body with hers in one swift stroke.

He reveled in muted triumph when her arms and legs wrapped around him, holding him, keeping him close, clinging to him as though she never wanted to let him go.

Rejoicing, because he never intended to let her.

He rocked in the cradle of her body, whispering endearments in her ear, showing her with his lips and his fingers and his flesh how much he cherished her. How much he'd love her if she but let him.

Her body quivered and shook as he slowly brought her to completion. Then he started all over again. Determined to please her. Determined to imprint the feel of his body on her flesh, the scent of him in her nostrils, the coaxing of his voice in her ears, so much so she'd never be able to make love to another man without thinking of him.

No!

So she'd never make love to another man at all. Ever.

He rolled her on top of him and placed her knees by his hips. "Open your eyes," he ordered. Forcing her to look down at him—*him*—as he slid her onto his thick length.

"Rio," she whispered, clasping him with her inner muscles.

"Make love to me," he said. "Show me how much you want me."

And she did.

She took his breath away.

He thought he'd experienced bliss before, but it was nothing like this. Never like this. Her sweet lips, her trembling fingers, her shy, eager tongue, they drove him to the brink of madness before at last she cried out and tumbled over the edge again, her long hair curling about their faces and shoulders in a pale, fragrant halo. But he held himself back.

He spun back on top and put her under him, covering her completely with his body. He wanted to possess her totally. He wanted her breathless and helpless beneath him. He wanted to claim her over and over, to rob her of her power and her will, and fill her with his own.

So she would stay with him.

She called his name, again, and again, sobbing it with gasps and moans, sighing it with blissful adoration, swelling his chest and his sex and his heart.

"You're mine," he told her again on a growl.

And God help anyone who tried to take her away.

Rio was relentless.

Sass meant to resist. Honestly she did. But it was impossible. He made love to her like a demon, now wild and passionate, now gentle and achingly sensitive. She could but cling to him and hope to survive the onslaught.

She did. But her heart didn't. Sometime during the tumultuous evening she gave it to him, wholly and unreservedly.

How could she not?

He made it clear that he wanted her. Clearer still that he intended to have her, regardless of her fears.

What woman could resist such an intensity of feeling? Especially if her whole life she had been starving for just such a love? What woman would not surrender completely to the man who felt that way toward her?

She could deny him nothing. So she laid herself bare, and gave him everything. Everything she had, heart and soul.

And did her best to ignore the growing certainty that disaster loomed just around the corner, waiting to knock on their door and steal him away from her.

And the even greater certainty that if she lost him, this time she wouldn't want to survive.

A loud, sudden pounding on the hatch door jerked Sass out of a deep sleep and had her lunging for her weapon.

She slammed into Rio, who was doing the same thing, just as disoriented in the bright morning sunbeams coming in from the portholes. She swore as her Walther skittered across the slippery sheets. He caught it and tossed it to her before grabbing his own automatic, whipping the top sheet around his waist and running at a crouch into the salon.

The pounding grew louder.

"Gerard! Gun! Where the hell are you?"

Rio lowered his weapon and glanced at her wryly. "I gotta get out of this business," he muttered between curses. "What do you want?" he yelled through the hatch.

"Mr. Dawson needs you up at the mansion!"

Recognizing the voice of one of Dawson's six remaining

bodyguards, Sass relaxed. Good grief. If this had been another enemy attack, they'd both be dead or dying.

Through the partially closed door, Sass listened as the guard jumped down the ladder and exchanged words with Rio. Apparently the shipment was arriving soon. And Dawson missed their company.

How touching.

"I'll wait with the golf cart while you two get dressed," the guard said, eyeing Rio's sheet and Sass's hastily thrown on kimono as she walked out to the galley.

"I'm not going anywhere before I get my coffee," she declared with Gun's best snooty attitude.

"Forget the coffee," he said testily. "There's a full spread waiting at the mansion."

"Well, thank goodness the cook survived," she said with a toss of her head. "Did you ever find out who those commandos were?"

"We assume it was Betty's crew from Romania," the guard said. "But, except for the wireless laptop, communications are still knocked out so we haven't been able to confirm that."

"No communications?" Rio raised his eyebrows. "What about the shipment? How'll they find this place?"

"Dawson still has his cell phone. Besides, it's all been prearranged."

Rio's lips pursed and she could practically hear the cogs turning in his head. "With who?"

"You'll have to take that up with Mr. Dawson," the guard said, and climbed topside, leaving them some privacy.

"What equipment am I going to need?" she whispered when they were back in the stateroom. She peered at Jules's gadgets, which she'd laid out next to her overnight bag.

Rio pulled some clothes from his dresser. "Better bring it

all. He'll try to get the cameras up and running again today so we have to move fast."

She nodded and checked that everything was safely secured inside its disguising toiletry item. Afterward she shook out her hands and rubbed them together in an attempt to quell the nervousness that skittered through her limbs.

"You okay?" he asked, noticing the gesture.

She blew out a determined breath. "Yeah. Just hadn't expected to have to go back in." She gave a weak laugh. "I've decided I don't like this undercover stuff all that much. Think I'll stick to plain old burglary from now on. Hell of a lot safer."

He walked to the shower and turned on the water. "You honestly enjoy breaking and entering?"

She smiled. "Yeah. Have to admit I do. I'm just happy I can do it for a good cause."

"And you like working for the Bureau."

"Wouldn't do anything else."

"So you keep saying," he mumbled. "Come shower with me. Don't know how long the hot water will last."

"Not sure I'll fit," she said, eyeing the postage-stamp-size stall. But looking forward to the squeeze.

"You'll fit," he assured her with a wink. "Even if we have to share the same space."

And so they did.

Sass and Rio's host stared at them over an elegant breakfast table set with crystal, fine porcelain and silver, teeming with a multitude of brunch delicacies. Sunshine streamed through the mullioned windows, making the ornate dining room glitter in gold and silver like a fairy palace. Soft music played in the background. The scents of cinnamon, vanilla and fresh-brewed coffee wafted from the sideboard.

Sass smiled at Dawson and helped herself to another blintz. "Miles, you do set the most incredible table."

She was working hard to deflect his continued fury over the stolen trigger. Using every means available.

She leaned over and languidly licked powdered sugar from Rio's lips, making sure Dawson was watching. "I especially love the beignets," she purred.

Not that he'd taken his eyes off them since they'd sat down. Sass had made sure of it. She figured watching their outrageous love play might put him in a better mood.

Rio went right along, lingering over their kisses between bites and sips. The way he gazed at her with his indigo bedroom eyes, it had to be obvious to anyone what they'd spent the night doing.

Dawson cleared his throat. "I'm disappointed you chose to stay on your yacht last night," he said. "Tonight you'll stay here."

"Sure," Rio said, continuing to look at her rather than him. "As long as the cameras aren't working. Otherwise forget it."

Dawson's coffee cup slammed down on the saucer. *Damn. So much for a better mood.*

"They're not," he spat out. "Those gorillas did a real number on the electronic equipment. It'll take days to get everything up and running properly." He drilled a hand through his hair. "Don't s'pose either of you knows anything about computers?"

Rio snorted. "You're kidding, right?"

Sass ran her fingers up his arm and trailed her tongue along his jaw. "But, Rafe, *älskling,* you're brilliant with computers! Remember that time I couldn't get my e-mail to work and you fixed it?" She gazed up at him worshipfully, then skimmed her lips over his. "Maybe you could fix Miles's, too?"

With a chuckle, he caught her face between his fingers and

gave her a long, wet kiss. "Baby, have I told you how sexy you look today?"

Even with Dawson watching, she felt her nipples tighten in response to Rio's low-spoken declaration. He'd told her at least half a dozen times at breakfast and before, but she still said, "Not that I recall," and kissed him back.

They'd made love all night and again in the shower this morning, but she still wanted him with a physical longing that made her throat ache.

They finally parted lips to find Dawson's reptilian eyes on them over the rim of his coffee cup. "I'll quadruple what Interpol is paying you to come work for me, Gerard."

Rio laughed, going back to his breakfast. "You couldn't pay me enough, Miles. I like my setup just as it is. Besides, I'll make a hell of a lot more money for you this way. Speaking of which, we heard the shipment is coming in soon."

"Within an hour or two."

"So, when are we going to find out what it is? My client was very disappointed about losing the triggering device. Not sure I can talk him into anything else."

Dawson dabbed his mouth and put down his napkin. "He'll want this. I guarantee it."

"How 'bout a hint?" Sass said, batting her eyelashes.

Dawson gave them a Cheshire cat smile. "All in good time. Meanwhile, shall we relax by the pool?"

Back in their room, Sass changed into one of Gun's micro-bikinis, then assembled her catsuit and equipment, readying them just in case she and Rio got an opportunity to slip away.

"This is going to be tricky," she said as he pulled on his swimming trunks.

"Yeah. This time we'll have to find an excuse for both of

us to leave." He rolled his eyes. "Without him wanting to tag along and watch."

She gave him a wry smile. "Sorry I'm not better with computers."

"Sorry I'm not better at picking locks."

Her smile turned into a grin. "I really will have to teach you one of these days."

He smiled back, but it held more than a touch of wistfulness. "Yeah. That would be fun."

But she knew it would never happen.

Suddenly, the day looked a whole lot bleaker.

Hell, her whole life looked a whole lot bleaker.

Setting her jaw, she swiped up her mesh beach bag. "Let's go down and get this over with. I want off this damn island. *Today.*"

They'd barely gotten settled on their chaise lounges when Ellis came out and announced the arrival of the speedboat with the mysterious shipment.

"It's tying up in the marina."

"Very good. Show them out here to the pool when they get to the house. And Ellis? Make sure they are heavily guarded. I don't want any incidents."

"Yes, Mr. Dawson." Ellis pulled out his walkie-talkie and turned back into the house.

Sass exchanged a look with Rio.

"Finally! How exciting," she said to Dawson with false enthusiasm. "Now will you tell us what it is?"

"You can see for yourself soon enough," he responded.

She waited with dread. She couldn't imagine what it might be, but she was pretty sure she didn't want to know. The things she was tasked to steal for the FBI had thus far been fairly benign: computer discs, incriminating videos and papers, the occasional pouch of raw diamonds or collection of contraband components. Never anything dangerous in and of itself. Or anything terrorists might use to do their dirty work.

She had a feeling whatever was in this shipment wasn't so innocuous.

The loud clump of heavy soles echoed stridently through the mansion as the guards escorted the delivery to them at the pool. For every step they came closer, Sass's pulse ratcheted up another notch.

The door burst open and she almost jumped from her chaise.

Dawson's guards strode in, surrounding one lone man who was carrying a square metal case handcuffed to his wrist.

Her breath whooshed out and she felt Rio's hand capture hers in a gentle squeeze. How was it he always knew when she needed his support? That just a touch from him made her feel safe and empowered?

"Who are they?" the man with the briefcase immediately demanded, pointing at her and Rio. He had an accent. Russian, maybe?

"The buyers," Dawson answered blithely, rising to his full height.

"Maybe," Rio said. "Depends on what you've got."

The man narrowed his eyes. "He doesn't know?"

"Thought I'd let it be a surprise. If they're not interested, I've got plenty of others who are."

"You trust them?" Suspicion dripped from every heavily accented syllable.

"I trust no one. However, they did save my life yesterday, so I owe them. Show us what you've got."

After a slight hesitation, the man carefully set the briefcase on the glass-topped table and unlocked the handcuff from his wrist, then made quick work of the combination locks. Slowly, he lifted the top.

Inside, in a nest of foam padding, sat a single test tube filled with liquid.

Rio's breath hissed in.

Almost against her will, Sass leaned forward. "What is it?"

Rio's tense voice cut into the absolute silence that followed. "Smallpox."

Chapter 15

Sass jumped back, nearly upsetting the chaise. "What do you mean, smallpox? How can it be—"

Rio's pulse stalled, then roared in his veins as everyone turned to him. *Damn it to hell. He should have guessed, should have tipped Macon last night to the possibility.* Where was his brain?

Unfortunately, he knew exactly where it had been for this entire mission.

"It's a vial of smallpox virus," he said somberly. "Stolen, if I'm not mistaken, a few weeks ago from a government medical testing facility near Paris."

"Very good, Gerard," Dawson said approvingly.

"How did you know that?" the delivery man sputtered. "Even the press hasn't gotten wind yet."

"Mr. Gerard works for Interpol," Dawson drawled with a smug curl to his lips.

The other man blanched. "Interpol! What the hell—!"

"Shut up, Gryzmski. He's not here to arrest us. Now. Shall we work out the details?" Dawson turned to Rio and Sass. "You'll excuse me for a few moments?"

"Sure. We'll just have a swim," Rio said. Sass looked shaken; he figured a little cold water couldn't hurt.

As the two men headed for the French doors, followed by Dawson's guards, Rio slung his arm around her and pulled her into the pool with a splash.

"Damn it, Rio—" she hissed.

"Rafe," he whispered warningly. Her eyes widened and she glanced around to see if anyone had heard her slip. Luckily they were totally alone by now.

She squeezed her eyes grimly shut. Water trickled down her face to her rigid jaw and he gently swiped the drops off with a thumb.

He could plainly see how upset she was. How over her head this whole operation was for her training. She'd already done far more than anyone should have expected of her. This was asking too much.

"I'm getting you out of here right now," he said, making a quick decision. "We'll tell them our client's not interested. Let's go."

She dug her heels into the bottom of the pool, surprising him with the fierceness of her stance. "No. We can't leave. We haven't finished what we came for."

"Baby—"

"Don't baby me," she whispered intently, her face screwed into a determined scowl. "They've got a vial of *smallpox*, for chrissakes. No way am I letting that get out into the world. Not a chance in hell. *I'll die first*."

The impact of her words hit them both like a hollow-point

bullet in Kevlar. He didn't argue, didn't even respond. He knew better.

She was serious. This was serious.

He moved his arms along the surface of the water making small waves that skimmed to the edge of the pool. Fighting the instinct to drag her out of there by the hair if necessary. Because she was right. And he had to stop thinking like a lover and think like the FBI special agent in charge of this op.

"Any suggestions?" he asked. "I have no experience with biologicals. No idea how to neutralize the virus. Do you?"

She shook her head. "We'll have to buy it. Secure it and make sure that briefcase doesn't leave our possession."

"I don't know. Those weren't Macon's orders," he reminded her. "He gave the diary top priority."

"Macon didn't know what was in that shipment," she pointed out, rightly.

The thought of carrying around a vial of deadly smallpox virus held no appeal to him. But he couldn't let fear or emotion cloud his judgment. Not about this.

On the other hand, his orders were clear. And he saw no reason to go against them.

"Knowing what was in the shipment wouldn't have made a difference to Macon," he said.

"How can you be so sure?"

"He said so himself."

"But—"

"I'll plant the tracking bug with the virus, like he said. Then we'll do whatever it takes to get the diary. Today. Once we have that, Macon can bring down the whole operation before nightfall. Dawson won't be able to send for a new buyer that soon. The virus isn't going anywhere."

She didn't look happy, but nodded reluctantly. "I suppose you're right."

He set his jaw. "Trust me. This is the best strategy."

At least he hoped to hell it was.

He gathered her in his arms, treading water as they floated together into the deep end of the pool. He tipped up her chin and held her eyes. "We can do this."

"I'm scared," she whispered so low he barely heard.

"Me, too, baby." He kissed her, and felt a light tremor sift through her body. So he deepened the kiss, hoping to distract them both. At least for a little while.

Because for now, there was nothing they could do but wait.

Dawson returned to the pool a while later looking very pleased with himself. "Well, then. What do you think of my newest offering?"

"Very impressive," Rio answered, fixing his expression to match. He was reclining on his chaise lounge in the sun sipping a bottle of water. "Can't tell you what a tizzy the frogs were in when their little vial turned up missing."

Dawson snickered. "I can imagine."

"Every law enforcement agency on the planet is looking for it."

"All the more reason to conclude our business quickly." He looked thoughtful. "You wouldn't be thinking of betraying me, would you? Recovering it would put quite a feather in your cap."

Rio gave him a withering look. "Let's see." He raised his palms to either side of him like a scale. He lifted one higher, "Feather?—" then the other "—million bucks. Gosh, it's such a tough decision."

Dawson chuckled. "Point taken. When will you call your clients?"

Rio consulted his watch. "Our contact time is in a few minutes."

"You think they'll be interested?"

"What, are you kidding? Even if they never use it, the worldwide blackmail value alone makes possession of it invaluable."

"My sentiments exactly."

Just then Ellis came out and passed a cell phone to Dawson. "It's the call you were expecting, sir."

"Ah, good. Hello?"

Sass strolled over to perch on the side of Rio's chaise, handed him a tube of suntan lotion and presented him with her back. He pretended not to listen to Dawson's conversation as he squirted the cool liquid on her skin and leisurely rubbed it in. But neither of them spoke.

"Perfect," Dawson said into the phone, idly watching Rio's movements. "The price is quite acceptable… Yes, I took care of that. My men planted the bomb on his boat while he was up here at the house… A cell phone detonator, as instructed. Hang on." He snapped his fingers and Ellis handed him a small piece of paper. "It's 843-555-7229… That's right… My pleasure. I'll be in touch."

With that, Dawson handed the phone back to Ellis.

Rio's blood chilled. The delivery man was to be blown up? Yet another example of Dawson's cold ruthlessness. He shouldn't care. The man was a terrorist, complicit in the sale of a weapon of mass destruction such as the world hadn't experienced since the near-annihilation of Native Americans by the very same agent. And yet, bile filled his stomach.

What would happen to him and Sass if *they* were caught? Especially Sass…

He didn't even want to consider it.

He finished with the lotion and lifted her fully onto the chaise between his legs, not wanting to let her go. Needing to feel her safe in his arms.

Her words from last night echoed in his mind…

Terrible things will happen. Dawson will get to you and do some horrible thing to you. You'll die!

No. That was nonsense.

He shook off the eerie feeling of impending doom.

No way. This operation was the culmination of a career spent chasing this evil man and men like him. Rio would win. There was no other option.

And he wasn't about to let anything happen to Sass.

"Ellis, give Mr. Gerard the phone. It's time to contact your clients," he said, turning to him.

Rio made a show of consulting his watch again. "Yeah, okay. But I prefer to use my own cell phone."

"Where is it?"

"On the *Mermaid.*"

"Then I'm afraid it won't be possible. I can't let you leave the mansion before having your answer."

And if it wasn't the answer Dawson wanted, no doubt there'd be a nasty surprise waiting on the *Mermaid* after they'd sailed off into the middle of the ocean. Like the delivery man.

Rio set his face in a rigid frown. "It appears I have no choice." He accepted the phone from Ellis, punched in the number Macon had given him last night. And sent up a swift prayer.

"Yes?" It was Macon on the other end, thank God.

"The new shipment came in."

"And?"

"It's the item that was lost in Paris a few weeks ago."

There was a long silence, then Macon said, "Okay. We weren't expecting that. But it should work nicely into our plans."

"How high are you willing to go?"

"Whatever it takes. Don't lose this one."

"Not to worry. We'll get it," Rio assured him.

"You and your wife are enjoying your stay?" Macon casually asked.

"Looking forward to spending our hefty commission," he said, avoiding the phrase "We're fine."

"Good. Let me know when to expect delivery." Then the line went dead.

Rio hung up and passed the phone back to Ellis.

Dawson's brows lifted. "Well?"

Rio leaned back and laced his fingers over Sass's abdomen. "It's a go. Name your price."

"All in good time," their host said with a menacing smile, then turned to Ellis. "Contact our man and have that call traced," he ordered.

Rio's feet crashed to the patio tiles and he jerked forward, making Sass squeak with surprise. "Wait a minute!" he snarled. "You can't do that! My clients require anonymity. They'll be furious!"

"Not if they're not told," Dawson said levelly, and stood. "You have to understand, I must know who I'm dealing with."

"I saved your freaking life! You don't trust me?"

"I believe I made it clear that I trust no one. It's what's kept me alive and in business. Now, if you two will just go to your room and wait, this shouldn't take too long."

Rio spat out a string of invective as he lunged off the chaise, dragging Sass up with him by the waist. "I can't believe this stinking treatment! You just lost yourself a powerful ally, my friend."

Dawson shrugged, unaffected. "I doubt it. In the end all that matters to you is the paycheck, and we both know it."

"Now, *älskling*," Sass said in Gun's soothing Swedish accent. "Miles is just being cautious. Which is a good thing, *ja?* We don't want to be caught in a setup, either, do we?" She stroked his face with a tender hand.

Rio pretended to be somewhat mollified, but muttered, "I still don't like it."

"Come now. I'm sure we can think of something to occupy our time upstairs," she purred, and gave him a kiss.

He let himself be persuaded. Hell, Dawson was playing right into their hands. This could be exactly the opportunity they'd been waiting for to get that diary.

"All right, fine." He stalked after her as she sauntered past Dawson, through the French doors and up the stairs to their room. He noted they were being followed.

Rio closed the bedroom door firmly behind them and blew out a breath, whispering, "He's posted a guard outside."

Sass shrugged. "Doesn't matter. We're going through the bathroom window."

They both sprang into action, changing out of their pool attire and quickly plucking up the equipment they'd assembled for their run on Dawson's computer.

Rio didn't mind admitting he was a bit nervous. He was strictly a front-door man. Being a cat burglar was something he'd never aspired to. Nor had he ever crawled over the roof of a three-story building or dangled thirty feet up from a wire thin enough to floss his teeth with. He just hoped he didn't discover a heretofore hidden fear of heights.

"The good news is we won't have to worry about cameras or outside guards," Sass murmured as she slid open the window and did a quick check of the grounds below to confirm

the perimeter guards had been among the casualties yesterday. "All clear. Ready?"

"Wait," he said, and grabbed her Walther from the waistband of his black pants, leaving his own Glock tucked in
place. Dawson had become remarkably lax about their weapons. "You'll need this."

She shook her head. "I never carry when I work."

He wasn't about to take no for an answer. He pressed the
weapon into her hand. "You've never been up against Dawson before."

She pushed out a breath and nodded once, taking the gun. Zipping it into her fanny pack, she indicated the window. "Ready?"

Rio nodded confidently. He'd never been more ready in his
life. He was determined to find Dawson's diary quickly and
get himself and Sass the hell out of there before it was too late.
He had a bad feeling Dawson was even now making plans to
eliminate his newest best friends.

Sass was out the window in a flash. Rio shook out the jitters and followed close on her heels. Hoping with all his
might they weren't crawling right into a trap.

Pausing on the crest of the roof, Sass turned her head to
make sure Rio wasn't having trouble shadowing her movements. He winked at her, just a few feet behind. She grinned
and gave him a thumbs-up.

She had to admit, he was a pretty game dude to try this. She'd
seen the misgivings in his expression as he'd taken the plunge
out of that bathroom window and into her world. SAC or no,
there weren't a lot of other agents who would have done that.

"Quite a view," he whispered when he joined her at the top,
glancing around. They could see the entire island from their
vantage point high above the treetops.

It was insane, but she couldn't help taking a brief moment to drink it all in. "Awesome," she murmured. The bright blue ocean sparkled like a million sapphires in the noon-day sun, surrounding the small, uneven circle of junglelike greenery that arose from the waves. Here and there, white sails dotted the horizon.

"When we get out of here, I'll take you sailing in the Keys," he murmured softly, and threw her a glance. Daring her to refuse.

She didn't. "Look forward to it," she whispered, brushing her lips over his.

Then she jigged over the roof peak and backed down the other side. After securing the pulley hook and wire to an eave beam, she beckoned him to the edge.

"I'll go first and get the window open. I'll signal when I'm in and you can follow."

"No way," he whispered, shaking his head. "What if there's a guard in the office? I'll go first."

She shot him an exasperated look. "And how do you propose to get in?"

He frowned, a battle playing itself out in his eyes—his macho side versus his logical side. "We'll both go."

"Yeah. This hook is really going to support both of us. You'll be lucky not to end up in the rose bushes as it is."

That shut him up. His mouth thinned to a line and he wagged a finger at her. But he didn't object—verbally at least—when she slid her sneaker into the stirrup loop and started lowering herself down with the hand winch.

Skirting the side of the office window, she halted, peered inside, and let out a sigh of relief when she saw it was empty.

In three minutes they were both inside Dawson's office.

"Thank goodness the laser matrix is still down," Rio said.

"Makes things a lot easier," she agreed and pointed. "Computer's in the armoire."

"Now comes the fun part," Rio said, cracking his knuckles. "Okay to open it?"

She nodded, having finished her inspection of the large piece of furniture. "Unless there's a trip wire I'm not seeing, you're all set. Think I'll just move along to the other side of the room…" She showed her teeth when he drilled her a look.

"Funny."

She couldn't believe it, but she was actually enjoying herself. No doubt an indication she was on the edge of hysterics.

She'd always assumed working with a partner would irritate her and drag her down. Rio did neither. He was right there on the ball with her. It was kind of nice to have company.

She didn't want to be a pest, so she made herself scarce while he brought the computer to life and stuck some kind of portable drive from his pocket into one of the ports. She watched admiringly as he bent to his task with a frown of concentration, working the keyboard as if it were a Steinway, coaxing soft beeps and whirs from the CPU.

He definitely looked like he knew what he was doing.

"Yes!" he whispered, and glanced up. "I'm in."

A sense of pride washed over her. Dumb. His success had nothing to do with her. But there it was. She couldn't be prouder if she'd done it herself.

She needed to stay alert, listen for any indication of approaching guards or other dangers. But for the next fifteen or twenty minutes she found it hard to focus on anything but Rio's broad shoulders and the endearing way his hair curled up in the back just a tiny bit.

Oh, yeah. She had it bad.

"Think I've found something," he finally murmured.

"The diary?"

"Possibly. Let me take a closer look."

Thank God. That meant they were nearly home free. And they could blow this pop stand.

Then suddenly she remembered. Once they left…it would be all over with Rio.

Lord, what would she do then? When the case was closed and they returned to Washington, D.C?

Sailing trips to the Keys aside, their lives would take very different roads. And long distance never worked, even if they wanted to try. Which she didn't. For all the reasons she'd been brewing about since they'd become lovers. But still, the thought of losing him so soon…

She stifled a sigh, barely noticing when his gently sloping back straightened with a jerk. He hissed out a swearword, more virulent than she'd ever heard from his mouth.

She jumped up and took a step toward him. "What is it?"

He swung around with a glare, making her falter in her tracks. His face was a mask of hatred.

"Rio?"

He stared at her for an endless moment in silence.

"What did you find?"

She could see his teeth clench and unclench, the muscles of his jaw roiling under the skin. She took a step back. *What the hell?*

"I found the diary."

"That's good," she said uncertainly. "Right?"

He drilled a hand through his hair. "You aren't going to believe what I stumbled onto."

"Tell me." She ventured a step closer.

He turned back to the computer monitor. "Over the years it's become a reflex to check out the time around my father's death when I first open a new line of enquiry. With a perp, or an old-timer cop I meet, or if I find old files during a case. Anything and everything I run across. And as you may recall, there were rumors his death was connected somehow with Dawson."

She stood over his shoulder and searched the screen. "There's something in Dawson's diary about your father's death?" she asked in cautious amazement.

"You could say that," he said tersely. "Just what I've been looking for for eighteen years. The name of the man who betrayed him."

Her jaw dropped. "Oh, Rio! You're serious? But how…why would that be in there? What's the connection?"

"Apparently the bastard worked for Dawson. I can't believe this."

She peered harder at the choppy sentences on the screen, grouped into neat paragraphs preceded by a date.

Suddenly, the hair on the back of her neck rose on end.

Those dates…

"Oh, my God," she whispered as the eerie familiarity of the month and year hit her straight in the gut. "It can't be…"

Hurriedly, she scanned through the passage Rio's gaze was glued to. And had to grab his chair for support when the name she'd been dreading to see jumped out at her from the screen, big as life.

"Clive Burton," Rio echoed with a growl.

She gasped, shaking her head.

"This is it, all the evidence I need—" Rio stabbed his finger at the monitor angrily "—*to hang the bastard*. And not just Dawson."

Sass's hand went to her mouth as she suppressed a cry. "No! You don't mean that."

"I do," he hissed. "Now I have his name it'll take me about five seconds to find him and boot his ass into prison. And then I'll—"

"He's already there," she whispered.

"What?" Rio whirled on her, his eyes narrowed. "What are you talking about?"

"You don't have to worry about catching him. He's already in jail."

"And you know this how?"

"Because," she said, her heart shriveling with misery, "Clive Burton is my father."

"Your *father?*"

Rio's face shuttered in revulsion and it was all Sass could do to keep from throwing herself to her knees and begging him to stop the thoughts running through his head. But it would do no good. She knew that.

"Rio, please. Don't look at me like that," she whispered.

"You *knew*," he spat out accusingly. "You knew all along! How could you touch me, knowing—"

"No! I swear I had no idea."

But suddenly she again recalled the odd question Clive had asked her about Rio in their last phone conversation before she left.

By any chance was Rio's father, or brother, a Fed?

Her shaking fingers shot to her lips. What was the name he'd mentioned…?

"Oh, my God. Was your father's name…Spencer? Spencer Rio?"

It obviously was, for his son's beautiful blue eyes went flat and cold. He swung away from her in disgust, leaving her heart hanging in shreds. "You're a real piece of work, Hawthorne, you know that? And to think I almost—"

She flinched as though he'd slapped her hard across the face. Pain razored through every cell of her body.

The words he'd left unspoken echoed big as life in the bitter silence. *—trusted you? —forgot you were a thief? —fell in love with the daughter of my father's murderer?*

"Rio, please," she pleaded. "Listen—"

He had to be mistaken. *Clive couldn't have done it.*

"Let's just get this over with," he interrupted, pounding keys with a vengeance. The computer sprang to life, a bright blue download bar zooming across the screen. "I have to get the hell out of here."

And away from her.

Out of her life.

Forever.

Her vision swam in a sea of anguish, but she nodded. "Yes. That would be best."

And it would. It was better this way. Far better. With no possibility he'd ever want her back. A clean, final break from Rio would make it so much easier to go on with her life. Without him. Because even if this misunderstanding had never happened, her life could never be spent with him. *For his sake.*

Really. It was better this way.

No matter what he thought of her.

She watched in quiet misery as he efficiently finished up with the download, slipped the portable drive back into his pocket and shut down the computer. He was just closing up the armoire when all at once the office door banged open with a loud crash.

Two guards charged in, machine guns aimed at their heads.

Behind the guards Dawson stepped into the room, hands on his hips.

"Well, well, well. And what do we have here?"

Chapter 16

Rio spun to face Dawson. Icy hatred burned in every fiber of his being. He'd waited half a lifetime for this moment.

Clive Burton's betrayal had led to his father's death, but it was *the man standing before him* who'd issued the order to take him out; Rio was now certain of it. Burton was simply Dawson's stooge.

Instinctively, Rio jerked Sass behind his body to shield her. She might be a thief and a liar, but she was still his responsibility.

For a split second his heart exploded with pain. Ruthlessly he suppressed it. He couldn't think about Sass now. It hurt too much.

"Ah, how sweet. You think you can protect your wife. But you're really only sparing us bullets."

Rio's civilized veneer shut down and all he knew was a burning need for vengeance. Vengeance and blood. With one vicious act, this man had taken from him the two people he'd loved most in this world—his father and Sass. He would pay for that. Even if it cost Rio his life, he would pay. Because right now, Rio had nothing else left to lose.

It was a good day to die.

"You had my father killed," Rio said, so softly Dawson had to cock his head to hear.

"What's that? Your father?"

"Special Agent Spencer Rio," he helpfully supplied.

Dawson frowned, clearly taken by surprise. His frown deepened as the possibilities flared through his eyes. "Ah," he finally said. "I see I've been thoroughly deceived. Congratulations, Gerard—or whoever you are. Not many people have been able to do that. Unfortunately for you, none of them have survived to tell about it."

Behind him he felt a slight movement. The Glock slid smoothly from the back of his waistband.

"Do your worst, Dawson," he growled. "But I warn you, if I go, I'm taking you down with me."

The barest breath of a whisper sounded in his ear. "One… two…"

Dawson gave a bark of laughter. "Brave words from a man with two Uzis pointed at his head. Brave, but stupid. You haven't got a—"

Instead of *three*, an ear-shattering double blast of gunfire burst through the room. Rio dived to the floor. Stray machine gun spatter popped around the room as the muscles of the two stunned guards, blood spurting from their chests, spasmed in death.

In the split second that followed, Rio rolled to catch a falling Uzi before it hit the floor. Kicking the other across the room, he leaped to his feet and jammed the machine gun at Dawson's forehead before he could react.

This was the second occasion Rio had found himself in this exact same position.

But this time he didn't intend to waste the opportunity. Macon would probably have him drummed out of the Bureau for killing a collar who had as much information to spill as Dawson did.

But he didn't care.

"Say goodbye, bastard."

"*No!* Wait!" Sass stepped right in Dawson's face. Still holding a gun in each hand, she stuck both muzzles in his gut. "Don't kill him yet. Not until he answers our questions."

Rio fiercely suppressed his need to pull the Uzi's trigger, and lowered the aggressive position of the weapon. Sass was right. He had to think beyond his own need for revenge and keep the bastard alive. So he could answer for everything he'd done. To Rio. To his country. Death was too good for him.

"Tell us what happened," Sass demanded of Dawson, her voice quivering with anger. "Why did you have Spencer Rio killed?"

He snorted. "That Fed was an interfering troublemaker. But what makes you think I had him killed?"

"Your own diary," Rio ground out, and shoved the Uzi back up against his temple. "This is a waste of time."

"You don't read very well," Dawson drawled, seemingly unconcerned that any second he could have his brains spattered all over the wall. "That was someone else on my payroll, a thief who'd rolled on me to the Feds. *He's* the one I ordered taken out. Rio just got in the way. A fortuitous accident."

Rio froze. *What?* In his peripheral vision, he saw Sass go chalk-white. He also noticed the arm of her catsuit was dripping crimson droplets onto the carpet. God, she'd been hit!

"What thief?" she asked, her voice strangled. "Who was it?"

"I don't remember." Dawson lifted a shoulder dismissively and Sass's guns rammed hard into him. "Tell me! Or by God, I swear I'll let him kill you instead of waiting for the Feds. In fact I'll help. But I'm not as good a shot as he is. It might take this whole clip to find that black heart of yours. Starting with—" She jammed the Glock between his legs, making the sucker gasp.

"All right! All right! Burton. His name was Clive Burton! The damned snitch. He deserved to die! Too bad the job never got finished."

Rio finally got his mouth to work. "You're saying Spencer Rio wasn't the real target that night? *Clive Burton* was?"

Dawson's eyes narrowed in memory. "Burton'd gone soft. Bought a house and wanted to settle down with the wife and kiddies. Get out of the game. I told him no way." His mouth twisted into an ugly snarl. "I taught him good, though. *No one* crosses me. I thought he'd learned his lesson, but a few years later he went crawling to Rio and his partner. Wanted to get out again. Said his little girl deserved a normal life." Dawson snorted derisively. *"He turned informant."*

There was a silent pause, then Sass's throat gave out a bloodcurdling growl. *"No!"*

At the same time, Rio heard a commotion downstairs. *The other guards?*

He grabbed her arm as she stuck the Glock against Dawson's throat. "Sass, no. We need him alive."

"Screw that. Get out of my way, Rio."

Heavy boots were now running up the stairs. "Damn it! We've got company."

"He killed my mother and sister!" she hissed, struggling harder against his hold on her gun arm. "They'd done nothing! They were innocent! He was going to kill my father, too! And he *did* kill yours!"

"I know, baby, I know. And he'll pay for it. All of it."

The boots were almost to the office and Rio was getting desperate. He glanced from Sass's enraged, tear-streaked face to the trail of blood dripping from her hand, to Dawson's smug smile.

He'd been wrong, so damned wrong, about her.

About everything.

"He'll pay, if it's the last thing I ever do," Rio muttered, and lifted the Uzi back to the bastard's temple. Throwing a choke hold around his neck, he swung him around to face the door. "Get behind me," he ordered Sass, shielding her as best he could. "Say your prayers, Dawson, cause I'll see you in hell before I let you get away."

Four men in full SWAT gear rushed through the door, aimed their weapons and halted in a defensive formation. Nobody moved.

"Room secure," one of them shouted.

Agent Macon walked in, followed by Jules Mannheim.

"Good work, Rio, Hawthorne," Macon said, his sharp gaze taking in the situation at a glance. "Stand down, you two. We and the federal prosecutor will take it from here."

Letting out a long sigh, Rio stood on the deck of the *Mermaid,* beer in hand, and stared up at the bright canopy of stars.

The mission was an overwhelming success.

By sundown Dawson had been whisked away, no doubt to several lifetimes in prison, at the very least, his employees rounded up—except for Ellis, who'd phoned Rio's contact number while tracing it and warned Macon what was happening, so he could come to the rescue, in exchange for a deal— and Dawson's worldwide terrorist contacts were in the process of being severely compromised by the tracking devices they'd planted, and the computer files Rio had downloaded.

Even at midnight, accolades and commendations were pouring in from as high up as the President. Rio could now retire in his well-earned blaze of glory.

So why didn't he feel in the least like celebrating?

He gazed down at the bare finger on his left hand. They'd taken the wedding bands along with the other equipment earlier. He felt naked without it. And that just made him even more depressed.

He gave another sigh and tipped his bottle up for a long swallow. He knew exactly why.

Because he'd lost Sass. Driven her away with his knee-jerk reaction and ugly words.

This afternoon, seconds after Macon and Mannheim's timely arrival, Rio had rushed to Sass to put a supporting arm around her as she sank into a chair, weak from blood loss. But she'd turned her back on him and let Mannheim take care of her until the medics arrived.

Rio's heart and throat ached with the memory of her rejection. But he was pretty sure it was nothing compared to the pain he'd given her with his blind lack of trust.

You're a real piece of work, Hawthorne. He cringed inwardly. How could he have said that, or thought those awful things about her? Even for a single second?

Because even if Clive Burton had held the gun that killed Rio's dad and pulled the trigger himself, that still wouldn't have a damn thing to do with Sass.

She was a victim in all this, just as he was.

He could see that, now that he was rational. But in the heat of the moment half a lifetime of prejudices had swamped him and he'd lashed out at her in the most unfair way possible.

He was a class-A jerk. He didn't deserve her. Or her love.

He threw himself down on the aft bench and leaned his head back on the hard fiberglass of the deck behind it. What could he do? He'd tried to apologize, but she wouldn't speak to him. She'd said it was over and they had nothing to talk about.

He didn't agree. He had plenty to talk about.

If only she'd listen.

He pulled his cell phone from his pocket and for the dozenth time punched in Mannheim's number.

"How is she?" he asked when Mannheim answered. He and Sass were still at the hospital across the water in Charleston. Rio had wanted to go with her, but she'd said no. And Mannheim was being his usual bossy, protective self.

"Same as half an hour ago," the other man said impatiently. "And if you don't stop calling I'm going to turn this phone off. I'm not supposed to have it on in the hospital anyway. The nurses threaten me every time it rings."

"You're a federal agent. Tell them to stuff it," Rio retorted just as impatiently. "I want to know how she really is."

Mannheim pushed out a breath. "Fine. As I told you a hundred times already, the bullet went right through her upper arm, no real damage. She's gotten her stitches and a heavy sedative. She's going to sleep. So stop calling."

"Let me talk to her."

"As I told you the last *seven thousand* times, she doesn't want to speak to you."

"Fine. I'll do all the talking. Give her the phone."

There was some static and a low conversation, then Mannheim came back on. "Sorry. No go."

"Put the damn phone to her ear and hold it there! Tell her she's going to hear what I have to say," he yelled, "or I'm coming over there and *making* her listen!"

After a moment Sass's groggy voice came on the line. "What do you want?"

Suddenly, he didn't know what to say. There was so much he needed to get out, and she might only give him a few seconds. His mind worked frantically, trying to come up with something, anything, that would bring her back to him.

In the end, he just blurted out, "Please, Sass, I'm so sorry. I'm on my knees here, begging for mercy. Baby, I love you. I don't want to live without you. Please, honey, come back to me."

Silence greeted his plea, and his heart crumbled.

He tried again, even knowing he was fighting a losing battle. "I know I was wrong. I was just so shocked. I should have trusted you. At least talk to me. Cuss me out. Anything. Baby?"

Mannheim came back on the line. "Sorry, buddy. The sedative must have kicked in. She fell asleep."

Under his breath Rio cursed the doctor and his damn drugs, his own stupidity and his dumb, rotten luck. The one and only time he'd ever said those three little words to a woman...

He gathered himself, and said, "When she wakes up, tell her I love her." He had no doubt Mannheim would be there through the night.

"I will," the older man promised, oddly unconfrontational for once.

"She could do worse than me," Rio said, petulance rising through the hurt that it wasn't him sitting at her bedside.

"A lot worse," Mannheim agreed, really taking him by surprise. "I'll give her your message."

Then he clicked off.

Rio stared at the phone in his hand for a long time. "Well, that was the kiss of death," he finally muttered.

You knew you were dead in the water when your main rival started feeling sorry for you.

With one last, long sigh, he made his way down to the state-room and flopped on the scarlet-sheeted bunk. He doubted he'd sleep, but at least he'd be surrounded by the scent of her and their lovemaking as he lay there dreaming of what could have been.

And wondering if he'd ever see her again, the woman he loved.

The next morning, Sass awoke feeling tired and cranky. Her arm hurt and her mouth felt as if a herd of elephants had trampled through it. Dirty elephants, with disgusting stuff on their feet.

"It's the meds," the doctor said when she grimaced in dis-taste. "Now, let's take a look at that wound, shall we?"

"I'll pass," she muttered, closing her eyes. "But you go right ahead."

The doctor chuckled. "A sense of humor. Always a good sign."

After the exam, she was pronounced fit and ready to be checked out if she wished.

She wished.

"We can hop the next plane to Washington, D.C.," Jules said from the chair he'd occupied all night by the look of him. He pulled an e-mail printout from his pocket. "I've got the de-parture times—"

"I need to talk to Rio."

She vaguely remembered hearing Rio's voice on the phone last night, just before she passed out from the sedative. She'd thought at first she must be dreaming. Wishful thinking. Be-cause he'd said he loved her. But then Jules had given her his message this morning, confirming it. Shocking her. Giving her a brief burst of hope. But in the end making her regret even more bitterly what she had to do.

"I can't leave him like this. He deserves…a better ending."

Mannheim pursed his lips. "Yeah. Whatever." He gave her a funny look. "Do you love him?"

Her eyes widened and she stammered, "N-no, of…of course n-not."

"Don't lie, Sass. You never were any good at it."

She squeezed her eyes shut. "Fine. Okay, I love him. But…it can't possibly go anywhere. He doesn't trust me. He'll always think of me as a thief. Always associate me with his father's death. And clearly, bad things happen to those I love."

"I think you may be wrong about that. He's apologized a dozen times for his single moment of doubt. I know this man's reputation. He wouldn't be saying he loves you if he didn't mean it. And none of what happened to your family was your fault, you know that."

"Whose side are you on, anyway?" she mumbled, giving him a doleful glance.

"Yours, sweetheart. You know I love you almost as much as your own dad. I want to see you happy. And I'd hate to see you throw away an opportunity to find that."

"You're starting to sound like Clive," she groused. "Speaking of whom… You knew didn't you." It wasn't a question.

"Knew what?"

"Rio thought it was me. But it was really you. You did all this on purpose, didn't you?"

"Did all what?" But his innocent face didn't fool her for a second.

"You're no better a liar than I am, Jules. You sent me and Rio in together to catch Dawson. You knew we'd find out about the connection between our fathers."

He puffed out his cheeks. "Maybe." At her raised brows, his posture deflated. "Okay, yeah. I did. It was probably self-ish. But I've been carrying around that burden of guilt for a long time. Until now it had been convenient having Rio think his father was betrayed by a thief—it made him extra good at his job. But since he started talking about retiring…"

She stared at Jules incredulously. "Why would you feel guilty about Spencer Rio's death?" Then it struck her. "Oh, my God. You were his partner!"

He nodded. "I was pretty certain that bullet was meant for your dad, not Spence. But if I'd said anything…"

"The Bureau's investigation might have stalled."

"I wanted the bastard caught. Your dad knew exactly what had happened, but unfortunately he also knew that he'd live a lot longer if he didn't open his mouth about any of it. So the investigation never went anywhere anyway."

"And that's why you've taken care of me all these years."

Jules smiled. "Nah. I just saw your potential. I wanted you on our side."

She smiled back, knowing in her heart it was probably true.

"Now, about you and Rio," he began.

She cut him off before he could start in on her again. "You're wasting your breath, Jules. It's not going to work out."

"And why is that? The man loves you. And you just admitted you love him. So what gives? Not that 'bad stuff happens' crap."

She shrugged. She really didn't want to go into it. Not even with Jules, who was more likely to understand than anyone.

"If for no other reason, he's retiring and moving a thousand miles south," she said reasonably. "Out to the middle of nowhere. I love my job at the Bureau. I'm not ready to quit."

"Who says you'd have to quit?"

She glanced at him skeptically. "What are you talking about?"

"You're a specialist, Sass. It doesn't matter where you make your home base. Not in this day and age of instant communication and high-speed travel."

She blinked uncomprehendingly. "You're saying I could move to Timbuktu and still keep my job?" For a brief, amazing moment her heart soared. *Or Podunk…*

But then she remembered the other part. And wanted to scream and weep at the unfairness of it all.

Instead she shook her head sadly. "Anyway, there's a lot more to it than the job, Jules. It just…isn't going to work."

He rose to his feet. "Well, you know I'll support you whatever you decide."

"Thanks. I appreciate that," she murmured as he gave her a hug goodbye. "I'll try to catch a later flight to D.C."

"Take all the time you need," he said with a warm smile, and left.

Afterward, the nurse bustled in offering to help her dress and pack up for discharge. Wearily, she went through the motions. Dreading the coming confrontation with Rio. It wasn't going to be easy, convincing him it was because she loved him so much that she had to let him go.

Maybe she'd get lucky and he'd already have gone. She knew he'd volunteered to sail the *Mermaid* north to a Coast Guard impound facility in Virginia, pending DOJ orders to have the yacht auctioned off.

But avoidance was the coward's way out. Aside from just delaying the inevitable. If Rio had told Mannheim he loved her, he wasn't going to stop trying until he heard from her own lips she didn't want to see him again.

She fervently hoped she was a better liar than Jules gave her credit for.

She rented a car and drove from Charleston south to Seven

Moon Island. She figured she'd hire that boat captain—Jenna? Bobby Jo?—at the boat charter place to ferry her out to Dawson's marina. And hope Rio was still there.

To her surprise, as soon as she turned into Seven Moon Island Charter's parking lot she spotted the *Mermaid* docked at the jetty.

What was Rio doing here?

She switched off the car engine and leaned back in the bucket seat. Thinking about the three pretty women who owned the charter boat company, a twinge of jealousy twisted through her.

Which she had no right to feel. She was about to hand the man his heart on a platter. What he did with it afterward was none of her business. If he wanted to ask the perky little Jenna or sultry Bobby Jo out to dinner, Sass had nothing to say about it. Nor about anything that might follow that dinner.

She squeezed her eyes shut and fought down a feeling of nausea and despair. The thought of Stewart Rio with another woman made her physically ill.

He was *hers.*

Her man.

Her lover.

Her—

No. He wasn't.

She wouldn't have him hurt. Not for anything in the world. Why, look at what had happened after just a few days together! Dawson had nearly killed him! Rio could be dead right now. They both might.

All because of her. Her background. Her father. Her jinx.

"You came."

She jumped at the deep, unmistakable voice from outside the car. "Rio!"

"I wasn't sure you would."

"I probably shouldn't have."

"Did you get my message?"

She nodded, looking down at her lap.

"Any reaction?"

She licked her bottom lip, biting the inside trying not to blurt out she loved him, too.

Her door swung open and her seat belt popped off. He grabbed her hand and pulled her up into his arms.

"Will you ever forgive me? Baby, please, I know I don't deserve it, but—"

"Yes," she whispered. "I forgive you. I don't want you to think that's why—"

"Thank God," he murmured.

Before she could protest his lips were on hers. He was kissing her, holding her tight. Breaking down her willpower with every persuasive stroke of his tongue and gentle touch of his hand.

She forced herself to pull back. "Rio, you have to stop."

"Damn. I'm sorry," he said contritely, eyeing the white bandage bisecting her upper arm. "I'm hurting your arm."

"No, it's not that."

"Then what? You don't like kissing me?" he murmured, bending close to brush his mouth over her lips, her cheeks, her eyelids.

"You know I do," she whispered on a moan, clutching at his shirt.

"Then what?"

"Oh, Rio, please don't torment me like this. You know what."

He held her away from him. "Baby, please tell me this isn't about your crazy fear something bad will happen because you want to settle down."

"I know you think it's nuts, but—"

"I don't think it's nuts, it *is* nuts. You can't possibly—"

"I'm not willing to take a chance with your life," she blurted out. "I love you too much."

There. She'd done it.

"You do?"

His mouth curved into a blinding smile. She gasped as he pulled her into his arms and swung her around, mindful of her injury but laughing and hugging her. Oh, God, he wasn't taking her seriously!

"Rio, you have to stop! I really can't be with you! It's just too dangerous."

"Bull," he said succinctly. She opened her mouth to disagree but he cut her off. "Maybe you could make that argument before, but things have changed now." He set her on her feet and put his hands on her cheeks, forcing her to look at him. "We know who caused all those bad things to happen in your life. It wasn't you wanting to settle down, it was Dawson not wanting to let your dad go and lead an honest life. Dawson did all of it, and now he's behind bars. He can't hurt you anymore. Ever."

Rio's words sank in, echoing through her mind. *He can't hurt you anymore.*

Was it really true?

She wanted so badly to believe it. Did she dare?

He was right. It *was* Dawson's fault. Dawson had given the orders behind all the horrors of her life.

That one simple fact rearranged all she'd endured into a kind of awful, logical sense.

One that exonerated her from responsibility for the disasters.

"Am I really free?" she whispered. *Free to love and settle down? Free to have a real family of her own someday?*

"Free as you want to be," Rio said, smiling down at her with love and adoration. "But I'm hoping you won't want to be free of me. Not for about a hundred years."

"Oh, Rio, never." She slid her arms around his neck. "Not if I have to follow you to Podunk, South Carolina."

He shook his head. "No, sweetheart, I know how much your job means to you. I could never ask you to give it up. I'm still retiring, but I'll stay in Washington, just as long as you want."

"No need," she said, hugging him happily. "Jules said I can work from anywhere I want."

Rio's eyes flared in surprise. "Really? Anywhere?"

"Even Podunk."

Then they went soft and mushy. "You'd do that? For me?"

"I'd go anywhere for you, Stewart Rio. And do anything at all to keep you."

"Yeah?"

"Yeah."

"In that case, marry me."

Her mouth dropped open in surprise. "But…but…we've only known each other a couple of days! I mean—you know."

He looked crestfallen. "Is that a no?"

"No, it's not a no!" She grinned up at him, the most unbelievably wonderful man in the world. The man she'd once thought her enemy. She'd marry him tomorrow—heck, today!—if he really wanted to.

"It doesn't have to be right away," he hurriedly said. "We could have a long—" he shrugged "—ish…engagement. If you need more time to get to know me."

"Like how long?"

"Well, like…you know—" his eyes twinkled mischievously "—a week. Or maybe even two."

She choked on a laugh. "That long?"

"Only if you're really uncertain."

"Somehow I don't think that'll be necessary."

"Then say yes."

Kansas Hawthorne had done a lot of crazy things in her life. But this was probably the craziest of all.

"Yes."

However, it didn't feel crazy. It felt like the sanest thing she'd ever done in her entire twenty-nine years.

His lips came down on hers and he swept her into a deep, powerful kiss, full of promise and hope and love.

Long moments later, he raised up and gazed into her eyes. "So, today, then?"

"Today, what?" Then his meaning sank in. "To get *married?*"

He consulted his watch. "We can probably make it in to Charleston in—" He halted. "Damn. Unless you need a ring? They took our rings and I don't have a ring." He swore.

"Oh, I definitely need a ring," she assured him, doing her best to keep the teasing out of her tone.

"Of course you do. We both do." Consternation flavored his declaration. "You can't get married without rings—your *own* rings."

"My dad once gave me the security codes for the back door of Tiffany & Co.," she ventured. "He was thinking of doing a—"

"No!" Rio said, horrified. "Don't even—" He suddenly halted, then wagged a finger. "Why, you little—you are so going to get it."

He grabbed for her and she jumped away with a squeal. Laughing, she took off at a sprint. He chased her, as she knew he would. Shrieking with laughter and giddy with anticipation over what would happen when he caught her, she ran. Right into a For Sale sign stuck in the ground. The spindly wooden stake cracked at the base and it went down, along with her. Followed by Rio.

He landed on her with an "oof" then proceeded to kiss the living daylights out of her.

Not that she objected.

"It must be a sign," he murmured when they finally came up for air.

"A For Sale sign, actually," she said, grinning.

"No. I mean you running into it like that."

"How's that?" she asked, already knowing what he was about to say. She'd known it from the first moment he'd laid eyes on this place—rickety dock, run-down shack and all— and had gotten all googly-eyed over it. Kind of the same expression he'd had the first time he'd unzipped her catsuit.

"I want this place."

"Yeah, I know."

"You don't mind? As I recall you weren't too enamored of the property's condition."

"If you like it, I like it, too."

Besides, it would keep him busy when she was off on her missions for the Bureau.

He smiled like a man who'd just gotten everything he'd ever wanted.

Well, almost.

He leaned down for a warm, slow kiss. "Don't s'pose you'd like to go back to the boat and celebrate? Gerard's got quite a nice collection of champagne in the galley fridge."

"Don't you think you should make an offer first?"

"I thought I just did."

She smiled. "For Seven Moon Charters."

"Oh." He smiled back. "Nah. I have a feeling it'll still be for sale tomorrow."

"You think?"

"Smartass."

Her smile widened. "Are you insulting me?"

"The mother of my future children? Hell, no. I love your ass. And all the rest of you. Every inch."

She gazed up at him, the love of her life, and her heart melted at his expression. "I love you, too, Rio. More than you'll ever know."

She was the thief, but he was the one who'd scored the biggest heist of all. He'd stolen her heart, utterly and completely. And her life would never be the same again.

Thank God.

"Come on," she whispered. "Let's go celebrate."

"I'll get the champagne," he whispered back.

She batted her eyelashes coyly. "Who said anything about champagne?"

* * * * *

INTIMATE MOMENTS™

Bad-boy government officer Simon Byrne
avoids relationships. By-the-book tech
officer Janna Harris won't get involved.
Pairing these two could only lead to
trouble and a passion so strong it
could risk their lives.

Breaking All the Rules

by **Susan Vaughan**

(Silhouette Intimate Moments #1406)

*Available February 2006
at your favorite retail outlet.*

If you enjoyed what you just read,
then we've got an offer you can't resist!

Take 2 bestselling love stories FREE!

Plus get a FREE surprise gift!

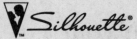

COMING NEXT MONTH

#1403 HIGH STAKES BRIDE—Fiona Brand
Dani Marlow doesn't have time for another dead-end relationship,
but is quickly thrown back into the arms of her ex, Assault
Specialist Carter Rawlings, when she is linked to a series of
fires...first as a suspect, then as a victim. Now Carter is faced
with the biggest challenge of his life: keeping Dani safe while
convincing her that their love is worth another chance.

#1404 WILD FIRE—Debra Cowan
The Hot Zone
Firefighter Shelby Fox can't remember the details of a murder
she witnessed, most importantly the killer's identity. With her life
on the line Shelby turns to her best friend, homicide detective
Clay Jessup, and discovers a growing desire that could forever
change—and possibly destroy—their friendship.

#1405 DEEP BLUE—Suzanne McMinn
PAX
Evidence linked to her twin sister's disappearance leads
Sienna Parker to the Florida Keys, but she's not the only one
fishing for clues. Posing as a renegade treasure hunter, PAX agent
Cade Brock knows Sienna is a link to uncovering a terrorist plot.
And he's in deep water when he realizes he is head over heels for
the unsuspecting twin.

#1406 BREAKING ALL THE RULES—Susan Vaughan
Bad-boy government officer Simon Byrne avoids relationships.
By-the-book tech officer Janna Harris won't get involved, either.
Pairing these two ex-lovers in a high-risk investigation will test
their boundaries...and the passion that could threaten their lives.

SIMCNM01